"Gentlemen! If I could have your attention, please! The brokerage house of Schuyler & Schuyler today departed from a time-honored tradition of Wall Street secre—, of Wall Str—"

The speaker suddenly raised both hands to his throat and swayed forward. Those surrounding him leaped to his assistance. Voices rose in a discord of confusion.

"He's sick. Get a doctor!"

"It must be a heart attack!"

"He's collapsed!"

"Clear that couch!"

But as the couch was cleared, Nat Schuyler rose to his feet and commanded the room with his voice.

"I'm afraid he's dead."

It wasn't a heart attack, it was poison. Only John Putnam Thatcher could discern who had a real motive among the people gathered to drink to each other's health or death.

the sound to involve himself with Tom Abercrombie. Bowman lowered his voice while the other looked frankly enthralled.

"No, although I know Vin is broken up. He's not a

Books by Emma Lathen

Ashes to Ashes
Death Shall Overcome
Double Double Oil and Trouble
The Longer the Thread
Murder Without Icing
Pick Up Sticks
A Place for Murder

Published by POCKET BOOKS

EMMA LATHEN

DEATH SHALL OVERCOME

PUBLISHED BY POCKET BOOKS NEW YORK

**POCKET BOOKS, a Simon & Schuster division of
GULF & WESTERN CORPORATION
1230 Avenue of the Americas, New York, N.Y. 10020**

Published by arrangement with Macmillan Publishing Co., Inc.
Library of Congress Catalog Card Number: 66-21159

ISBN: 0-671-83675-7

First Pocket Books printing December, 1974

10 9 8 7 6 5 4 3

POCKET and colophon are trademarks of Simon & Schuster.

Printed in the U.S.A.

Contents

DEATH SHALL
OVERCOME

thanks to the Air Force. You were a sitting duck. If it hadn't been for that sonic boom, you wouldn't be here now, talking about hunters and teen-agers. That threw

1 · Fling Out the Banner!

ABOVE ALL, Wall Street is power. The talk is of stocks and bonds, of contracts and bills of lading, of gold certificates and wheat futures, but it is talk that sends fleets steaming to distant oceans, that determines the fate of new African governments, that closes mining camps in the Chibougamou. In the world's great money market, power has forged massive canyons through which thousands of men and women daily hurry to work, hurry to lunch, hurry, hurry, hurry in the shadow of towers tall enough to defy the heavens. Depending upon your point of view, Wall Street is either awesomely impressive or appalling.

No one has ever called it beautiful.

John Putnam Thatcher, Senior Vice-President of the Sloan Guaranty Trust (and, incidentally, a man who had sent plenty of tankers to the Sulu Sea in his day), paid the taxi driver and inspected his portion of Wall Street, which happened to be Exchange Place, with profound satisfaction. It had been turned an exceptionally dirty gray by low-lying November clouds. The chilled hordes streaming past the entrance to the Sloan were an unaesthetic spectacle. Nevertheless, Thatcher felt the real contentment that comes, so we are told, from the sight of an authentic work of art.

"Which proves," he told himself as he struggled into the Sloan's lobby, "that it is all in the eye of the beholder. Morning, Billings."

"Good to have you back, Mr. Thatcher," said Billings, with as much dignity as if he were still presiding over the magnificently begrilled oak elevator that had served executives in the old Sloan instead of a pneumatic pillbox.

"Did you have a good trip? It was India, wasn't it?"

"Poona," said Thatcher. "Yes, it was a good trip, but I'm glad to be back."

"I'm sure you are. Here we are, sir."

As he rode up to the sixth floor and the Trust Department, Thatcher considered the warmth in Billings' voice. Was it possible that Billings too had been in Poona?

Miss Corsa, as busy in his outer office as if Thatcher had never been away, had not visited Poona. She welcomed her employer back from foreign parts with her usual calm, then interestedly inspected the length of sheer golden silk he produced from his briefcase.

"It's a beautiful scarf, Mr. Thatcher. Thank you very much."

"Scarf?" Thatcher replied. "It's a sari, Miss Corsa. I noticed that it enlivens an office considerably when the secretary wears something like that. I anticipate coming in one morning to find you looking like a bird of paradise."

Involuntarily Miss Corsa glanced again at the transparent shimmer of the silk. Then she carefully refolded it, stowed it in a drawer, and got down to business.

"And I've clipped the articles in the *Times*, Mr. Thatcher. And the pictures . . ."

"Miss Corsa, it is my intention to forget these past two weeks as rapidly as possible."

Miss Corsa ignored the interruption and made a mental note that foreign travel reinforced her employer's regrettable tendency to levity.

"*Newsweek* had a very good photograph of you in that furry hat. When you were up in the mountains."

"Furry hat!" he repeated irascibly, proceeding into his own office. Banking careers have drawbacks as well as compensations, but not until last week had John Putnam Thatcher added exotic headgear to the list.

"Remind me to send a memo to the chairman this afternoon, will you, Miss Corsa?"

It was the Chairman of the Board, George C. Lancer, who had put Thatcher into that furry hat. He prided himself on a statesmanlike view of the Sloan's far-flung financial commitments, which currently included modest participation in a vast hydro-electric project some two hundred miles northeast of Poona. It was, Lancer pointed out, only fit and proper that the Sloan Guaranty Trust and the United States of America be represented at the opening ceremonies.

"Certainly," Thatcher had replied. "When do you . . .?"

"Unfortunately, I'll be representing the bank at the launching of a trawler fleet in Ghana," Lancer had said with a straight face.

Since Bradford Withers, the president of the Sloan, had accepted a luncheon invitation to the White House during the relevant period and the head of International Division was en route to a trade conference in Dubrovnik, it was John Putnam Thatcher who went to Poona, and to an endless round of functions centering on the importance of waterpower—including several religious observances—that culminated in an exceedingly uncomfortable trip to what should rightly have been inaccessible mountain fastnesses. The motley crew of dignitaries accompanying him did not improve the situation.

"Yes. I want to be sure to tell Lancer that the United States was represented by the ambassador, poor fish. And don't let me forget to mention that the Russian technicians outnumbered the Indian officials. *That* will give International something to think about!"

Miss Corsa shook her head disapprovingly, indicated the business at hand, tempered her welcome by pointing out that she had not expected him until the next day, which accounted for the disorder he found (Thatcher's desk was a model of mathematical precision), then withdrew.

With a sigh of relief, Thatcher sank into his own chair, at his own desk. At long last, he had regained the peace and order of the Sloan that had sustained him through the worst moments in India—among which he was inclined to number his own ribbon-cutting remarks.

Almost immediately, reality intruded. Whether from Billings or those members of the staff he had encountered in the hallway—but certainly not from Miss Corsa—news of Thatcher's return roared through the sixth floor like a forest fire. Most of the sixth floor, it soon developed, had urgent need to consult him.

Fittingly enough, Walter Bowman, Chief of the Research Section, was the first to receive tidings of his return, and lumbered in, ostensibly to welcome Thatcher back, actually to argue the merits of Northern Kansas Utilities which he hoped to present to next week's Investment Committee. After this matter had been thrashed out, Bowman solicited Thatcher's impression of the Sloan's Paris branch, visited in passing.

It was not high.

"Just as I thought," Bowman said. "Tell you what, John. I'll send them a list of our reports, and ask for one of theirs. That way, we'll find out what they're doing—if they know."

"Clear it with International, Walter," Thatcher replied. "And remember that Withers' nephew is over there."

Bowman looked innocent as he heaved his great bulk out of the easy chair.

"I'll be tact itself, John. You know that. Well, you'll want to get caught up so I'll go. By the way, I thought India was hot. Why were you wearing that fur hat in the pictures?"

"Oh, take your tactful self out of here."

This set the pattern. One by one, Thatcher's subordinates cajoled their way past Miss Corsa to lay their problems on the desk of their returned chief.

"I thought Charlie Trinkam was supposed to be keeping the Trust Department running," said Thatcher aloud as he sped Kenneth Nicolls on his way. "And why is young Nicolls looking so tired?"

"I understand that he's been working nights," Miss Corsa replied, depositing a mountain of correspondence on his desk.

"Splendid," said Thatcher brutally.

"He's helping to build a cooperative nursery school in Brooklyn Heights," she continued. "Mr. Nicolls is doing the cabinetwork."

"Another illusion shattered," Thatcher commented. "Miss Corsa, do you think you could manage to keep the rest of the staff out of here. . . .?"

"John! Talk about timing!"

Radiating enthusiasm, Charlie Trinkam stood in the doorway. A man devoted to milking life of the enjoyment it held, he was also a fine trust officer, if unorthodox in method. The unalloyed pleasure in his voice made both Thatcher and Miss Corsa look up with surprise, but Trinkam advanced into the room like a cat stalking a canary. Just beyond him was Everett Gabler, the oldest and primmest of Thatcher's trust officers.

Thatcher narrowed his eyes. Not only was Everett Gabler a born fusser, he was also section chief of Rails and Industrials. This meant that, professionally as well as temperamentally, he was invariably at sword's points with Trinkam (Utilities).

Yet here he was, happily polishing his glasses.

"Well, well, well! It is good to see you back, John." He glanced at Trinkam. "You know, Charlie, I think this solves all our problems nicely. Very, very nicely."

The normal crises that arose when Trinkam assumed nominal authority during Thatcher's absences could never have effected this rapprochement. For a moment Thatcher studied Trinkam and Gabler, both beaming at him with uncharacteristic heartiness, then decided to tread very warily.

"That will do, Miss Corsa. Yes, I got back a day early."

"Great!" said Trinkam.

Thatcher said nothing.

"Have a good trip?" Everett Gabler inquired after a pause.

"Excellent," said Thatcher.

It was noteworthy that Charlie Trinkam did not inquire about Paris.

Thatcher let his eyes stray to his heaped in-box and saw Trinkam and Gabler exchange conspiratorial glances. Charlie cleared his throat.

"Ah . . . John, the reason we're glad that you got back a little early is that we've got a problem on our hands."

"Nothing serious. Things have been going very smoothly," Gabler interpolated.

He was a man in whose jaundiced view things never went smoothly.

"Yes?" Thatcher said courteously.

"You know Schuyler & Schuyler?" Trinkam continued.

Unlimited patience was not John Putnam Thatcher's forte. His voice grew testy.

"Of course I know Schuyler & Schuyler, Charlie. Will you two get to the point, or get out and let me do some work?"

Neither Trinkam nor Gabler budged.

"Had the rumors about Schuyler & Schuyler started before you left?" Gabler asked.

"Rumors? No, I haven't heard a thing. But they can't be in trouble," Thatcher replied, interested despite himself.

Schuyler & Schuyler was a small, well-regarded brokerage firm. Old Nat Schuyler, one of the founders, still ran it with an autocratic hand that guaranteed Schuyler & Schuyler's capital reserves were always well above the required minimum.

"Not the kind of trouble you're thinking about," Trinkam assured him soberly. "No, for the last week or so there's been a lot of talk. Schuyler & Schuyler want to take in a new partner and get him a seat on the Exchange."

"So?"

"He's a Negro," said Everett Gabler quietly.

Thatcher raised his eyebrows. Only someone who had spent almost forty years on Wall Street, someone who knew the Stock Exchange, the investment banks, the great law firms and the brokerage houses could immediately appreciate how much talk there must have been.

He smiled wryly.

"It's Nat Schuyler all over," Charlie said admiringly. "A real damn-your-eyes aristo, isn't he?"

"With a green thumb for money," Thatcher added. "If he can pull it off, it will mean a lot of business."

"He's a smart old cooky," Trinkam said. "But that's a mighty big 'if.'"

John Thatcher sat lost in thought for a moment. Then he asked, "Who's the man?"

Gabler pursed his lips. "That's it. For a while there were a lot of wild rumors . . ."

"I'm sure there were," Thatcher replied, amused.

"He turns out to be somebody named Edward Parry. Walter tells me that his family set up Savings and Loan Associations in Atlanta and Richmond. Worth millions . . ."

Thatcher tilted his chair appreciatively. Not only could he see the furor this must have caused on the Street, he could see the furor growing and growing. He could make a fairly good guess at Nathaniel Schuyler's frame of mind —the man had always played the *enfant terrible* and he obviously proposed to continue doing so even though he must be near eighty. And with some clarity, John Putnam Thatcher could see the shoals looming up before the Board of Governors of the New York Stock Exchange.

"But for the life of me," he said aloud, settling his chair, "I cannot see why this should create problems for the Sloan Guaranty Trust."

Again Everett Gabler exchanged a look with Charlie Trinkam.

"Schuyler & Schuyler sent invitations to most of the big firms on the Street—'To Meet Edward Parry,'" he said. "There's a reception this afternoon."

"The old devil," said Thatcher, after he had considered this. "I wonder if he can pull it off. Well, if anybody can, it's Nat Schuyler. I take it that he's sent an invitation to the Sloan, and you two think you're going to saddle me with it."

"Not quite," said Gabler gently.

Simultaneously Trinkam said, "Hell, no, it's worse than that!"

Gabler proceeded:

"Bradford Withers has accepted the invitation. The chairman has . . . er . . . urgently requested that Charlie or I . . . er . . . accompany Withers . . . to be sure that there won't be any statements . . . uh . . . from the Sloan that aren't what we would want."

Speechlessly, John Putnam Thatcher stared at him. Bradford Withers' role as president of the Sloan was largely ceremonial and, as such, ideally suited to a man whose outstanding characteristic was that he never saw what the trouble was. This rendered him liable to utter, publicly, comments that were hair-raising in their grand disregard of implications. Understandably, it was house policy at the Sloan to keep a weather eye on Bradford Withers in any situation other than the severely social.

"Ev and I don't want to do it," Charlie pointed out reasonably. "And you know, John, you're the only one who can control Brad." He paused to let this sink in, before adding, "And this could get very tricky."

John Putnam Thatcher bowed his head, acknowledging the truth, however unpalatable. In so doing, he caught sight of his wristwatch.

It had taken precisely two hours and fourteen minutes at his desk to transform Poona into a haven of peace and quiet.

2 · Once to Every Man and Nation

To the untutored eye, all large Wall Street functions seem to be repeat performances played by the same cast. The familiar faces from the big banks, brokerage houses and law firms are everywhere. But in slight fluctuations of personnel, in minute shifts in representation, the experienced eye can read its own lesson.

If, without a word of warning, some astounding feat of levitation had wafted Thatcher straight from the Jockey Club in Poona to the dark-paneled room overlooking Pine Street where he and Bradford Withers found themselves later that day, he would have taken one look, sniffed suspiciously and immediately realized that he was attending a Very Special Occasion.

The first three people he saw were all Governors of the New York Stock Exchange. Further inspection revealed that the Curb Exchange, the commodity brokers, and the over-the-counter houses had satisfied themselves with nominal attendance, as if to emphasize that this was a family problem in someone else's family. The Big Board had their best wishes, oh certainly, but anything more would smack of intrusiveness. And as for the Big Board—the suspicious density of senior partners suggested that many an executive felt with Thatcher that, if a blunder were to be made, he himself would make it, not some middling-to-junior subordinate.

A small, stocky man in his forties had pushed his way to their side.

"Thatcher! I'm glad to see you got back in time. We didn't expect you."

As Thatcher introduced Withers to Arthur Foote, one of the partners at Schuyler & Schuyler, he reflected that Nathaniel Schuyler had organized this affair carefully enough to document the movements of some three hundred men. The old goat must be enjoying himself thoroughly as he prepared once again to shock the Street with a display of his brilliant strategy.

"Look, why don't you come and meet Ed Parry now?" Foote was continuing. "There'll be a mob around him after our official announcement."

Glad to get this accomplished while Bradford Withers was still mindful of the cautions urged on him, Thatcher plodded along in the wake of the other two men.

Edward Parry stood in an alcove with Nat Schuyler. Like everyone present, he looked simonized for the occasion. The lurking fear of television had triggered a wave of five o'clock shaves and clean shirts. In all other visible aspects, Parry was a credit to Nat Schuyler's acumen—that is, he was a replica of a Wall Street financier with a dark skin. The net result was that his teeth and shirt looked cleaner than anybody else's. His slow, considered speech and steady handclasp as he acknowledged their greeting confirmed the impression of integrity, reliability and conservatism. A man of property at every point. In a happier era he might have been a Republican.

The whole thing went like clockwork. For five minutes they chatted on innocuous subjects, thereby edifying the room with a public demonstration of the Sloan's lack of racial bias. That, after all, was what they were there for.

Then Arthur Foote's glance strayed over Thatcher's shoulder to the doorway.

"Excuse me. There's someone who wants to meet Ed."

Thatcher turned to his companion, only to realize that once again he had been caught off base by Withers' vagaries.

"A forty-six-foot hull, you say? That's pretty small." Brad shook his head dubiously.

"Yes," agreed Parry. "But plastic makes all the difference. It's not fiber glass, you know. Something completely different. This boatyard in England . . ."

Withers was moved to animation. "I'd like to see that."

The conversation started to bristle with references to the Americas Cup Races and the Bermuda Races. Thatcher's eyes met those of old Nat Schuyler. Above cadaverous cheeks, a distinct twinkle could be seen. Thatcher sighed. His worst fears were confirmed. Schuyler was having a hell of a good time.

"Come on, Brad," he said. "We can't monopolize this corner. Foote is bringing some people over."

Detaching his reluctant superior, Thatcher fought a path to the bar and supplied himself with a Scotch and water. Withers, never one to change course easily, was describing the forty-six-foot paragon to some crony from the Century Club. Vigilance could be relaxed.

A voice broke in on his meditations.

"What are you doing, Thatcher? Making up a roll call?"

Thatcher turned to find Stanton Carruthers at his elbow. He was the trust and estate man for one of the big law firms.

"Counting," replied Thatcher truthfully. "The first thing I saw was three member Governors. I wondered how many turned up."

"Fourteen." Carruthers' reply was prompt. He too had remarked the overpowering display of institutional solidarity.

"What happened to the fifteenth? Dissenting opinion?"

"Oh, no! Slipped disk. Poor Bentley is doubled up like a croquet hoop."

Carruthers wriggled sideways to give someone access to

the bar. Snatches of small talk could be heard from all
directions. Was a corporate reorganization going through
and, if so, what would be its effect on second mortgage
bondholders? Was Miller, Pierce and Dwyer moving uptown? Was it true what they were saying about the price
of landscaping in Mamaroneck? Nobody was talking about
the Stock Exchange, its membership—or Edward Parry.

"This," announced Thatcher, "is a very decorous meeting."

Carruthers looked at him speculatively.

"You've been out of town, haven't you?" Then he ven-
tured further. "There isn't going to be any trouble, here.
Owen Abercrombie's still making a last minute effort to
get Schuyler to withdraw. The trouble will start after the
formal application has been filed."

Thatcher nodded. Owen Abercrombie was Wall Street's
most vocal ultraconservative.

"And when will that be?"

"Of course I don't *know* anything," said Carruthers
cautiously, "but I understand that Schuyler & Schuyler is
going to make a statement about that right here."

Yes, that fitted in. Nat Schuyler would want to throw
his glove down before as many people as possible. Pref-
erably when they were all nervously on their best behavior.

Not only the guests were nervous. A barman, no doubt
overcome by the oppressive atmosphere, let a bowl of
ice cubes crash to the table. The ensuing hush was broken
only by the tinkle of breakage and one shrill voice carrying its remarks over into the silence by the impetus of its
own defiance:

". . . suddenly acting as if they've got a right to be
treated just like us . . ."

The speaker stopped abruptly and then compounded his
error by flushing fiery red as he became the cynosure of
all eyes. Desperate conversation arose from seventy determined voices.

"Couldn't be more unfortunate," said Carruthers with
placid detachment. "Thank God we don't act for them.
They must be having their hands full." He shuddered

delicately at the thought of clients barreling along out of control.

"Who is he?"

Thatcher looked at the speaker disapprovingly. Only sandy hair and the back of a red neck met his inspection.

"Young Caldwell, from Schuyler & Schuyler."

"You mean he's one of Nat Schuyler's partners?" asked Thatcher incredulously. "I don't remember him."

"Well, he's not a partner," conceded Carruthers, admitting some slight meliorative. "But he's their senior analyst. Been giving them a lot of trouble these past two weeks, talking indiscreetly. He's from Alabama," he concluded darkly.

"What about the partners? Let's see. Besides Nat, there was his cousin Ambrose, of course. That's the vacant seat. And then there are Vin McCullough and Arthur Foote. Is there anybody else?"

"No, you've got them all." Carruthers smiled as if encouraging a promising pupil. "It's a small house, and Nat always dominated it. Foote is backing him on this all the way, they say."

"And McCullough?"

"He's by no means enthusiastic about it. But what chance has he got, once Schuyler's made up his mind. And naturally he wants to be careful not to be associated with Abercrombie's group. Oh, hello, Clark. Hello, Robichaux. Just get here?"

Lee Clark, a broker from one of the largest houses, agreed quickly that they had just arrived and went on to ask a question of his own.

"What was that about Owen Abercrombie? Has he been up to something again?"

"Not to my knowledge."

"Well, he will be," said Clark sourly. "As if things aren't bad enough without the John Birchers wanting to burn crosses or something. It's gotten so that you can't get anybody to understand reasonable objections because they've had to listen to some lunatic outpouring from Abercrombie."

Tom Robichaux, who had been busy at the bar, thrust a glass into Clark's hand.

"No use getting worked up," he said sympathetically. "Here! Drink this and calm down."

Lee Clark shook his head irritably. "It's all very well for you, Tom. You don't have a penny at stake. Robichaux & Devane can just sit back and watch the fun."

"Now, that just shows how wrong you are," said Robichaux, stung by the injustice of life. "Francis is keen on moral conscience. I spent the afternoon unloading twenty thousand shares of Stevenson Can at a loss. So we're neither of us feeling funny about anything."

Clark started to explain that there were different ways of losing money, but Arthur Foote had sighted the latest arrivals and was bearing down on them.

"Hello, Lee. Glad you were able to make it." He shook hands cordially and then, with a fine show of indirection, turned to Carruthers. "Stanton, you haven't had a chance to meet Ed Parry. Why don't we get you a fresh drink and go over? Bourbon, is it? And maybe Lee would like to come, too?"

"Oh, for God's sake, Arthur! You don't have to be so subtle about it," grumbled his target. "You know perfectly well that I don't have anything against Parry himself. But I do say, and I'll say it to anybody, that Nat Schuyler is pulling a damn raw deal. And if he thinks that I'm just going to stand still while he jerks the rug from under me, he's got another think coming . . ."

"Well, that's just fine, Lee," replied his host hastily. "That'll be one bourbon and soda and one tomato juice," he added to the barman.

"Tomato juice?" queried Robichaux sternly as the barman complied with the order.

"Ulcers," Foote explained sadly as he led his charges off without further display of hostility.

"He didn't have ulcers last week."

Thatcher inspected Robichaux, an investment banker and lifelong friend. There was no point, he knew, in trying to introduce a new subject of conversation until Tom had settled to his own satisfaction whatever doubts and suspicions had been raised in his butterfly mind by Foote's order.

Finally the tight look of concentration that had been narrowing Robichaux' eyes relaxed.

"You know what? I'll bet all this fuss about Parry has had him worrying. He probably *has* got ulcers. I mean, there's no reason to suppose that going teetotal has got anything to do with all this."

He waved his arm largely to indicate the gathering they were attending.

"Certainly not." Thatcher's tone was bracing. "Particularly as Parry himself was ordering a refill on his Bloody Mary when I left him. You can drink your Scotch in peace without wondering whether it's a clue to your racial sympathies, if any."

Robichaux looked at his companion suspiciously.

"I don't have to have any feelings about this sort of thing. Francis takes care of all that," he explained simply.

Not for the first time Thatcher found himself wondering how that militant Quaker and humanist, Francis Devane, managed to put up with his partner's determined blindness to all extra-curricular obligations except wine, women and song.

Come to think of it, it was surprising that Devane was not playing a leading role in this drama.

It turned out that he was. Arthur Foote, busy on another errand, bustled up. "Have you seen Devane?"

"He's over by the window," said Robichaux. "Said he was going to stay put, in case you wanted him."

Thanking him, Foote sped off in the direction indicated. Robichaux followed his trail with interest.

"I guess the balloon's going up," he said. "Francis is representing the president of the Stock Exchange today. Ponsonby had to go down to Washington."

"Then Nat Schuyler is going to announce that he's filing an application to transfer his cousin's seat to Parry, I suppose," said Thatcher.

"Yes. There's going to be a public statement, with a potted biography of Parry. The Exchange wanted to keep everything quiet, but Schuyler persuaded them that a prepared statement to the *Journal* was better than a lot of inaccurate publicity."

Thatcher said that there were no flies on old Nat Schuyler.

"A buck's a buck," said Robichaux philosophically. "And Nat's little sprees usually bring him a pretty profit."

As usual, when it was a question of money, Robichaux was dead right.

"There they go," he continued as a parting in the crowd revealed Arthur Foote and Francis Devane standing together by the window. Foote was waving across the room to the alcove where Thatcher had been earlier. In response to his signal Edward Parry and Nat Schuyler were advancing to join him. Parry had taken a sheet of typewritten paper form his breast pocket and was carefully unfolding it. Schuyler, bring up the rear, looked jaunty and triumphant.

"You have to hand it to old Nat," said Robichaux, echoing Thatcher's unspoken thought. "He does manage to get a kick out of things. Look at him. Everybody else there is handling that release as if it were dynamite, but he's full of vinegar."

"My God, have they gotten to the press release already?" demanded a new voice.

Two men had entered from the foyer while Thatcher and Robichaux had been watching history unfold. Expressionlessly Thatcher greeted Owen Abercrombie and Vincent McCullough. What was a partner of Schuyler & Schuyler doing with Abercrombie, today of all days?

As if answering the question, Vin McCullough hastened to dissociate himself from his companion.

"Owen and I caught the same elevator. I'd better get over there and join the firm. Grab yourself a drink, Owen."

Unconsciously straightening his tie and running a hand over his close-cropped graying hair, McCullough advanced to the support of his partners, present and presumptive. Foote, putting on horn-rimmed glasses to study the release which had been handed to him by Francis Devane, threw a questioning glance at McCullough and then at Abercrombie. Thatcher knew McCullough would be explaining the unfortunate proximity in the elevator even before he came to a halt.

"What do you mean, a press release?" Owen Abercrobie's question was literally hurled at Tom Robichaux.

Robichaux repeated his explanation.

"That's absurd. I went out of my way to make an appointment with Schuyler for tomorrow morning to try and bring the old fool to his senses." Abercrombie's bushy eyebrows lowered into a scowl of astonishing ferocity. "He can't get away with this."

"Well, it's not my party, Owen," replied Robichaux mildly. "If you've got any complaints, make them to the management."

"That's what I intend to do! Schuyler & Schuyler will regret this, you take it from me!"

Without further parley, Abercrombie plunged off to the windows where he could be seen haranguing Nat Schuyler. Within seconds he could be heard also. The phrase, "no sense of decency," came winging its way back.

"Wonderful how above-it-all Francis looks," murmured Robichaux appreciatively.

And indeed, Francis Devane, his handsome white head inclined, had engaged Edward Parry in discussion of some point in the release that they were both holding, thereby contriving to protect Parry from Abercrombie's onslaught and to emphasize his own detachment.

Suddenly it all came to an end. From nowhere, Lee Clark and Dean Caldwell materialized. For a moment there was a swirl of activity; then they emerged leading Owen Abercrombie. The altercation attracted the attention of the entire room although a few hardy souls were still doggedly discussing rising office costs.

Arthur Foote took advantage of the near silence to clear his throat and raise an arm.

"Gentlemen! If I could have your attention, please!"

The babble of voices stilled.

"We at Schuyler & Schuyler have asked you to come here this afternoon in order that the financial community may have the earliest intimation of the action we contemplate. I am happy to announce that, together with representatives of the New York Stock Exchange, we have prepared a statement explaining the proposed disposition of the seat on that Exchange held by the late Ambrose Schuyler. If you will bear with me for a moment, I will read that statement to you, and then be happy to answer any questions which you may have."

Everybody settled into receptive postures. Nat Schuyler and Francis Devane handed Foote the release with gestures that seemed to indicate some emendations to the original draft. Foote nodded comprehendingly, took a revivifying gulp of his tomato juice, and started to read:

"The brokerage house of Schuyler & Schuyler today departed from a time-honored tradition of Wall Street secre—, of Wall Str—"

The speaker suddenly raised both hands to his throat and swayed forward. Those surrounding him leaped to his assistance. Voices rose in a discord of confusion.

"He's sick. Get a doctor!"

"It must be a heart attack!"

"He's collapsed!"

"Clear that couch!"

But even as the couch was cleared and men crouched to lift Foote from the floor, Nat Schuyler rose to his feet and commanded the room with his voice.

"I'm afraid he's dead."

3 · Fruitful Let Thy Sorrows Be

THESE CHILLING WORDS echoed through the room as Nat Schuyler's pronouncement was repeated, doubted, then accepted. Yet, after the first instinctive shock, Pine Street was gripped not by sorrow, but social perplexity.

It was easy enough for the members of Schuyler & Schuyler, who knew what was expected of them. A grave Nathaniel Schuyler positioned himself correctly, like a chief mourner, as he awaited the arrival of the doctor.

A step or two behind him stood Vin McCullough beside Edward Parry. Both men looked appropriately solemn.

Dean Caldwell, deputized to handle details, which included obtaining a tablecloth to shield Arthur Foote's sightless eyes, looked shaken as he returned from the telephone to station himself in the formal array. And this, too, was as it should be.

The rest of the room, however, had milled away from the focus of interest, uncertain about the respectful thing to do. It was difficult to shift into formal funeral manner, although there seemed to be tacit agreement that immediate departure would be in poor taste. Accordingly, small groups of uncomfortable men were left to exchange brief, meaningless remarks in hushed voices. After initial confusion, the bartender nodded to his acolytes, and waiters sped through the room, removing half-empty glasses, overflowing ashtrays and other evidence of conviviality. Within a matter of minutes, the atmosphere was that of an extremely awkward wake.

Schuyler & Schuyler's reception for Edward Parry had not been a comfortable social event. Arthur Foote's untimely collapse, however, had injected a new element of anxiety into the assemblage. For the moment, at least, the problem of racial attitudes was displaced by incipient hypochondria.

"But, my God, how old *was* Art?" Thatcher heard a hoarse voice ask.

Fully twenty per cent of the guests, he was prepared to wager, would present themselves for medical examination within the week. Heart attacks among one's colleagues are always unsettling; among one's younger colleagues, they can be downright apocalyptic.

He inclined his head to Watson Kingsley's solemn banalities, while letting his attention range more widely. Across the room, he saw one member of the Board of Governors of the Stock Exchange deep in earnest converse with another. Sad a commentary as it was, he thought as Watson Kingsley mentioned the word "blessing," the fact was inescapable; those of the late Arthur Foote's friends and acquaintances not brooding about their own cardiac conditions were feeling the inconvenience, rather than the tragedy, of his method of going.

"Well, at least this should hold up Nat's scheme about that Negro!"

The voice was suitably low; the sentiment, given the circumstances, was universally offensive. Involuntarily Thatcher and Watson Kingsley (who had moved on to "inscrutable designs of Providence") turned to identify the author. Not surprisingly, it was Owen Abercrombie, still energetically scowling over his own grievances.

Abercrombie was talking to Lee Clark, who was embarrassed. His normally pallid countenance was slightly flushed as he registered the disapproval emanating from their neighbors. He said something inaudible to Abercrombie, who shook his head vigorously.

"No. Nat won't have time to go on with this crackbrained foolishness, Lee. Our troubles are over."

He sounded quite reasonable, a man stating the facts as he saw them. That his way of looking at the facts was brutal had not occurred to him.

It had occurred to Clark, who again murmured something inaudible and moved away with more haste than courtesy. Abercrombie surveyed the room, then strolled through the crush to inflict his brand of reasonableness on other acquaintances.

Thatcher turned to find that Tom Robichaux had joined him. The *bon vivant* looked apprehensive.

"Francis wants me to stand by," he rumbled gloomily. "You know, there's such a thing as carrying Christianity too far . . ."

Thatcher felt a certain measure of sympathy. The highminded, who gladly shoulder burdens themselves, have a fatal propensity to do so on behalf of their associates as well. However, this was not the time to criticize anyone willing to support Schuyler & Schuyler through the trying formalities surrounding sudden death, so he turned the subject to something that had been puzzling him mildly.

"What's Lee Clark up to?" he asked.

Cooperatively, Robichaux abandoned his own trials and, in his own way, responded.

"You've been away," he said accusingly.

"So people keep reminding me," Thatcher replied. "You'd think I'd been on a desert island for two years."

Robichaux pursued his train of thought to an interesting conclusion.

"I'd like to get away myself," he said with a glance at the funeral party. "But you can't deny it. If you're away from the Street, you lose touch."

"Lee Clark," Thatcher reminded him.

"Oh, that's simple enough."

As usual, once the question came within his professional orbit, Robichaux rose to heights of coherency bordering on the intelligent. He reminded Thatcher of Clovis Greene Bear & Spencer's major coup of some ten years earlier—an expansion into Harlem with plush offices, massive advertising budgets and colored customer's men. This move, for which Lee Clark had been mainly responsible, paid off. Clovis Greene began to enjoy a virtual monopoly of Negro investment in the stock market and became Clovis Greene Bear Spencer & Clark.

"And nobody else ever moved into Harlem," Robichaux continued. "Wasn't worth it with Clovis Greene so big. But it Schuyler & Schuyler gets a Negro partner, then Clovis Greene has had it. And so has Lee."

Thatcher nodded. Really, there were no heights unworthy of Nat Schuyler. It would be a shame if fate had boobytrapped his enterprise by anything so fortuitous as Arthur Foote's heart attack.

"I remember. That's why Clark is so edgy about Abercrombie, isn't it?"

"Well I ask you," Robichaux replied reasonably. "Would you want the Sloan mixed up with someone who wants to send Negroes back to Africa, abolish Social Security and drop the hydrogen bomb on Cuba?"

Thatcher said that he saw Lee Clark's point.

"And then," Robichaux continued reflectively, "I don't think people liked the sound of that trouble up in Katonah. Of course they tried to hush it up—but the story got around."

"What trouble?"

"Abercrombie and Parry both live way up in Westchester, Katonah. When the Parrys built their place a couple of years ago, Owen tried to stir up trouble. Well, nasty letters to the local papers are one thing—but there was talk about pressuring the contractor, and paying off the building inspector and dumping garbage at night. I tell you, people are beginning to wonder if Abercrombie is respectable."

Thatcher, who had been privileged to hear Abercrombie's views on foreign policy ("Send in the Marines!") and fiscal problems ("Abolish the income tax!") tried to picture him slinking around at night with a truckload of garbage.

It was impossible.

It was not impossible, however, to visualize Abercrombie ordering some handyman to do it.

Owen Abercrombie must be causing saner heads at Dibbel Abercrombie considerable discomfort.

This thought reminded John Putnam Thatcher of his own responsibilities. He took leave of Robichaux and hurriedly began to search the room for Bradford Withers.

When he finally located him in a distant corner, however, he discovered his fears had been misplaced; death, like birth and marriage, found Withers at the top of his form. Impeccably formal, he stood exchanging unexceptionable commonplaces about morality with old Bartlett Sims.

As Thatcher approached, Withers eyed the Schuyler & Schuyler staff still standing guard over their fallen 'comrade.

"I want Nat to know he can count on us," he said. "But this isn't the time to disturb him."

Thatcher was happy to be able to report that Francis Devane (and his colleagues) were taking care of that. As he spoke there was a stir in the doorway and a small clutch of men hurried into the room. Either Dean Caldwell had been too agitated to report the situation accurately, or the doctors felt it politic to hurry into so august a gathering of Wall Street dignitaries. In either event, their arrival clearly signaled release.

"Why are doctors always too late?" Withers mused. "Well, it's a sad affair, but you know, I think we could slip away."

In no other area did John Putnam Thatcher accept Bradford Withers as arbiter but, in matters like this, he was peerless. Thatcher followed him as he made his way, without unseemly haste, to the door. As others joined them, a general exodus began. Within minutes, only the Schuyler & Schuyler contingent, Francis Devane and the luckless Tom Robichaux remained near the corpse.

The hallway was a relief.

"Thank God that's over," somebody near him said with feeling.

Wall Street being a conventional community, Bartlett Sims immediately replied, "Terrible thing."

"Terrible," everybody dutifully chorused, gratefully going their way.

Fortunately, it was not until they had reached the privacy of a taxi that Bradford Withers shed his public manner for confidences.

"You know," he said, "I can't help feeling that this is a bad sign."

Bradford Withers would not be alone in attributing symbolic importance to the recent catastrophe. Therefore, when they had adjourned to Luchow's for an early dinner, Thatcher listened to his chief with more than usual interest. But, out of touch or no, he learned very little about Wall Street thinking from Bradford Withers' disjointed remarks. Arthur Foote's death was profoundly significant, Withers felt, but he could not specify, to Thatcher's satisfaction, precisely what it signified.

"Well, it's tragic," he concluded with his Linzer torte. "Of course, Nat Schuyler really needs new blood in the office now. Parry sounded very able to me. Did you hear what he said about those new megachrome hulls. . . ?"

"Owen Abercrombie doesn't seem to think that he'll be an addition to the financial community," Thatcher remarked.

Withers put down his cup indignantly.

"You know, Owen is beginning to get positively eccentric. If he were a woman, I'd say . . ."

"What do you think the Board of Governors will do about Parry?" Thatcher intervened to inquire.

Bradford Withers' chief virtue, as well as his most outstanding defect, was transparent truthfulness.

"I haven't the remotest idea," he said with enough hauteur in his voice to suggest that the Board of Governors of the New York Stock Exchange was not the sort of group that a Withers cared to understand. "You know, John, I'm sorry you didn't have a chance to see Jahoda. The maharajah could have given you some fine shooting . . ."

What Thatcher did want to see, after dinner, was his own office. A few hours spent dictating might bring him abreast of the arrears that the Schuyler & Schuyler reception had further delayed. This decision was received by his dinner companion with incomprehension. Going to the office in the morning was, under certain conditions, perfectly reasonable behavior to the president of the Sloan Guaranty Trust. Going there after dinner smacked of the bizarre.

Nevertheless, John Thatcher parted from Withers with less impatience than usual. The Sloan's president was limited, to put it mildly. But he was not an Owen Abercrombie.

Thatcher rather suspected that in the days to come, this might be enough.

He was midway through a letter to a small Massachusetts electronics firm which had recently changed its name and corporate structure in the apparent belief that its stockholders would simply evaporate, when Walter Bowman, who did not share Withers' views on after-hours work, appeared in the doorway.

"I thought I saw you go past. What's this I hear about Art Foote?"

He listened to Thatcher's account of the happenings at Pine Street without revealing how he had received such prompt news of the tragedy. Lost in thought, he lowered himself into the easy chair.

"This might make a difference," he said thoughtfully. "Foote was cooperating with Nat Schuyler to the hilt, you know. He told me he didn't care if Parry was black, blue or green, he'd be worth a million dollars in commissions from Harlem within six months."

With one of the first twinges of amusement he had felt in some hours, John Thatcher mentally saluted his chief researcher. Come typhoon, the return of the ice age, or an epidemic of cholera, Bowman's interest would remain unfalteringly centered on profits and losses. Clearly, here was the man to fill in the lacunae in his own information.

Without regret, he abandoned the ingenuous electronics specialists on Route 128 and did what he guessed much of Wall Street must be doing: considered Schuyler & Schuyler, and Edward Parry.

"Nat did his picking carefully," he observed. "Edward Parry is quite impressive. Did Gabler tell me he had money?"

Bowman grunted.

"Impressive is right. And money, too. I happen to know that Schuyler has been planning this move for months, but to tell you the truth, he couldn't have done better if he'd been beating the bushes for ten years. Parry is the oldest son of Sylvanus Parry. You know, the Savings and Loan man. But he was a millionaire before that—made a fortune out of Atlanta real estate. The son is everything anybody could ask for; he rowed for Yale, he collected almost every medal the Army gives. Then he got a Rhodes Scholarship and spent two or three years in England. Absolutely brilliant, they tell me. Since then, he's been running the family businesses with one of his brothers. And just about doubling the old man's pile."

Thatcher digested this no-doubt abbreviated, and possibly colloquial, but undoubtedly accurate version of the press release on Edward Parry that had not been distributed.

"Tell me, why hasn't this paragon been in the public eye before?" he asked curiously. "God knows, I feel that I've read the life history of every Negro lawyer on the

East Coast in the past few years. And minister, too, of course."

Bowman nodded understandingly.

"That's what I wondered. Gus Townely—he's one of our auditors—comes from Atlanta," he said.

Apparently he could not pass on detailed information about Georgia without citing authority.

"He says that the Parry family is simply old money—no publicity, pretty conservative. They're big in community good works—but no politics."

In fact, Edward Parry, spiritually speaking, was another Bradford Withers—with brains, of course. John Thatcher did not say this aloud. What he did say was:

"Really, I've never given Nat Schuyler his due. The one thing that can be said against Parry is that he's a Negro. Is it going to be enough, Walter?"

Like Withers, Walter Bowman did not know.

Neither did Everett Gabler when he drifted in with regrets for having dispatched Thatcher to what had been, in effect, a deathbed.

"It's very hard to tell," he said when Thatcher asked his opinion. "You see, until today, there have only been rumors. Some of them were unfortunate, I grant you, but everything remained vague. The climate of opinion won't jell until Schuyler & Schuyler makes formal application. . . ."

Authoritatively, Walter Bowman corrected him.

"You're wrong, Ev. This is just between the three of us, but I happen to know that Owen Abercrombie has begun circulating a petition. He's just approaching people he's sure of, but they tell me that he's got some important signatures. Including one from Schuyler & Schuyler."

Everett Gabler looked horrified.

"You don't mean McCullough, do you?" Thatcher said. Who had told him that Vin McCullough opposed Nat Schuyler's plan? He forgot. But surely McCullough was too sound to involve himself with Owen Abercrombie.

Bowman lowered his voice while Gabler looked frankly enthralled.

"No, although I know Vin is burned up. He's got a

big Southern clientele. Scared to death that a Negro partner will blow his accounts to hell! But basically Vin is decent. He wouldn't get involved in anything ugly. No, it's that Caldwell kid—I don't know if you met him?"

"Briefly," Thatcher said. "Do you mean to tell me that nonentity has been fool enough to ally himself publicly with Owen Abercrombie—against the head of his own firm?"

Walter Bowman's normally good-natured expression gave way to a singularly disagreeable smile.

"He's the last fading flower of the Confederacy. He's . . ." Bowman continued his definition in emphatic terms, finally ending, "He's the kind who likes to call Parry a 'nigra.' Behind his back, of course. The little rat! They tell me Art Foote gave him hell! But I don't think Nat knows about it—yet!"

"Disgusting," Everett Gabler said. "Absolutely disgusting."

There was a moment of silence, then Walter Bowman said, "And I can't help thinking that Art Foote's death is a bad sign."

Suddenly, John Putnam Thatcher felt a surge of impatience.

"Well, this is one bank that's not going to get drawn into somebody else's Roman Circus!" he declared emphatically. "I can see that we can all spend hours on this —but we're not going to. I think we'll have a review meeting of the trust officers tomorrow. At nine o'clock! That should remind the staff of precisely what our business is!"

4 · There Is a Balm in Gilead

THE NEXT MORNING, while John Putnam Thatcher was bringing the Trust Department to its senses, Edward Parry was explaining to his wife how Arthur Foote's death might affect the immediate plans of the Parry family.

"Do you mean Nathaniel Schuyler may back out now?" asked Gloria Parry.

"Oh, no. But I wonder whether he might not want to delay things. That's two partners gone in less than four months. The work load will have more than doubled in the firm. He'd have some justification if he decides that he just can't afford to spend all his time politicking up and down the Street right now."

His wife frowned thoughtfully into her coffee cup.

"And what would a delay mean?"

"It's hard to tell. The whole point of Nat's bulldozer approach was to take everyone by surprise. A delay would give the opposition time to organize. And in the end," he paused a moment, reluctant to continue, "it might mean a face-saving way for Nat to withdraw."

At this ominous conclusion, his wife's frown cleared and she laughed softly.

"You're up to your old games, Ed. Trying to prepare for the worst. But I've met your Mr. Schuyler, and I've seen the two of you together. So it's no use trotting out a lot of rational excuses for him to back out, or for you to back out. The fact is, both of you decided to be thoroughly irrational more than two months ago."

Ed Parry looked up in sudden protest. "Now, Gloria, I know you haven't been very enthusiastic about all this—"

"No, I wasn't," she interrupted. "But now—I wouldn't have you stop for anything. What's more, Nat Schuyler isn't used to losing battles, and, in your own quiet way, honey, neither are you. More coffee?"

With a profound sigh of relief, her husband shook his head. "No, I've got to catch the 9:42. I told them I'd be in to see how we stand. You're right, I've just been trying to anticipate the worst. I wouldn't back out for anything now. And while I'm doing battle with Wall Street, how are you going to pass the time?"

"I promised Mrs. Hickey I'd drop by and sign the petition to the Air Force about these sonic booms."

Her husband grimaced ruefully. "One way or the other, we seem to be spending all our time protesting."

"Well, Mrs. Hickey has a problem with all those greenhouses, and I suppose it was decent of her to ask us. It's only right to try and help her."

"Does she have any concrete suggestions as to where the Air Force should take its jets?"

"Of course not. She just wants them to go away. It's not only a question of the glass. She says the petunias have never recovered."

Ed Parry was still laughing as he put on his hat and coat and went to the garage. But it was not just the thought of the Air Force's elaborately polite response that lifted his spirits. It was the knowledge that Gloria, at first reluctant to accept the inevitable rupture of their privacy which his association with Schuyler & Schuyler portended, had at last decided that the game was worth the candle. Her slowness to come to this decision did not bother him. Gloria was one of those people who, unwilling to disown burdens, have learned in self-defense not to shoulder them lightly.

He was whistling as he came to a conscientious full stop at the end of his driveway before turning onto the county road. As he started to make this turn, all hell broke loose.

It was the grandfather of all sonic booms. It was as if the heavens, rent by some internal fury, had smashed down on him. He flinched against the seat, the windshield starred, and the car swerved. A triumphant reflex brought his foot heavily down on the brake.

The next thing he knew he was canted across the left lane, his bumper locked into that of a school bus. Hastily he scrambled out of the car. He called to the bus driver, asking shakily if the children were hurt.

"Nobody here but me," was the satisfactory reply. "The kids are all at school. I'm taking the bus back to the depot."

The driver climbed down to view the damage.

Looking at his trembling hand, Ed Parry felt a gust of fellow-feeling for Mrs. Hickey's petunias. He was not at all sure that he would ever recover. He would sign any number of petitions to the Air Force, he decided, as he wanly agreed with the driver that that had been one hell of a boom.

"But we're going to have to file a report, all the same," grumbled the driver. "Your grill is all smashed and mine don't look so hot. Probably thousands of reports. You know insurance companies."

Parry joined him to see if they could manhandle the bumpers apart.

"I don't see how they can say it's anybody's fault," he said, bending over to get some purchase. "If the Air Force is going to go around smashing windshields while people are driving, they have to expect—"

"Smashing windshields?"

"Yes. What do you think sent me into that skid? Not only windshields . . ." He was about to detail the depredations committed upon Mrs. Hickey's greenhouses but he was again interrupted.

"Mister! Have you looked at your windshield?"

Parry looked up. The driver had abandoned the bumpers. He was standing bolt upright pointing an accusing finger. Following his gaze, Parry saw that all the cracks in his windshield radiated out in a circle.

In the exact center was a neat round hole.

For two hours he tried valiantly to fight the evidence of his senses. The state police, summoned to the scene by phone, listened, investigated and quietly demolished his theories one by one.

First, he insisted that the windshield must be some freak breakage caused by the boom. Perhaps there had been a structural fault, some weakness in the glass at that particular point which had reacted to stress in this fashion.

The police dug a rifle bullet out of the upholstery in the passenger seat.

Then he suggested that possibly a passing hunter had made an ill-advised shot and, appalled by its consequences, had fled in panic.

"Look, Mr. Parry," said the police lieutenant heavily, "we've got to be sensible about this. You know as well as I do that there are 'No Hunting' signs posted all over the township. And, anyway, what would a hunter be shooting at? You can't tell me he was chasing a deer around here."

He waved his hand at the surrounding landscape. Carefully manicured lawns and clipped hedges rolled back from the road on both sides, with groupings of shade trees dotted at strategic intervals. On the right, set on the breast of the sloping hillside, was the modern Parry house. On the left the Bollingers' Colonial rambled over its level setting.

Ed Parry looked at the scene with discomfort. It was difficult to believe that a bona fide hunter could have fired a shot across this supremely domestic compound. The formal facade was broken only by the Bollinger swimming pool which, together with its surrounding terraces and Colonial cabanas, dominated the front aspect of their house. Parry's own pool lurked modestly in the rear, out of deference to his neighbors' sensibilities. Its placing had been the occasion of considerable discussion with Gloria. She had maintained that the respective wetness or dryness of their skins was irrelevant; the overwhelming fact was the presence. But he, raised in a Southern community which had been shocked to its back teeth by the first sight of colored legs in madras Bermuda shorts, had been anxious to avoid a possible proliferation of irritants.

Now, two years later, he bowed to Gloria's higher realism. He had been guilty of the single eye, seeing only the problems centering on himself, and thereby had done his fellow townsmen—with the single exception of Owen Abercrombie—a considerable injustice. The looming menace of a housing development (for thirty thousand dollar homes) preoccupied them to the exclusion of all other anxieties. They were perfectly prepared to embrace any one-home builder, provided only that he was a multi-millionaire.

A minute later and he was wondering if the police lieutenant had been thinking along the same lines. It would be a help if the man let any expression appear on his face.

"There was some trouble here when you people were

building, wasn't there?" the lieutenant asked in a tone suspiciously free from all inflection.

Parry wondered if he were becoming morbid. The man hadn't used any inflection when he asked about the sonic boom.

"There were some minor incidents," he said carefully.

He did not know it, but his voice was the very twin of the lieutenant's.

"Garbage was thrown," said the officer severely. "Paint drums were overturned."

"Nothing more than you could expect," Parry insisted dully. He wondered if he could make this man understand that no Negro had the right to be indignant about garbage while Sunday schools were being bombed.

The lieutenant gazed unseeingly at the horizon. "We don't tolerate that here."

Useless, he supposed, to explain that the Westchester police were not the Birmingham police.

During the ensuing silence, in which both men canvassed and rejected the possibility of further communication, a trooper came running up and drew his superior over to a lane running up the side of the Bollinger property.

Parry was left to his own reflections. He had asked Gloria to stay inside and, on the principle that activity would keep her from worrying, asked her to call the Oldsmobile people about getting the car fixed and sending an estimate to the insurance company. When she predicted that their quiet life was over, she had been right with a vengeance. Reluctantly his thoughts turned to Owen Abercrombie. The police would be asking about him soon. What a mess! This was not the kind of fight anticipated by old Nat Schuyler. Was it possible? Offhand, Parry would have thought not. Abercrombie was not the type to do his own dirty work. But, Parry gloomily admitted to himself, he did not understand the Owen Abercrombies of the world.

He squared his shoulders. The lieutenant was coming back. He would make one last-ditch attempt to have the whole thing passed off as one of those inexplicable freaks of life that occur in the best-regulated communities.

"Lieutenant!"

"Yes, Mr. Parry?"

"I've been thinking. What about a teen-ager? You never can tell. He might have seen a rabbit or something and taken a pot-shot just for the hell of it. There are rabbits around now and these kids aren't very responsible, particularly if they've got a new rifle."

The lieutenant shook his head. "It's time we got down out of the clouds. You'd better come and see what we've just found."

Together they walked over to the lane. A clump of trees screened it from the Bollinger lawn, and the unpruned shrubbery straggling along its side completed the cover. The area was larger than it seemed from a distance. When they arrived Parry was surprised to see that the little copse had four or five troopers carefully searching the ground. A patch had been cordoned off, and it was to this spot that he was led.

"See those three holes?" The lieutenant pointed to the clearly marked depressions.

Silently Ed Parry nodded. He knew what the explanation would be.

"Those are the marks of a tripod. And we've found some matches and cigarette ashes, not to mention the cartridge. It's as clear as daylight. This sharpshooter"—and his voice was ironic—"set himself up here, took a bead on the end of your driveway, and settled down to wait. He must have had his car turned around, ready for a getaway up the lane. You say you came to a full stop before turning?"

"Yes. That's right." The words were like the tolling of a bell, evenly spaced, evenly accented.

"Well, that gave him his chance to line you up in his sights."

"I guess so."

"I tell you one thing, Mr. Parry. You owe a vote of thanks to the Air Force. You were a sitting duck. If it hadn't been for that sonic boom, you wouldn't be here now, talking about hunters and teen-agers. That threw him off. But he may get his nerve back and try again. You understand that?"

Parry took a deep breath. In a way it was almost a relief to have it out in the open. This was not careful deliberations by a membership committee, or whispered mutterings in a locker room. This was something that there was a word for.

And the word was murder.

His voice was steady when he replied. "Believe me, I'd like to help, Lieutenant. After all, I'm the intended victim. But what can I do about future attacks?"

"It would be a start to find out if there have been any past attacks. Now, I know all about the garbage and paint and the building inspector. But you've been living here now for a couple of years. Has there been anything you tried to shrug off? Or anything you didn't realize was important? Accidents to the car? Fires starting in the outbuildings? Or even," he paused wryly, "even careless hunters?"

Soberly Ed Parry reviewed his life in Westchester. "No, I really don't think so. For the life of me, I can't remember anything."

"It *is* for the life of you," the lieutenant reminded him grimly. "Of course, this character may just be working himself up to shooting. What about your wife? Has she had any trouble?"

Parry bit back the automatic reply. Not any more than you would expect. No, that wasn't what this policeman was after.

"I'll ask her. But I don't think so. Nothing that she's mentioned, anyway."

"We'll *both* ask her." He held up a hand at Parry's gesture of dissent. "I know. You don't want to have her worried. Well, that won't answer. If there's some crackpot with a gun around, the more worried you both are, the better. What about your kids, anyway? Are they here?"

The children were away at school, Parry told him. Both men looked happier for the news.

"O.K. We'd better go up to the house. I'm going to want you both to figure out what sort of individual grudges you might have started. Anything that might have happened in the last month or so to trigger this off. There's usually something specific if people have been here for a couple of years already."

The suggestion of previous experience with the problem heartened Parry. They were not alone then. After all, Westchester County was a big place. Here and there, scattered among its suburban amenities, were pinpoints of corruption, discharging venom into the community. The police would know all about them, would have records and files charting the outbreaks and subsidences. They would know what to do.

The first thing to do, apparently, was to ask endless questions. It seemed to Edward Parry that he and Gloria told the lieutenant every action and movement in their lives for the past three months. The restaurants they had eaten at, the parties they had gone to, the golf courses they had played at, the stores they had patronized.

At the end of two hours they were all exhausted, confronting each other with blank, defeated faces.

So intent had the lieutenant been on their experiences in Westchester, that only then did he remember the contents of the morning paper.

"Say, weren't you at some party in the city yesterday? Something to do with Wall Street. And there was an accident of some sort?"

"No, no." Parry hastened to reassure him. "It wasn't anything of that kind. Someone dropped dead, a broker. But it was just a heart attack. That's all."

Ed Parry was trying to tell the truth, but he lied.

The twelve o'clock news was the first broadcast in New York City to carry the item about the Westchester shooting. It received only second billing.

The leading bulletin was the announcement that Arthur Foote's death had been caused by nicotine poisoning.

5 · Were You There . . . ?

WHATEVER SUCCESS John Thatcher's nine o'clock meeting had in turning the minds of his subordinates from the problems of Edward Parry to the affairs of the Sloan Guaranty Trust was of so limited a duration as to rob it of any significance. The contents of the twelve o'clock news broadcast were disseminated the length and breadth of Wall Street by the time the last trust officer returned from lunch, and formed the sole topic of conversation.

Poison, eh? Well, that was a new wrinkle. And shootings in Westchester, too. You couldn't say that Schuyler & Schuyler didn't manage to grab the headlines—one way or the other.

Nor was Thatcher himself setting a very good example of austere devotion to duty. He was idly discussing these latest dramatics with Charlie Trinkam, when Miss Corsa entered to announce that a Detective Sergeant Frazier would appreciate a few moments of Mr. Thatcher's time.

Charlie was the first to react.

"You know what, John?" he demanded, with every evidence of satisfaction. "You're a witness. We may have the joy of seeing you testify at a trial."

"You already have seen me testify."

Trinkam waved away Thatcher's appearance as expert witness on the question of the value a going business in McKeesport, Pennsylvania, would have had, if its contractual commitments had been such as were represented to the purchaser.

"I don't mean that sort of thing," he said loftily. "If this Foote business ends up in a trial, it will be for good, old-fashioned murder."

"Yes, and I won't be the only witness," said Thatcher,

43

carried away in spite of himself. "Every bank and broker-age house down here has someone involved."

Charlie grinned. "And a pretty picture it makes, too. I'm beginning to be sorry I missed the fun. What kind of detective do you think the police department has come up with to grill you and Owen Abercrombie and Nat Schuyler?"

"You can see for yourself as you go out," Thatcher suggested pointedly. "All right, Miss Corsa. You can bring in Sergeant Frazier."

The appearance presented by Sergeant Frazier suggested that someone at Centre Street was thinking. He was a clean-cut, serious-looking young man, probably older than he looked. He wore civilian clothes (and natural-shouldered charcoal gray at that). His mode of address was politely deferential, with a formality that for some reason immediately recalled the FBI in its unending round of security clearances. It developed, as time went on, that he was also a skilled interrogator.

He made no attempt to create a relaxed atmosphere. Instead he opened the proceedings by asking gravely if Thatcher had heard the midday news.

"I didn't hear it myself," Thatcher replied accurately. "But everybody is talking about it. They say Arthur Foote was murdered with nicotine poison."

Sergeant Frazier was even more scrupulously accurate.

"The autopsy makes it clear that Mr. Foote died from the ingestion of nicotine in toxic quantities. We have not yet ruled out the question of accident or suicide. But, as the poison was certainly taken while Mr. Foote was at the reception yesterday afternoon, we are naturally anxious to get as clear a picture as possible of his movements there."

Thatcher appreciated the prudence of the police department in refusing to confirm informal announcements of murder. But still, he felt the sergeant's statements were unduly circumlocutory. Probably there was no proof that the poison had been in Foote's glass. After all, there had been that swift clearing up of the premises to remove the unseemly signs of festivity. On the other hand, there was no point in abandoning common sense out of an exaggerated instinct for caution. Lethal doses of poison do not appear at Wall Street gatherings by accident, and Arthur Foote would not have chosen such a locale for suicide. The police in their own good time would, no doubt, produce proof rising to the precision of mathematical logic that neither of these eventualities had occurred. In the meantime, Thatcher was quite content to take a short cut.

"Yes, I can see how you would be interested in Mr. Foote's movements. But I'm afraid I won't be of much help to you. We arrived rather late, and I had only intermittent contacts with Mr. Foote."

"Of course," agreed Frazier earnestly. "Nobody present will be able to give us a minute-by-minute account of the victim. We'll have to arrive at that by making a composite of all the statements. Perhaps you could start by telling me about your own movements at the party, and then we can go into detail on the critical points."

Accordingly, Thatcher cast his mind back to the fateful moment when he and Withers had entered the room and been accosted by Arthur Foote. It was surprisingly easy to conjure up the events of the previous afternoon. Things which he had not consciously noticed returned with startling clarity. The center-piece on the bar, Nat Schuyler's jaunty posturing as he followed Ed Parry across the room, a little dribble down the side of a bottle of bitters, the tie that Tom Robichaux had been wearing. He spoke slowly, making a conscientious attempt to include the position of every person whom he had noticed at any time.

The sergeant let him complete his recital without interruption.

"That's very good, sir," he said at its conclusion. "Very helpful and clear. Now, if we could just go back over a few points." .

They went back to the moment when Foote had waved Schuyler and Parry over to join Francis Devane and proceeded in exhaustive detail down to the moment of Foote's collapse.

Thatcher found himself wondering what there was in

his testimony capable of producing such spellbound attention.

"That's very interesting. Let me see if I have everything clear. You say that Mr. Schuyler toasted someone as he crossed the room?"

"Well, it was more of a salute. A gesture, you know. Mr. Schuyler was being playful, I think."

"Yes, of course. And what was in his glass?"

Thatcher was startled. "I don't know. Whisky, I would imagine. Anyway, it was a highball glass."

"And Mr. Parry was unfolding the press release?"

Thatcher nodded.

"And then the press release was passed around and Mr. Devane and Mr. Foote put down their glasses to read it?"

"Yes. And Mr. Foote put on his horn-rims."

Why all this interest in the press release, Thatcher wondered? Surely there was no elaborate theory of its folds containing a minute dusting of powder or something equally exotic.

The sergeant now produced his blockbuster.

"Then, Mr. Thatcher, if I understand the position correctly, there were four men grouped together around this press release, and there were three glasses standing on the table by their side."

"Three?" Thatcher looked up intently. "I'm afraid I don't follow you, Sergeant."

"But you said that Mr. Parry was unfolding the release as he walked over, carefully unfolding it. I take it that he was using both hands to do that?"

The picture was very clear in Thatcher's mind. "Oh yes, he was using both hands."

The sergeant nodded to himself in approval. "Then he couldn't have been carrying a drink, and we have established that no further drinks were delivered to that corner."

Thatcher eyed the sergeant with respect. The damning facts had been extracted from him very neatly. He had an uneasy conviction as to what the next question would be.

"You say you were next to the bar when Mr. Foote

ordered his last tomato juice. Did you happen to notice what kind of glass it was served in?"

Oh yes, Thatcher remembered that all right. "It was a double old-fashioned glass."

"Then," said the sergeant as if he were leading a class to the last remorseless line of a Euclid theorem, "the three glasses standing on that table were two highball glasses, containing some kind of whisky, and one cocktail glass with tomato juice in it."

"That is correct."

Confidently Thatcher waited for a battery of questions about Edward Parry's Bloody Mary, although only one mattered—did it look like tomato juice in a cocktail glass? The answer to that was, yes.

The sergeant cleared his throat, smiled blandly and abandoned the party of the previous afternoon completely. How long had Thatcher known Arthur Foote, when was the last time he had seen him before the party, did he know whether Foote had any enemies, had he heard about the ulcer before Foote mentioned it yesterday, what did he know about Foote's drinking habits?

Thatcher explained concisely that he had known Arthur Foote professionally for at least ten years. He had done some business with him by phone in recent months, but had not seen him in person since the preceding spring. He knew nothing about his enemies or his ulcer, and could recall nothing prominent about his drinking habits, which meant that Foote was an ordinary drinker.

Sergeant Frazier punctiliously thanked Thatcher for his cooperation and took his departure, leaving Thatcher prey to a host of questions.

It was clever of the police to have spotted the business about the glasses. And cleverer still, not to press the obvious. Thatcher reviewed his testimony. The last glass of tomato juice must have been the one that had been poisoned. The police were certainly proceeding along those lines.

What had happened after Foote supplied himself with it? Stanton Carruthers and Lee Clark had gone over to meet Parry. Then there had been the huddle over the press release and the more-or-less wholesale abandonment of their drinks by the principals. Then there had been the late arrival of Vincent McCullough, followed by the eruption of Owen Abercrombie and his removal by Lee Clark and Dean Caldwell. During that swirl of activity, anything could have happened. Everybody was trying to pretend that nothing was going on. Half the room could have slipped over and tipped something into one of those drinks.

And most people had been introduced to Parry earlier, when he was rather obviously drinking Bloody Marys. A poisoner, in the natural agitation of the moment, might easily have looked at those three glasses and assumed that Foote's tomato juice was Parry's drink. Particularly if he were familiar enough with the drinking habits of the three regulars so that he would automatically disassociate them from the contents of the old-fashioned glass. In other words, a habitué of Wall Street.

Well, thought Thatcher, that didn't change the picture. Habitués were the only people present, with the sole exception of the guest of honor, who now seemed to have been cast for the role of victim.

John Thatcher was not the only one whose routine had been disturbed that afternoon. Up Wall Street, down Pine Street, along Broad Street, a whole army of serious, polite young men had been making inquiries. In their wake, they left many disturbed executives who, after a round of fruitless introspection, found themselves reaching for a phone. Not surprisingly, some of these calls were to John Thatcher.

The first caller was Bradford Withers.

"John? Somebody from the police has been in my office," he said, rather as if expecting his senior vice-president to send along the fumigator.

"Oh?"

"He wanted to ask me all sorts of questions about that damned party yesterday," the president of the Sloan went on in accusing accents.

Thatcher was soothing. "That's too bad. But I guess we had to expect it, Brad."

"Naturally, I did my best to help him," said Withers, suddenly reverting to his role of responsible citizen. "Don't know why he wanted to know who I talked with. But he did, so I told him."

"Good," said Thatcher hastily. "I'm sure he appreciated that."

"Oh yes," Withers perked up. "And he was interested in that forty-six-foot schooner. He agreed that they've really got something there."

"Fine."

Withers was not easily silenced. "But the hell of it is, John, that it turns out that fellow Foote didn't have a heart attack. They seem to think he was poisoned."

Grateful that Withers had been spared any appreciation of the horrors lurking before them, Thatcher made appropriate noises of sympathy.

"We've never had that sort of thing before," Withers continued disapprovingly. "I tell you, John, I don't like it."

Cradling the phone, Thatcher had time to reflect that many people were going to join Withers in those sentiments, before he was again summoned by the bell.

"John?"

It was Tom Robichaux, at his most conspiratorial.

"Yes, we've had the police here, too," said Thatcher, stealing his thunder.

"Oh? Did they ask you all that business about the glasses?"

Continuing his policy of ruthless shortcuts, Thatcher replied, "They seemed to think that Parry might have been the target."

"Did they ask you where you were this morning when somebody tried to shoot Parry?"

"Good God, no!"

"They asked us," said Robichaux with simple pride. "Francis was very upset."

Thatcher was perfectly prepared to concede Tom the sensation he had earned. He tried to picture Sergeant

Frazier, or one of his ilk, asking Francis Devane for an alibi. He could just manage it. All done very deferentially, with an old-fashioned respect for age and station.

"I can well believe it," he replied. "But why did they pick on you?"

"Actually it wasn't me, it was Francis. I suppose because he's been seeing so much of the whole Schuyler & Schuyler bunch lately."

"Yes," said Thatcher slowly. "I suppose he has been."

"And besides, Francis recommended a doctor to Art Foote. So he knew all about the ulcer."

"What is all this about an ulcer?"

"I didn't know about it myself, until yesterday," said Robichaux, gratified at this proper interest in the tribulations of Robichaux & Devane. "But Foote had been having all sorts of stomach trouble, and then he went to this doctor of Francis' for the tests. So, once they knew it was an ulcer, he started on that whole regimen they have. You know what it's like. God knows, there are enough of them around down here. He gave up drinking last week. Nat says he stuck to it, too, which is more than a lot of them do. Usually he just didn't have anything. And he didn't yesterday either, until he got that glass of tomato juice just at the end. Shows you what drinking that sort of thing can lead to," he concluded on a sepulchral note.

Undeterred by this tempting side issue, Thatcher wanted to know if they had seen Nat Schuyler that day.

"Oh yes, he was closeted with Francis for two hours this afternoon. Don't know what it was all about, yet. You know Nat. He likes to pretend he's organizing the landing at Leyte."

Thatcher agreed that Schuyler liked to be secretive about his plans and asked to have his sympathies conveyed to the much-put-upon Francis Devane. Before hanging up, he asked one further question.

"Tell me, Tom. What did Foote drink before the ulcer? Do you know?"

"Martinis," was the prompt answer. "And brandy after dinner."

There followed, in rapid succession, calls from Watson Kingsley (who wanted to arrange suitable attendance at Foote's funeral), Stanton Carruthers (who *understood* that the police had not been able to dig up a single motive for anyone wanting to kill Arthur Foote. "Makes you think the man must have been abnormal, doesn't it?") and Bartlett Sims (Monstrous! Monstrous! He didn't know what the Street was coming to.).

At this point, Thatcher firmly replaced the phone, told Miss Corsa he would take no more calls and swept Charlie Trinkam off to have a drink with him.

Charlie, while sympathetic, was not encouraging.

"Things have barely begun to hot up," he said as they walked half a dozen blocks north. "You can look at it one of two ways. Either somebody has decided to liquidate all of Schuyler & Schuyler—and you wonder why some broker's customer hasn't thought of *that* one before—or else somebody's making a dead set for Ed Parry. Either way it means more fun and games."

"Unless the poisoning here and the shooting in Westchester have nothing to do with each other," Thatcher advanced.

"I don't believe that, and neither do you," said Charlie briskly. "Anyway, it wouldn't make any difference if they were unconnected, so long as people think they are. What people think is what's going to make the stink."

Thatcher paused before the revolving doors to consider this. His raffish subordinate had an unerring finger for the pulse of popular conviction.

"Yes, I see what you mean. And either theory will result in an uproar down here."

"Naturally," said Charlie with unabated cheerfulness. "It means one of our little buddies is wandering around with poison and a gun and some unfinished business. For all we know, he may try knives or strangler's rope next time. Just to introduce a little variety."

Oppressed by this catalog of coming delights, Thatcher marched unseeingly into the gloomy interior. It was not until they were hailed that he realized he had been bearing down on a table occupied by Nat Schuyler and Vin McCullough.

"Join us," urged the octogenarian. "We're celebrating."

Vin McCullough pulled out a chair hospitably and grinned. "*You're* celebrating, Nat," he emphasized. "I've got too much sense."

Thatcher and Charlie Trinkam seated themselves, ordered and asked what the celebration was about.

"And," added Charlie, "why is it so ill-timed?"

If Trinkam was hoping to embarrass Nat Schuyler into the realization of a faux pas, he was reckoning without the armor acquired during eighty years of hard work as the bugbear of his more conservative colleagues.

"Naturally, we are both sincerely shocked by Arthur's death. Nor would I countenance anything in the way of a carnival downtown. That's the reason we came up here. But, still, I think that the moment deserves some recognition."

Thatcher preferred Nat Schuyler in his blunter moments. To encourage a return to simple statements, he asked a simple question.

"What have you done?"

Schuyler smiled demonically. "I have just filed a formal application to transfer Ambrose's seat to Ed Parry."

Charlie whistled appreciatively, and McCullough sighed.

Thatcher, who had not lost sight of Nat's goals for a minute, said smoothly, "I don't know anyone who capitalizes on free publicity the way you do, Nat."

"It is not just a question of publicity," said Schuyler with dignity. "After Owen Abercrombie's action, I do not see that I had any choice. Even Vin here agreed with me."

McCullough looked more discouraged than ever.

"What's the old bastard been up to now?" said Charlie, courageously voicing Thatcher's unspoken thought.

Schuyler drew himself up. Ten generations of established New York family could be heard in his voice.

"Owen had the effrontery to present himself in my office this afternoon, with a so-called petition. This petition, after reciting the known facts of the attacks on Arthur

and Ed Parry, went on to blame me for—and I quote—
'letting loose violence in the streets.' It then ordered me
to cease and desist from further attempts to disrupt our
American way of life, or be responsible to my conscience
and to my fellow citizens for the consequences of my
subversive activities."

There was an impressive pause. Schuyler allowed it to
prolong itself for the maximum dramatic effect before
continuing mildly:

"I showed this document to Ed Parry when he arrived
in the office after the assault on him this morning, and
we were in entire agreement that we should press forward
immediately."

"One can scarcely blame him," said Thatcher
reflectively.

Charlie looked accusingly at McCullough. "And you
wanted them to hold back?"

"Look, I can understand how Ed feels," Vin McCullough protested. "First, he's shot at, and then he comes
in to town to find Abercrombie and his bunch are accusing him of being responsible for violence. But I've already
lost a couple of Southern clients, and I was holding on to
a bunch of others by the skin of my teeth. If we did this
slowly, I could bring them around. But this way, it will
hit them like a bombshell, and they'll be withdrawing their
portfolios before the week is out."

His superior shed his magisterial quality.

"I know this isn't doing you any good, my boy. But we'll
make it up to you with other accounts. It will take some
time to arrange things, but I'll see that you don't lose out
in the long run. And you're wrong in your idea of tactics,
you know. I've been through a good many battles on Wall
Street, and that's always the best way to hit people—like a
bombshell."

"Oh, come off it, Nat," urged Charlie with a grin. "It
may work out as the best way when you're involved, but
mostly it's simply the way you enjoy doing things. And
speaking of bombshells, people are going to get a bellyful
of them. Have the police been around to you yet?"

"Certainly. They were with us this morning," said

Schuyler, clearly thriving on a day that had consisted of police inquiries about the murder of one of his partners, the arrival of a potential partner fresh from another attack, an exchange of broadsides with Owen Abercrombie and an extended session with an outraged Governor of the New York Stock Exchange.

Thatcher found himself hoping for a similar wellspring of vitality when he was eighty. No doubt being a professional gadfly helped. He would have to explore the matter.

"They asked a good many questions about the possibility of confusing Parry's glass with Foote's," he offered.

Schuyler was brisk. "Yes, I know. With us they concentrated on finding out how many people knew Ed drank Bloody Marys, before the reception."

"And did many?"

"Oh, almost everybody," was the unconcerned reply. "We've been having a lot of private dinners and lunches for Ed. I tried to get you for one, but you were out of town. So a good many people saw him drinking them—and he never drank anything else as a cocktail—and even more heard about it. I myself heard Abercrombie, at the Recess Club, complaining about it, as if it were some kind of added offense."

Having neatly conveyed the information that Owen Abercrombie had the requisite knowledge to be the murderer, Schuyler seemed prepared to let the subject of his interrogation by the police lapse. Thatcher wondered if he could be drawn further. Probably not. Schuyler, in spite of his surface unpredictability, always knew what he was saying long before the words left his mouth.

"Charlie and I were just discussing the interpretation that's going to be put on these two attacks. We agreed that it's a toss-up between a vendetta against your house, or a campaign against Ed Parry."

"Well, it's not the first," replied Schuyler. "You see, any program to eliminate Schuyler & Schuyler would start with me." He looked around the table with authority. No one contradicted him.

"But, it might start with the name," challenged Trinkam. "By the way, how did Ambrose die?"

Nat Schuyler's innocent blue eyes widened. Vin McCullough sputtered into his drink.

"Now, hold it . . ."

"Just a minute, Vin." Schuyler raised a monitory hand. "I suppose that was a logical question. To reassure you, Charlie, let me say that Ambrose was eighty-two and died of a heart condition that had been troubling him for fifteen years. He was treated by his own doctor on the occasion of his final attack, as well as three previous ones."

"That seems to settle that," admitted Trinkam unrepentantly.

"I should hope so. And now, I really do mean to celebrate the start of my war with Abercrombie. Why don't you all have dinner with me?"

There was a hasty review of plans for the evening. Thatcher immediately accepted. He would not dream of leaving Nat Schuyler while he was in so informative a mood. Charlie Trinkam decided to call up someone and cancel an engagement. Vin McCullough, who would have been a Banquo's ghost anyway, decided that, after one more drink, he would have to be getting home.

"Promised to help my wife," he explained. "We're moving back into the city, now that the youngest has gotten married."

"That's the trouble with all this moving," said Schuyler after McCullough had left to catch his train. "Makes people edgy. I can't understand why people sell their houses when the children go, anyway. We never did that sort of thing," he said, looking back over half a century with some difficulty. "But you can take it from me, that's why he's so impatient about our arrangements with Ed Parry. Really, he has enough to do at the office without dealing with real estate agents and getting rid of furniture. He couldn't have picked a worse time."

This transparent attempt to conceal the very real difficulties that Schuyler's plans were making for McCullough left both Thatcher and Trinkam unimpressed. Charlie spoke for both of them:

"If he thinks there's been a lot of trouble already, he's in for a shock. He hasn't seen anything yet."

6 · Who Follows in His Train?

WEDNESDAY, which in retrospect John Putnam Thatcher was to date as the beginning of The Troubles, provided convincing demonstration of John Maynard Keynes's celebrated dictum about the power of ideas. It was unfortunate, in the light of subsequent events, that so many of these ideas were wrong.

After twenty-four hours, the New York City press put two and two together, produced four, and promptly exploded.

"WALL STREET RACISTS ON KILLING SPREE," screamed one headline.

"POISON AND BULLETS TO KEEP BIZ WHITE," said another.

"WAVE OF TERROR ON THE STREET."

"It's disgraceful, absolutely disgraceful," muttered Everett Gabler.

So indignant was he that he had purchased the tabloids, which under normal circumstances he would not dream of touching, and was now flourishing them at Thatcher.

"Surely there must be some recourse against this grossly irresponsible journalism! Listen to this! 'Wall Street Racists . . .'—why, it's libelous!"

"A little too colorful, I admit," said Thatcher, examining one of the journals. It had managed to invest the murder of Arthur Foote and the attempt on Edward Parry with sexual overtones. Well, they had a specialty and they stuck to it.

"You have to expect the tabloids . . ."

"Hah!" Gabler crowed, thrusting an organ of unimpeachable conservatism at his chief. "And what about this!"

"BROKERAGE EXECUTIVE MURDERED," the headline said

chastely. Even the subheadline was restrained. *"Attempt
on Negro Candidate for Partnership,"* it read.

The article, unfortunately, did not omit the facts.

Wall Street rumors about proposals that a Negro acquire a
seat on the New York Stock Exchange were apparently
confirmed in violence Monday with the murder of Arthur
Foote, 47, a partner in the brokerage firm of Schuyler &
Schuyler.

Police are withholding comment on the case, but informed
sources report that an autopsy revealed that the victim suc-
cumbed to nicotine poison, probably administered during a
reception held by his firm for Edward Parry. Mr. Parry, 42,
is a Negro.

Although neither Mr. Parry nor the officers of Schuyler &
Schuyler were available for comment, it is understood that
the firm was expected to admit Mr. Parry to partnership,
and support his bid for a seat on the New York Stock
Exchange.

Officials of the New York Stock Exchange were not available for comment.

The collapse of Mr. Foote disrupted the reception, attended
by many financial luminaries. Barely twenty-four hours later,
it was learned that an attempt had been made on Mr. Parry's
life, as he was leaving his home in suburban Katonah.
(cont. on p. 24)

Thatcher looked up. "I don't know what else you can
expect," he remarked. "After all, Foote was murdered, it
appears. And somebody did take a potshot at Parry."

"Turn to page twenty-four," Gabler directed him sternly.

It was true. Page twenty-four (and page twenty-five,
for that matter) was excessive. In addition to the con-
tinuation of the front-page story, whose sedate tone was
perhaps attributable to the fact that its author was one of
the paper's stable of financial writers, there were: a brief
biography of Edward Parry (with photograph); a feature
article on the Board of Governors of the New York Stock
Exchange; for no apparent reason, a description of the

Harlem office of Clovis Greene Bear Spencer & Clark, including an interview with Andrew F. Trimmer, Office Manager. ("'I have no comment,' said Mr. Trimmer. Mr. Trimmer is a Negro.") There was a summary of Negro employment in the financial district, an excerpt from the Civil Rights Bill, and a glossary of technical terms. ("Seat: Membership in the New York Stock Exchange. Only Members can buy or sell securities on the Floor. Floor: The Floor of the . . .")

Unkindest cut of all, there was a list of firms "rumored" to have dispatched representatives to the ill-fated reception.

"'Rumored,'" said Gabler indignantly. "I tell you it's disgraceful. Well, I suppose I'd better get back to that Rail Summary. I don't know what Ben thinks he's doing out there in Chicago, but I'll write it up for you. I did want to bring all this to your attention."

"Thank you," said Thatcher courteously, letting his eye roam over the biography which substantiated Walter Bowman's informal information:

> . . . Mr. Parry interrupted his undergraduate career at Yale College to enlist in the Army in 1942. He was on active duty in the European Theater of Operations where he rose to the rank of major . . . awarded the Distinguished Service Cross for valor during the Battle of Anzio . . . later attached to the staff . . . Fifth Army . . . crossing of the Rhine . . . wounded . . . medical discharge. After graduating summa cum laude from Yale, where he rowed in the varsity crew of 1946, Mr. Parry attended Oxford University on a Rhodes Scholarship and achieved first class honors in politics, philosophy and economics. Mr. Parry returned to the United States after two years with the London *Economist*. In 1955 he joined his father and brothers in business in Atlanta. Mr. Parry is married to the former Gloria Cole of Philadelphia and has two children, a son Robert and a daughter Louise.

"Yes," continued Thatcher, "it's all very unfortunate." But Gabler was not settling for anything so tepid.

"Unfortunate!" He brooded darkly for a moment. "I tell you it's inflammatory."

He disappeared before Thatcher could inquire who was going to be inflamed. He was soon to be enlightened.

Miss Corsa arrived within five minutes, technically on time, but far off her own track record. Before she had doffed her raincoat, she too presented Thatcher with an exceptionally large bundle of newspapers.

"Mr. Thatcher, have you . . . ?"

"Yes, I have seen them," he replied gently. Then, because he was only human, he added:

"A little later than usual today, eh, Miss Corsa?"

"My mother didn't want me to come to work," she replied, withdrawing.

For a moment, Thatcher considered this non sequitur. Miss Corsa's large family rarely figured in her conversation. Presumably, then, her comment had been in the nature of an explanation.

"Why," he asked, going to the door to find her composedly settled at her desk, "why didn't your mother want you to come to work?"

Surprised, she looked up. "Why, because of all this trouble. That's why I'm late. I missed my transfer." She turned to the file, in effect dismissing him. If John Putnam Thatcher had time to waste, Rose Theresa Corsa did not.

He retreated into his own office.

"Inflammatory," Everett Gabler had said. "Trouble," echoed a Mrs. Corsa, somewhere in Queens.

"Hmm," said John Putnam Thatcher.

He was not wrong. Mrs. Corsa and Everett Gabler were but straws in a mighty wind. At one minute after nine, his telephone rang.

"Have you seen . . . ?"

"Yes," said Thatcher.

What unfortunate chance had willed that Bradford Withers should choose today, of all days, for prompt arrival at his desk, and for one of his rare perusals of the morning papers?

Thatcher feared deeply that he and the staff were in for one of Withers' captain-on-the-bridge days.

"Damn the Americas Cup," he said to himself.

"Don't like the way the clouds are gathering," said

Withers. "Do you think we should send our people home early today?"

"Good God, Brad!" Thatcher exclaimed.

"These things," Withers said simply, "can turn ugly. We have to think of the women and children!"

With commendable self-control, Thatcher did not reply directly. Instead he pleaded an urgent meeting.

But no sooner was the phone down, than Miss Corsa buzzed again.

"Mrs. Carlson," she announced.

His daughter sounded breathless. "Daddy, are you all right? Why don't you come out and stay . . . ?"

"Laura, what on earth are you talking about?" her fond parent demanded.

"The race riots, of course. Everybody's talking about them. I'm worried sick. . . ."

In this context, "everybody" referred to the Connecticut community where Laura, her doctor husband, and her three—no, four children—resided.

"As I recall," Thatcher observed mildly, "your immediate circle consists almost exclusively of small children and their attendants."

Like her mother, before her, Laura could utilize the pause to communicate impatience. Then she said, "Margo Hillyer called—her husband's at Clovis Greene, you know —and she said . . ."

In the subsequent three minutes, John Thatcher did not form a high opinion of Mrs. Hillyer. Mr. Hillyer, he was fair-mindedly inclined to dismiss because the evidence was so circumstantial. After hearing Laura out, assuring her that he was in no immediate danger, he rang off, prepared to settle down to a memorandum from the Research Department touting Slotkin Corp., an exceedingly dubious operation that purported to see fortunes to be made in secondary oil recovery despite their almost endearing lack of capital.

He had just penciled a question about Slotkin's suspicious ingenuity in the matter of depreciation allowances when the telephone again interrupted him. This time it was Tom Robichaux.

"If you've called to ask me if I've seen the papers," Thatcher began.

"The papers?" Robichaux asked vaguely. "Why should I . . . oh, you mean the excitement about Parry. It will all blow over. Always does."

But, since Thatcher had introduced the topic, Robichaux cast about for something to add. "Ran into Glover this morning. He tells me that Owen Abercrombie has gone crazy."

"How could he tell?" asked Thatcher with genuine interest.

"Says he's talking about a Wall Street Defense Council," said Robichaux. "With rifles. You remember they had to take his uncle Basil off the Floor in a straitjacket, in '29?"

"I didn't," said Thatcher, considerably entertained.

"Bad blood," Robichaux said. "Francis says that this whole thing is a tempest in a teapot. No reason to anticipate violence."

Normally, Robichaux conveyed his partner's more elevated pronouncements uncritically. But today, perhaps still smarting from having been dragooned into the mourning party, he added a comment of his own.

"Just between you and me, John, I don't think that's the line to take after one murder and one near-miss. But that's Francis' business."

His erratic interest in the subject exhausted, Robichaux reverted to his reason for calling. He had, it developed, a really interesting situation to describe to Thatcher. If he was free for lunch one day this week . . . ?

"What about today?" Thatcher replied.

"Today?" Robichaux was taken aback, as well he might be, since Thatcher normally resisted such bait. "Well, let's see . . . yes, fine, fine. At the Club?"

Only by lunching with Tom Robichaux, Thatcher was convinced, did he have any chance to escape a luncheon conversation centering on Wall street's emerging racial problems.

That, instead, he was subjected first to a disquisition on Bravura Chemicals ("Synthetic citric acid, John. Don't ask me why, but it's big."), then to one on the current Mrs.

Robichaux ("Celestine is sailing someplace with that Greek. Don't really like it, but there you are!") was a small price to pay, he reflected two hours later. It turned out, in fact, to be too small.

"Have you seen the statement the Board just issued?"

Lee Clark, pausing by their table, at least did not ask if they had read the morning papers.

"No," said Thatcher, while Robichaux leaned back, looking unutterably bored.

"A masterpiece," said Clark with a sour smile. "Be sure to read it." He stepped closer to let two men move past.

"I think you're wrong," one of them said angrily. "We could be another Bedford-Stuyvesant. I say that Nat should be . . ."

"Now hold it, Fred," his companion interjected.

As they passed beyond earshot, Lee Clark prepared to follow.

"I can tell you what I think should be done with Nat Schuyler," he said in an undertone.

They watched him disappear into the lounge.

"Letting things get him down," Robichaux commented without approval. He was a firm believer in never letting anything get him down. "Always a mistake to take your troubles to lunch. Now, about Bravura, John."

"I'm inclined to think that Bravura may be one of your troubles, Tom."

They were still disputing the point when they strolled into the lounge ten minutes later. It was unusually crowded. Instead of lunching, then hurrying on about business, Wall Street was sticking together today.

"Have you heard . . . ?"

"Did you see . . . ?"

"You heard about Owen . . . ?"

Somebody, seeking electronic solace, idly switched on the corner television set. Moodily, he stood watching the news. Suddenly, to nobody in particular, he said, "Look at this!"

Like so many Boy Scouts, they crowded around.

"Terrible reception," said Robichaux.

"Sshh!"

The reception, though terrible, was adequate to reveal a hysterical-looking youth draped in earphones and microphones, interrogating a portly, conservatively attired Negro.

". . . Richard Simpson, the well-known novelist."

Mr. Simpson lowered his eyelids briefly.

"And what is the purpose of cash, Mr. Simpson?"

"Cash, cash? Is this one of those quiz programs my wife is always watching?" asked somebody near Thatcher.

"Sshh!"

Mr. Simpson, noted for his simpleminded and successful novels about an expatriate in Paris and his beautiful relationship with a sylphlike busboy, had the resonant voice of an actor, and a firm grasp on the microphone thrust before him.

"The Colored Association of Share Holders," he said, enunciating distinctly.

"Oh my God!"

It was a cry from somebody's heart.

". . . or CASH," Simpson continued, "has been formed today to investigate and combat the gross inequities confronting the Negro in Wall Street."

From around John Thatcher arose a group keening.

"Tell me, Mr. Simpson, how does CASH propose to buck Wall Street?" the young man asked throbbingly.

"Who is that damned fool?" Fenster O'Dowd asked the world. "I've a good mind to call Bill and tell him . . ."

"Sshh!"

". . . using whatever means," Mr. Simpson declaimed. He paused, noted that the hysterical young man was framing another question, and pushed on. "The evidence that the New York Stock Exchange intends to remain lily white has been a shock to thousands upon thousands of patriotic American stockholders who happen to be colored."

Whatever his reception in the saloons on Third Avenue, Richard Simpson could not have asked for a more attentive audience than that standing with Thatcher and Robichaux.

"What are you going to do?" the reporter asked.

Mr. Simpson gave him a look suggesting that he shared Fenster O'Dowd's opinion, and said:

"We have not yet determined what methods are appropriate to counter the racist forces that are denying Edward Parry a seat on the New York Stock Exchange—solely and exclusively because of his color. We do not have our complete strategy mapped out in the face of the kind of anti-Negro forces that were responsible for the death of Arthur Foote, one of the great white men who was a consistent friend to the Negro stockholder. . . ."

He bowed his head. His rich voice was so moving that Thatcher distinctly heard someone murmur brokenly, "Poor old Art!"

"*But,*" Simpson continued martially, "I can promise you that America's Negro stockholders will present a dramatic and moving protest. Including, among our other weapons" —he broke off, staring piercingly into the camera—"including a March on Wall Street!"

"Thank *you*, Mr. Simpson. Now our High-Sky Patrol . . . crackle, crackle . . . an accident on the Long Island Expressway . . ."

At the Club, to use a technical term, all hell broke loose.

7 · Glorious Things of Thee Are Spoken

As MIGHT have been anticipated, Richard Simpson's ominous words, "A March on Wall Street," swiftly relegated the murder of Arthur Foote and the attack on Edward Parry to the mists of ancient history. A number of prominent financiers forgot their newly formed habit of carefully inspecting all nutriment served south of City Hall; in the same area the sales of the collected works of Richard Simpson quadrupled. The financial community, in an orgy of self-absorption, abandoned itself to emotional reactions, ranging from stark bewilderment through cold fury to mindless frenzy. The mighty institutions of lower Manhattan, galvanized by the tocsins of total war and mindful of extensive casualties yet to come, could no longer respond to the tragedy of individual death.

Or perhaps it was even simpler. The targets of Richard Simpson's crusade were the most powerful stockbrokers, the most influential bankers, the most important lawyers in the world. Daily they made decisions that shaped the destinies of men and nations. Naturally, they disliked feeling helpless in the grip of forces bigger than they were. Wall Street was enraged—and surprised—to discover that there were bigger forces. And so, voices were raised with more heat than had been evoked since the nation went off the Gold Standard, and men in expensive tailoring raged with unwonted vigor.

At the heart of the vortex around which these disturbances eddied, was the New York Stock Exchange. The Exchange is a complex body; its work is performed by eleven hundred employees and its ruling organ, the Board of Governors, consists of thirty-three men, twenty-nine representing the individuals and firms which are members of the Exchange, three functioning as nominal representatives of the public, and the President of the Exchange. The President is the Exchange's executive head; his main function is to steer an uneasy course past the demands of the Staff, periodically erupting with policies of its own development, the members mired in internecine politics and time-hardened customs of the trade, and the Board. The President breaks into print in two ways—in the glossy brochures published by the Exchange that cozily remind everyone that stockholders are just ordinary people, and in the public press during his frequent joustings with the Securities and Exchange Commission. The Governors representing the public emerge only when some more-than-ordinarily selfless statement is required. The remaining Governors try to stay on top of everybody else. It is rare indeed that any unanimity can be achieved among these diverse elements. But the specter of Richard Simpson succeeded in awaking several thousand people to a common need.

They wanted somebody else to hold the baby.

The Exchange was opting for a neutrality so rigid that it would justify ignorance of the passions roiling through the Street. In high places telephones began to ring and rolling phrases echoed through the marble halls of the mighty.

"If the financial community were to form a small, independent committee to . . . er . . . ensure that fairness and scrupulous disinterest will be the order of the day, it would be of inestimable assistance to the Exchange," said one of its spokesmen.

"The Exchange and the rest of the community must not be directly involved," said a kindred spirit. "Now a committee could . . . er . . . focus the attention of these dissident elements and allow the rest of us to continue with our work."

A more outspoken representative eschewed nobility for frank speaking. "God knows *we* can't talk to these people. And somebody has to. Now, if one of *your* partners were to be on this committee. . . ."

It says much for the insularity of Wall Street that by three o'clock the next day it had convinced itself that a committee composed of an outstanding broker, lawyer and banker, all Wall Street denizens, would commend itself to the rest of the world as fair-minded, independent and impartial. Absolutely impartial.

The Committee of Three had as its members Hugh Waymark, Stanton Carruthers and John Putnam Thatcher.

The three defenders of Wall Street had their first meeting in Stanton Carruthers' office, where they eyed each other resentfully.

Carruthers, who had spent a lifetime explaining to clients that he could scarcely be expected to act in the absence of specific instructions, felt the situation most keenly.

"I'll be damned if I can see what we're supposed to do," he said, in effect repeating the statement he had made to the assembled partners of his firm when he had been presented with their ultimatum.

Hugh Waymark hitched himself forward helpfully. While every bit as annoyed as his colleagues at being singled out by a malign fate, he was the only one to cherish any illusion that decisive action might yet cut away the difficulties and reduce his world to that satisfying condition of unchallenged somnolence from which it had been so rudely awakened.

"The way I see it, Stan, they want us to talk some sense into this Simpson. After all, what good would a March on Wall Street do? Has he asked himself that?"

"Pah!"

Even Thatcher was surprised at the noise forced from his lips by sheer irritation. "The buck has been passed to us, that's what. And how are we supposed to talk sense anyway? Do they expect us to hire billboards and sell the world on the proposition that Arthur Foote died of old age, and nobody has noticed Parry's color?"

Waymark looked hurt, but before he could launch a protest, Carruthers intervened:

"Nobody cares about Arthur Foote anymore," he said, sternly facing facts. "And, as for the rest of it, John is right. We're not supposed to do anything. We wait for something to happen. Then everybody blames us. That keeps the principals in the clear."

Fact facing never has a wide appeal. Hugh Waymark was still grumbling when the Committee of Three prepared to adjourn *sine die*, filled with high purpose and no program. In many ways a comfortable state of affairs . . . certainly more comfortable than what was coming.

There was a muted buzz from the phone and Stanton Carruthers held up a hand. "Would you mind waiting a moment? I told my girl not to put through anything unless it concerned our meeting."

Obediently Waymark and Thatcher halted their progress to the door. Carruthers swiveled around to reach the receiver. His subsequent comments, consisting almost entirely of a series of alarmed grunts punctuated with exclamations of surprise, brought no enlightenment to his audience, but Hugh Waymark glanced up frowningly at his conclusion.

"All right, all right. We'll come right over. Yes, we'll do what we can, but it sounds too late for talking."

Carruthers swung around and up in one urgent movement. He explained tensely:

"That was Clovis Greene. They say they've got a race riot over there. The trouble's down on the Street, and it started over an hour ago. We'd better hurry."

Such was the power of the vision created by these words, that they were down on the street without further questioning.

Stanton Carruthers' law firm maintained its cramped old-fashioned offices on Rector Street. Clovis Greene stretched in expansive grandeur over four floors at the corner of William Street and Wall Street, ten minutes away. Without a word the three trotted toward Broadway. Passing Trinity Church, its gallant spire dwarfed by surrounding colossi, they peered anxiously ahead toward their destination. As usual the vista was obliterated by a solid wave of humanity.

"I don't see any squad cars," muttered Waymark. "I hope to God the police have got things under control."

"Well, if they haven't, I don't see precisely what we are expected to accomplish," said Thatcher shortly.

For half a block, there was depressed silence. Then:

"The main thing is to keep it from spreading," said Waymark, mindful of his own brokerage house a scant three blocks from the disturbance.

Carruthers was more public spirited. "There will have to be some statements made. That's our job—to strike a calming note."

But Waymark, back in the days of his glory as a staff colonel, was viewing the terrain with a keen military eye.

"Good thing there isn't much glass frontage down here. Street fighting won't do much damage. The Chase will just have to take its chances, of course. And you can always raise barricades with cobblestones," he added breathlessly. The pace set by his two companions was incompatible with his figure, no longer what it had been in 1944.

"Are you suggesting that we dig up the asphalt with our bare fingernails?" Thatcher demanded acidly. He was becoming conscious of the spectacle they presented. Waymark's rotundity was balanced by Carruthers' lean length, now stretched forward in hawklike flight. They sped past the Stock Exchange at a lope. The three musketeers, thought Thatcher dispiritedly. And what wouldn't he give for a D'Artagnan, full of youth and fire, prepared to undertake all sorts of ill-advised actions! Carried away by this conceit, he had no difficulty in casting Waymark as Porthos. Carruthers, he supposed, was Aramis. That left him as Athos. Not, he concluded sourly, a congenial role.

Maybe he needed an assistant on this job . . . say, Ken Nicolls. No, he decided reluctantly. The whole point of the Committee was that it should operate personally, borrowing luster and commanding respect by virtue of its distinguished participants. Another objection lay in visualizing D'Artagnan spending his evenings setting up a cooperative nursery in Brooklyn Heights.

Carruthers, leading by a nose, came to a sudden halt at the Seventh Avenue IRT station with an abruptness that brought his two colleagues cannoning into him.

"Where is it?" he asked blankly.

"We'll have to look for it," said Waymark, nothing daunted.

"I thought race riots proclaimed themselves," Thatcher objected.

At this moment there was a slight gap in the scurrying crowds. Carruthers pointed into it.

"Do you think," he asked dubiously, "that *that* can be what they called about?"

He was pointing to a small band of weedy pickets parading before an entrance on William Street with assorted placards. They were treading their stately measure under the disenchanted gaze of three policemen.

"For God's sake! Do you mean this is all there is?" protested Waymark, making no attempt to disguise his disappointment. It was as if Kitchener had fetched up at Khartoum only to find everybody having a friendly hand of five-card stud.

Thatcher maintained a disapproving silence for so long that his colleagues looked at him. He was staring at the placards.

"Tell me," he said, "does it seem to you that these pickets are a long way from unity?"

The passing throng paid no attention either to the pickets or to the gimlet-eyed trio which now advanced to close quarters and soberly read each message as it revolved before them. Some people were rushing down into the bowels of the subway. Others were rushing up. Messenger boys from the printers were everywhere, delivering hot proofs of prospectuses, briefs and bank letters. A steady persistent trickle made its way to the small Roman Catholic chapel on Pine Street which provides support and solace for the faithful in the very shadow of Mammon.

Jostled and buffeted, the three musketeers remained motionless, enthralled by their reading. The first sign said that Clovis Greene was racially biased, while the second said that Schuyler & Schuyler were troublemakers. A third, rather confusingly, maintained that "Colored operated is not colored owned," while a fourth demanded simply: "Down with the Stock Exchange." An even more alien note was introduced by a lone theological student carrying a banner proclaiming: "White Turret Restaurant is Unfair."

Thatcher, rousing himself from bemusement, voiced a problem: "Why are they picketing Schuyler & Schuyler here?"

"Didn't you know? They're in this building, too."

"Fine. That's all we need. It makes one thing certain. If there's going to be any fighting, it is likely to be internal warfare among the pickets."

Waymark was eyeing a youth in a turtleneck sweater and beard. "They look like pacifists to me. Well, I suppose we ought to go up and see Clovis Greene."

"I'd like to see them," said Carruthers grimly. "There's work waiting for me on my desk. What do they think they're doing, pushing the panic button like this?"

"We may have to do more than give Clovis Greene a piece of our mind," remarked Thatcher, nodding at a car that was inching along the street amidst the pedestrian traffic. In the windshield appeared the grim legend: Press.

"Oh, for God's sake!"

"With luck, we have two or three minutes clear," said Thatcher, manfully overcoming the temptation to dive down into the IRT, shoot up to Grand Central and entrain for distant places.

Carruthers was brisk. "You're right. We'd better tell these pickets to address their complaints to us. I'll promise to interview the interested parties and bring them an answer."

Waymark, one eye on the car which now hovered by a truck engineering withdrawal from the curb, threw himself into the fray. "We've got to work fast."

Achieving something of their former urgency, the three marched over and assumed a commanding position. Carruthers raised a courtroom voice to gain attention and introduced the Committee, primarily for the benefit of the suddenly alert police. With an easy stream of professional fluency, he said that they understood the pickets were protesting certain actions on the part of Schuyler & Schuyler and of Clovis Greene, that the Committee would interview these firms and be back shortly with statements as to their contemplated actions. Masterfully silencing all attempts to break into speech and usurp any portion of his precious time, he urged the pickets to continue the responsible citizenship already demonstrated by their courageous, forthright and nonviolent conduct.

A speech embracing a diversity of activities and desires is necessarily generalized, but Thatcher gave Carruthers full marks for conveying the impression that the pickets were regarded seriously and that action was being taken.

The Committee then plunged into the building, timing their entrance so nicely that the closing of the glass door coincided with the descent of a horde of journalists onto the scene.

At the elevator, Carruthers paused in indecision. "Which first?"

"Schuyler & Schuyler, I think," Thatcher replied. "Most

of those pickets could be quieted by a statement from Parry. We might be able to get one."

"But what about the Abercrombie boys down there?"

"Nothing will quiet them. They're looking for trouble."

On the twenty-sixth floor, Schuyler & Schuyler was going about its business with a commendable absence of hysteria. Indeed, when they were ushered into Nat Schuyler's office, it was to disrupt a business conference between him and Vin McCullough.

"Come in, come in. Don't mind Vin. I'm snowed under at the moment, and I'm pushing all of poor Arthur's accounts onto him. Between Ambrose's accounts and Parry's application, I don't have a minute to spare."

He smiled up at them genially without mentioning the very substantial accounts in his own name. It was these accounts which had always supported Nat Schuyler's unwavering domination of his firm.

"I heard you three had been formed into some sort of committee. Don't understand what it's all about exactly, but we'll be glad to do anything we can for you."

Thatcher was in no mood to encourage witticisms on the subject of the Committee's mission.

"Tell me, Nat," he said, "do you realize that there are about twenty pickets parading up and down in front of this building?"

Guileless blue eyes turned to him. "Why, yes," said Schuyler thoughtfully, "yes, I believe someone did say something about it."

"And that Clovis Greene has whipped itself into a frenzy on the subject?" Thatcher pressed.

"Now that was what they were saying. That Clovis Greene was calling in the police." Schuyler beamed blandly at the room. "Very imprudent of them, I feel."

Carruthers brought his jaws together with an audible click, while Thatcher stared frostily at the man behind the desk. It was all too clear what was happening. Clovis Greene was being tempted to all sorts of rash, hasty reactions to their present dilemma—and, alas, succumbing to that temptation. Once they had been given ample opportunity to put themselves hopelessly in the wrong, Nat

Schuyler would waft himself downstairs and appear on the scene as a white-haired harbinger of peace and moderation.

Nor was any of this playacting aimed at those youthful pickets. Old Schuyler hadn't lost sight of the ball for one single second. It was the pulse of the financial community that he was following with his stethoscopic shrewdness. Given enough publicity, by tomorrow morning a large number of people on the Street would be feeling that Nat Schuyler was the voice of sweet reason. Because the people on the Street, like the residents of Katonah, were basically not interested in Ed Parry's problems; they were interested in their own. And how could you get on with business, if crackpots like Owen Abercrombie wanted you to shoulder a rifle, or oddballs like Clovis Greene tried to call out the National Guard because a couple of students were walking up and down the sidewalk?

At this point in Thatcher's meditations, the door opened and a familiar figure entered. It was young Dean Caldwell.

"Sorry, Nat. I didn't realize that you had people here."

But he was too consumed with the importance of his own activities to make more than a token apology. He continued without pause:

"Do you realize that the people have refused to do anything about what's going on outside? They say as long as the situation is orderly, they won't interfere. Christ! Why don't they admit they don't have the guts to do anything!"

"I wasn't aware that we'd asked them to do anything."

An ugly red tide suffused Caldwell's face. "Clovis Green has!" he snapped. "Lee Clark says he's going to take it right up to the Commissioner."

"Oh?"

Caldwell took several angry, stamping steps. "That's not the way to handle this sort of thing!" Suddenly he raised his eyes and looked directly at Schuyler. "You may as well know. I called Abercrombie, so he could send a couple of his own pickets over. That trash downstairs won't make any trouble, if they know there's someone willing to take them on."

Did Caldwell realize that he was playing Schuyler's game? Thatcher thought not. But a healthy instinct of self-preservation would have rung an alarm at Schuyler's next words.

"Did you, now? That was very thoughtful of you, my boy," he said, his voice silkier by the second. "Now that you've assured our personal safety, was there anything else?"

Caldwell stood his ground, but it was at Vin McCullough that he looked. "I've got those reports on the holdings in Art's accounts that you wanted. You can look at them now."

"I don't have time now. You'd better send them along to my office," replied McCullough, pointedly disassociating himself from the departing chief analyst.

Schuyler was amused by the exchange. "You'll have to look at those reports some time, Vin. And he'll make you go to him. So he can sound out your loyalties."

"He makes me sick," said McCullough suddenly.

"Yes. An object lesson to us all. But a very good analyst. The reports will make nice reading."

McCullough relaxed. "They'd better. I got three more cancellations from clients in Biloxi this morning."

"Don't worry," said Thatcher dryly. "I can scarcely believe that there isn't a lot of business heading toward Schuyler & Schuyler. I can almost hear it pattering down from Clovis Greene."

Vin McCullough grinned. He was hardened to Nat Schuyler's tactics but he enjoyed watching their effect on outsiders.

"But those will be Parry's accounts," he said.

"And it is about Ed Parry that we wanted to speak to you. Is he here by the way?"

"No." Nat Schuyler shook his head. "Do you want to see him?"

"Yes. We"—and Thatcher included the rest of the committee in a sweep of his hand—"would like to get a statement from him, urging calm and forbearance on the public scene."

"I think we can do better than that," replied Schuyler, who obviously had the whole statement already planned. "Mind you, I don't know whether Ed will agree to this. But you could suggest that he say he has every confidence in the integrity and fairness of the Stock Exchange. We filed our application yesterday. In the normal course of events, it will be reviewed by the Department of Membership Firms and then by the Board of Governors. Fortunately, Ed more than meets the personal and financial qualifications involved. That should make approval of the application a certainty, unless he has misjudged the spirit guiding the Exchange. I think he would be willing to say publicly that an imputation of such gross bias and inequality should not be made until the Exchange has had an opportunity to conduct its normal clearance activities."

Thatcher drew a breath.

"That will do nicely," he said firmly. "What you're saying is that all hell will break loose if they don't give him his seat. Our mission seems to be to keep things calm until the Exchange makes its decision. I am not prepared to cross any additional bridges. Right?"

Carruthers and Waymark indicated their approval, and an appointment was finally made for a meeting with Parry on Monday morning. On their way out Schuyler smiled diabolically and asked them to convey his regards to Lee Clark if they were stopping by at Clovis Greene.

"How did he know we were going upstairs?" asked Waymark resentfully.

"Because he's an old devil," said Carruthers, punching the button for the thirty-second floor. "And I am very glad I'm in the law business. We steal our clients from each other much more quietly."

Clovis Greene had the grace to be slightly abashed when its sins were firmly pointed out.

"I'm sorry if they made it sound like a riot, Stanton," said Lee Clark. "We're all on edge. The fact is, we really do have a near riot in our Harlem office. And when the pickets started to show up here we thought it was going to be the same thing all over."

Carruthers had not spent years cross-examining hostile witnesses on disputed wills for nothing.

"Exactly what is going on at the Harlem office?" he demanded.

"The police have got fifteen men there, and I can tell you that they're not putting out that kind of man power lightly. There's a mob in the street that's forced them to reroute traffic, the pickets are inside the office and there's been trouble with the help. And if that isn't enough, there's a line around the block of customers waiting to close their accounts." He ran a hand through his hair and suddenly looked very tired. "I don't know how they expect us to close all their accounts if they frighten the help away."

Thatcher found himself silently thanking heaven that the Committee's geographical jurisdiction might reasonably be held to end at Park Row.

"That is very unfortunate," he said as sympathetically as he could. He knew perfectly well that Lee Clark was looking old and tired because he saw his position at Clovis Greene going down the drain. "We all want to prevent an outbreak of that sort here. Particularly the line of customers withdrawing. Now, are you prepared to join Schuyler & Schuyler in a plea for peace in the streets?"

"Sure, sure." Clark waved his hand vaguely. "You might also say that we have no racial bias. We just don't happen to know any Negro millionaires we can pull out of our pocket."

Thatcher firmly reminded himself that he had already decided not being Owen Abercrombie was enough. Nevertheless the Committee would be wise to expect nothing better than self-pity from Lee Clark in the trying days ahead. He said as much as they drafted hasty bromides on the downward plunge.

"That's that," said Carruthers with satisfaction. "Now all we have to do is read this to those pickets outside. Then I can get back to work."

But outside was no longer what it had been. From no-where had come a fleet of trucks outrigged with booms at the end of which perched large cameras and small men. Yards and yards of cable festooned the street, while young men with deep, unctuous voices roamed up and down, microphone in hand.

"And this," said one of them in an oily voice of friendly doom, "is Miss Shirley Glauber from Brooklyn College. Tell our viewers, Shirley, why you have come here to picket Clovis Greene."

Miss Glauber tossed her pony tail and proceeded to harangue the network's listeners in tones destined to carry her far in the League of Women Voters.

Out of the corner of his eye, Thatcher saw two micro-phones heading for his nose. Well, he thought bitterly, at least he was not wearing furry headgear for his debut on nationwide television.

8 · Tidings from Afar

WHILE *Sturm und Drang* raged on Wall Street, peace and serenity reigned in Katonah, Westchester. That, of course, is why people live there. But Ed Parry, after an hour with the newspapers and mail, looked on his sunlit lawns with patent dissatisfaction. He had just come in from the hall phone.

"That was the office calling," he explained to his wife. "Nat's bringing Thatcher up here. They're on the way."

"We could ask them to stay to lunch."

"Yes." Parry shifted restlessly. Then he burst out: "It doesn't seem right. Maybe I should have insisted on going in to meet them."

"Oh, Ed!"

Then suddenly Gloria Parry started to laugh.

Her husband looked up in hurt bewilderment.

"What have I said that's so funny?"

She shook her head. "It's not what you're saying, it's what you're feeling. For forty-two years you've been feeling guilty because you haven't suffered with the problems of most Negroes. You've felt like a draft-dodger because money has protected you from most of the nastiness . . . finding a job, or moving into a garden apartment, or getting a decent education for your children. Now somebody's tried to poison you, you've been shot at, and eggs have been thrown at you. And what do you do? Do you stop feeling guilty?" She answered her own question by another gurgle of mirth. "Not a bit of it. You just shift your ground and start feeling guilty because you aren't suffering the tribulations of all the other brokers down on Wall Street. You are! Admit it!"

"It's not exactly that," he hedged. "It's just that I can't help realizing what I've stirred up. After all, I've been in the banking business all my life. I know what's going on at places like Clovis Greene. And all this doesn't help." He flicked a derisive finger at the front page featuring beatnik pickets and Richard Simpson outlining plans for his great March. "And then . . ." he halted uncertainly.

"And then?" challenged Gloria.

"And then I wonder what good it's doing. After all, there aren't thousands of Negroes waiting to buy seats on the Exchange."

"There you go again. Of course there aren't. But you know as well as I do that you can crack an institution much faster from the top than the bottom. It will make a big difference downtown if there's a prominent Negro at the top—a difference in hiring secretaries and customer's men and research analysts. And, Ed, even you can't deny that this has dramatized the question of potential Negro investment."

"I suppose so," he said gloomily. "But at the price of bringing discomfort to a lot of people."

Gloria's tone grew brisker. "There's always discomfort when you change things. Particularly to the people who don't want a change. And even to innocent bystanders. But so long as it's nothing worse than discomfort, the job you're doing is worth it. And, I hope you aren't wasting any of this sympathy on Nat Schuyler."

Suddenly her husband grinned. "No, I haven't lost my mind completely. He's having a grand time, and he knew exactly what he was taking on. The whole thing was his idea, and he's going to make a lot of money out of it." The momentary gaiety faded from his voice. "That seems like a hell of a motive for something like this."

"It's the motive for most financial moves," said Gloria dryly.

"You don't like Nat, do you?"

"It's not a question of liking him. I feel profoundly grateful to him."

"How's that?"

"He's the only thing that makes it all possible. You couldn't stand this if you had to deal with a burning zealot. You'd have to worry about him all the time. But with Nat, you're completely safe. If they dynamite Schuyler & Schuyler tomorrow, Nat will be dug out of the shambles chortling over how he can use the bombing in his next maneuver."

"I don't have to worry about anybody at Schuyler & Schuyler. Even Vin McCullough is going to make a pretty penny out of this, too, in the long run."

"And Dean Caldwell?" asked Gloria slyly.

Her husband frowned. "I may be soft," he replied, "but I'm not crazy. Dean Caldwell can take care of himself!"

"Good! Believe it or not, so can the Governors of the New York Stock Exchange. If you could only realize that they can live through the experience of having to make a lot of statements, and even walk through a picket line, you'd be much more comfortable about the whole thing."

Not for the first time, Ed Parry realized that his wife's armor was thicker than his. Gloria's father had been one of the first Negroes to be elevated to the federal bench—but she had grown up the daughter of a struggling colored lawyer without the protection of a healthy bank balance. The rewards that had come into the Cole family's life had come late enough to be the rewards of endeavor. Gloria Cole Parry bore no burden of guilt, and she had considerable experience with racial problems which her husband had been spared.

"I don't know that I have any right to be comfortable," he concluded glumly. "And I suppose I'm not being truthful with myself, or I'd admit that one of the things that bothers me is the loss of our privacy. I hate the idea of being a professional Negro man of distinction. For years I've gone out of my way not to have articles in the magazines or let myself be exploited by the State Department—and now, this!"

Gloria grinned. "Yes, there's been no nonsense about sticking your toe in to get the feel of the water. You dived in all the way."

She smiled at him with great affection.

Almost grudgingly, he started to return her smile.

"Yes. And I know what you're thinking—even if you don't say it. If I don't have the right to be comfortable, what makes me think I've got the right to be private? And if I get that seat, I will be doing some good."

"When," corrected Gloria firmly.

The smile broadened. "*When* I get that seat," he agreed. "And for somebody who was lukewarm about this whole affair, you certainly are turning into an activist."

"Oh, you'll see me marching with a banner yet."

She did not bother to explain that her motive for activism was the support and comfort of Ed Parry. That would probably make him feel guilty, too. Instead she nodded toward the window overlooking the drive. "That must be your visitors."

Two minutes later and Thatcher was being introduced to his hostess. Ed Parry started off by apologizing for making them drive to Katonah.

"It's the Police Commissioner," he explained. "There was a little trouble Friday night. He wants to give me an escort when I go into the city."

Everybody contemplated the spectacle of a potential member of the Exchange moving through New York under heavy police guard.

"You didn't go into any details about the trouble, Ed,

when you called," said Nat Schuyler bluntly. "Was it another shooting?"

No, it hadn't been anything like that. There had been a crowd of hecklers waiting for his taxi when he got to Grand Central. There had been shoving and a few rotten eggs thrown. The police had broken it up.

"Under the circumstances," concluded Parry mildly, "it seemed best to minimize the number of my visits to the city. For everybody's sake."

Thatcher was heartened by this display of self-control. He realized that the Committee, Wall Street and New York could congratulate themselves that they were dealing with sober, responsible adults, not fire-eating young lunatics. Like Gloria Parry, he was beginning to be profoundly thankful that Nat Schuyler, as prime mover of this drama, was so *dégagé* in his motives. Giving partial expression to these thoughts, he said:

"That encourages me to feel that you'll agree to a suggestion made by Mr. Schuyler. It would involve asking the Negro community to suspend judgment until the Exchange has had an opportunity to complete its normal review of your application for membership."

Now that the participants of the meeting were getting down to business, Gloria Parry made an excuse and started to rise.

"No, Gloria, don't go." Her husband waved her back and turned to the others. "This concerns my wife as much as it concerns me. I'd like to have her consider this, too."

The consideration turned out to be protracted, no doubt due to the alarming range of connotations that can be quickened into life by any single sentence in the English language. Happily the group was as one in deploring violence, but . . .

He was the last man in the world to condone mob rule, said Nat Schuyler blandly, but it was every American's God-given right to change stockbrokers. Transferring an account from Clovis Greene to Schuyler & Schuyler did not constitute a threat to the community. Particularly if the customer were moved by certain aspects of the whole man. . . .

It must be clearly understood that the Exchange is as far above a bribe as a threat, John Putnam Thatcher found himself saying. Its rarefied deliberations would pursue their stately course unswayed by both abstention from violence and the hideous specter of mobs chanting at the window. There could be no suggestion of a bargain with the Negro community.

The Parrys, not to be outdone, also had difficulties. They would willingly withhold judgment on the Exchange until presented with irrefutable proof of racial bias. In return, the Parry application must be treated as the normal exercise of a millionaire prerogative. Ed Parry was not approaching the New York Stock Exchange by the back door, hat in hand, humbly asking for a favor. And while he was prepared to plead for peace, he would countenance no suggestion that there had been any Negro violence.

"Because there hasn't been any," he said firmly. "Look at what has actually happened. Aside from a few pickets and a few speeches, there has been only one kind of violence."

"Exactly," chimed in Nat Schuyler. "A series of murderous attacks on Art Foote and on Ed. Not to mention a little egg-throwing."

Parry intervened. "The egg-throwing is a natural result of the situation, Nat. You can't hitch it up with the other two."

"All the same, it must have stemmed from Wall Street."

"Oh?" asked Thatcher.

"Certainly. Ed, here, isn't a household face, and his daily agenda isn't published in the newspapers. That gang must have had some grounds for believing he would be at Grand Central on Friday. Isn't that right, Ed?"

But Parry, who had seen where Schuyler's argument was leading, merely looked acutely uncomfortable.

"I still don't see how that ties in with Wall Street."

Schuyler leaned back expansively.

"Because Ed was going to a dinner with some bond dealers; that was common gossip in the luncheon clubs.

And there aren't many trains to Katonah after the rush hour. Anybody could figure out when Ed would be showing up at Grand Central. And, of course, a resident of Katonah would know—without even having to think about it."

"Why don't you say it, Nat?" Parry shook his head angrily. "You think Owen Abercrombie arranged that little reception for me at the station. For that matter, I wouldn't put it past him. But that doesn't have anything to do with slipping nicotine into Art Foote's tomato juice."

"You know perfectly well that the police think your Bloody Mary was the target for that nicotine. But I too find it difficult to see Owen fooling around with any sleight of hand with poison packets. He'd be much more likely to spray the room with a machine gun. I do wonder if somebody didn't tip him off about your movements last Friday. Maybe put him up to creating a disturbance. Because what you have to face is that we *do* have a murderer around here. And Owen Abercrombie would make a perfect stalking horse for him."

Unwillingly Thatcher was reminded that the house of Schuyler & Schuyler harbored at least one tipster for Owen Abercrombie. Was that what Nat Schuyler wanted him to think about? Dean Caldwell's name had been carefully kept out of the conversation—but not his image.

Ed Parry was not prepared to let the discussion center around personalities. In fact, thought Thatcher with growing amusement, he was much more the Exchange's *beau ideal* of a member than Nat Schuyler.

"In any event, I think we've made my point to Mr. Thatcher," he said. "What violence there has been has stemmed from the opponents of my application. And it has been directed against our brokerage firm, and not the Exchange, or Clovis Greene. Now, you say that the Exchange is concerned about stabilizing the market in the face of these wild rumors. I am concerned about that, too. After all, I have substantial investments myself. Anything that can be done by calming statements, I'm prepared to do. But I am not prepared to agree that the way to stop these slides is to wrap a curtain of silence over the question of Negro investments. The sooner people start to think about that, the better. Remember, the big slides have been started by attacks on us. If the market is going to dip every time somebody takes a bead on me, then the thing to do is stop this potshotting. There's nothing I can do about it."

Thatcher sighed. Everything that Parry said made sense. One more attempt on his life and the market would have to stop trading.

Gloria Parry came to the support of her husband's intransigence.

"Nor are we prepared to retreat to a cave for the duration. Ed is trying to cooperate with the Police Commissioner, but certain things we have pledged to do and those we'll go through with. You may as well know that we're patrons of the NAACP benefit night at Lincoln Center this weekend. And we're going to it, no matter how anybody feels. It won't be our people who start a riot there."

She looked around the room defiantly.

Curiously, it was Nat Schuyler who was moved to protest. He even started to ask a question, no doubt to emphasize the desirability of keeping the issue simple. Further examination of his hostess's resolute countenance persuaded him to remain silent. This silence was broken by the telephone.

It was for John Thatcher, from Hugh Waymark.

"You've got to get back here right away," said Waymark tersely. Thatcher hoped that his hoarseness was A.T.&T.'s fault. "All hell is breaking loose. The Exchange wants to talk to all three of us."

"I'm perfectly willing to talk to them this afternoon. But I can't leave now. We haven't even worked out a final draft—"

"The draft doesn't matter. This can't wait!"

"What can't?" demanded Thatcher, irritation yielding to curiosity.

Waymark laughed dementedly. "I can't explain. Just turn on your television set."

After hanging up, Thatcher turned to the others. This was no time to break the news that the Committee of Three was already beginning to crack at the seams.

"It seems," he said cautiously, "that something is going on. Could we turn on your television set?"

Gloria Parry obligingly walked over to a sleek walnut hi-fi arrangement and slid back a panel revealing the screen. "What station do you want?" she asked as she started to twist knobs.

But no further information was required. Even before the sound came on, it became apparent that all the networks were carrying the distorted, flickering image of Richard Simpson.

In the ghostly silence that persisted for several seconds, Simpson threw his arms out and opened his mouth in what must have been a bull-like roar. Clearly he was urging some form of Homeric action. In that brief interval of speculation, Thatcher rejected several possibilities as unduly dramatic. Reality for once surpassed his expectations.

". . . Star Chamber proceedings. We demand a fair and open hearing for Edward J. Parry. Let every man stand and be counted! Let there be an open ballot, so that we may know our enemies . . . those consumed by jealousy of the black man must be identified! I call upon you to join CASH in its first show of strength . . . not for us, the sit-in or the wade-in! We are shareholders! Ours is economic power! Use that power! Now is the time for our trade-in . . . each and every one of you must trade-in Vita Cola! Drive that price down! Bear your losses! These are money changers in the Temple!"

"My God!" said Nat Schuyler, awed by a capacity for freakishness outstripping his own.

"Why?" asked Parry, bewildered.

"I think," said Thatcher gently, "I think I'd better be getting back to town."

9 · They Call Us to Deliver

THE TRIP from Katonah to the Wheatmen's Mutual Building, where Waymark & Sims had their offices, took Thatcher exactly one hour and thirty-seven minutes to accomplish. It says much for the penetrative qualities of modern communications media that, by the time he arrived, Vita Cola had fallen four points.

"The boys over at the Exchange are going ape," announced Waymark, whose conversation these days was heavily salted with service jargon. "They keep saying there must be a law against this sort of thing."

Carruthers shook his head. "You mean they think there *should* be a law against it. What do they want the SEC to do? Prohibit the sale of stock?"

"No, no!" rejoined Waymark, his instincts as a broker coming to the fore. "How the hell could we make any commissions? But isn't this some sort of stock manipulation?"

"Not unless someone is making money out of it. It would be different if these people had sold short. But if they just want to sell their stock at a loss, no one can stop them. I suppose they look on it as a kind of donation to the NAACP."

"Well, that's a hell of a way to treat a portfolio!"

But the protest was a mere formality. Hugh Waymark regarded himself as a man on the firing line. To do him justice this had invigorated, rather than oppressed, him. The large modern office, with its paneled elegance hinting at a bar, sun lamp, vibrating chair and all the other amenities necessary to the demanding business of underwriting, seemed to harbor the whiff of grapeshot.

". . . what we've got to do is map out our strategy," he continued.

Before he could start unrolling maps, Thatcher thought it was time to bring some sanity to the issue before them.

"I admit this Vita Cola move is unnerving," he remarked, "but surely it's a little early for Simpson's supporters to have gotten their sell orders in and effected."

"That's just it," said Carruthers. "It can't possibly be them. They'll hit later today and tomorrow. The brokers and institutions must have started unloading."

Both men turned to look reproachfully at Waymark. "Well, naturally, no one on the Street wants to be hit by an avalanche," he explained glibly.

Under the circumstances, it was scarcely tactful to query the movements of Waymark & Sims in Vita Cola. Carruthers chose a roundabout approach instead.

"But that's just playing Simpson's game. Has it occurred to you what he'll do after he's forced Vita Cola into a real nose dive?"

Waymark stirred uneasily. "The Exchange was mumbling something about his going on to another stock."

His two colleagues nodded soberly.

"Of course, the whole thing may blow over before that problem arises," said Waymark halfheartedly.

"Blow over!" Carruthers sounded harassed. "You'll think twice about that once the word leaks out that we met here today."

Thatcher was curious.

"Are you having trouble at your place?" he asked.

"Pickets!" said Carruthers in tones of loathing. "We have forty of them carrying placards in and out of the reception room, choking up the elevator, parading through the lobby. It's a madhouse."

Idly Thatcher inquired about the message of the placards which had descended on Carruthers, Broadside & Pettigrew.

"That's just it!" said Carruthers with unusual heat. "Most of them simply said 'Justice.' And that's a fine thing to be parading around a law office!"

Gravely Thatcher concurred.

". . . naturally we didn't want to call the police," Carruthers explained. "But how can anybody work, when there are twenty people singing in the reception room?"

"I suppose . . ."

Carruthers shook his head. "No, John, it was not 'We Shall Overcome.' It was some new song."

Both Hugh Waymark and John Putnam Thatcher were conspicuously not interested in new songs. It was, then, with some surprise that they heard the normally polished Stanton Carruthers pursue the subject.

". . . a good strong tune, and some rousing lyrics, too."

"Fine," said Hugh Waymark. "Now, John . . ."

"I expect it may catch on," said Carruthers, speaking with his usual meticulous reflectiveness. "Not that I know much about these things, you understand, but my girl Fernanda seems to buy these records in carload lots."

Thatcher sympathized with the fleeting look of bewilderment that he saw on Hugh Waymark's face. It was gone in a minute; in that minute, Thatcher realized, Hugh Waymark had decided, for reasons known only to himself, that he had let his deep concern over *l'affaire Parry* (or was it *l'affaire* CASH? Or, *l'affaire Vita Cola*, for that matter?) cause him to commit a social solecism.

"Ah, yes, Fernanda. She's coming out next spring, isn't she?" he said chattily.

It was Stanton Carruthers' turn to look bewildered. But legal training gave him the edge when it came to seizing conversational gambits and bending them to his will.

"Yes, at my mother's place at Southampton. Now, the reason I mentioned the song is that I want both of you to be prepared."

He waited, satisfied himself that he had their complete attention, and continued:

"It's called 'The Three Wise Men.'"

There was a moment of silence.

Then, with real interest, John Putnam Thatcher said: "Catchy, eh? Tell me, what was the sense of the lyrics?"

"Confused," said Stanton Carruthers, repressively.

Hugh Waymark was manful in the face of adversity. Dismissing folk songs as the least of their current problems, he turned to Thatcher and asked if he had uncovered anything helpful in Katonah.

Thatcher considered the question, and replied truthfully.

"No."

He then relented and provided his colleagues with an abbreviated version of his interview with Edward Parry, together with a description of the statement that Parry had promised to issue.

They listened gloomily. Then, Waymark rose to a height of intelligence that Thatcher had previously felt beyond his reach.

"The real trouble isn't Parry. He's a good man, and he'll do what he can for us, but . . ."

With a short emphatic gesture he indicated the forces now rendering Wall Street hideous. They were indeed bigger than one man, even a man so impressive as Edward Parry.

". . . with open elections," Waymark continued, launching into a résumé of Richard Simpson's latest catalog of demands.

"That man has got the Board of Governors worried."

Possibly because of the folk singers, Stanton Carruthers was less imperturbable than usual.

"Well, I for one am delighted! The three of us are worried. The whole Street is worried. Why the Board should think that it can pretend to be above the struggle has always eluded me."

"You've made one mistake," Thatcher pointed out, recalling Katonah. "Nat Schuyler isn't worried."

"Nat Schuyler!" said Carruthers exasperatedly.

"I don't blame you," Thatcher said with a grin.

Hugh Waymark leaned forward: "Look, Stan, we all agree with you, but we've got to try to do something. I can tell you that the Board is very, very worried. Simpson is stirring up trouble right where they live. They've got their hands full with this new SEC study."

Recalling some of the salvos traded by the SEC and the President of the Exchange recently, Thatcher could well understand their alarm. Both in Congress and in the Commission itself, proponents of increased regulation always become more vociferous when internal policing measures of the Exchange prove inadequate to a crisis.

And if ever a crisis were running away from the optimists in Exchange Place, this was it.

Carruthers was thinking along the same lines. He frowned in thought.

"The Exchange is right to be worried," he agreed. "You know perfectly well that the SEC doesn't care what Simpson is doing. But it does care about the reaction downtown. If every member firm panics and dumps whatever stock Simpson mentions, then there's going to be a lot of talk about the need for government-imposed discipline. I hope to God they can count on the specialists."

All three men had professional reasons to remember the SEC investigation sparked by the behavior of one or two floor specialists on the day of the Presidential assassination. The job of the floor specialist is to promote orderly dealing in the stock for which he is responsible. In time of panic, he is expected to firm the market. Most of them do. But it takes only one exception to draw nationwide attention.

"And the Parry business won't help," Thatcher mused aloud. "It hadn't occurred to me before, but requiring that no seat can be transferred without the approval of the Board does make the Exchange look like a private club, doesn't it?"

Carruthers nodded. "Not just the seat. They have to approve any new partner in a member firm."

"And why not?" demanded Waymark. "You sound like this Simpson fellow. He's talking about public accommodations and demanding a right of appeal to the courts." A delicate shudder passed over his frame. "By God, you can see where that sort of thing might lead!"

Neither Thatcher nor Carruthers was prepared to stray down this tempting bypath. Instead they wanted to know what Hugh Waymark proposed.

"I've already put an idea of mine to the Board," he admitted. "If they're willing to go along, we could get cracking right away."

In the face of a noticeable lack of enthusiasm, he felt

the need to quote precedent. "Remember! Surprise is the essence of attack!"

This stirring battle cry evoked a profound silence which remained unbroken until Waymark's secretary opened the door to announce the arrival of the Exchange's emissary.

His jauntiness unimpaired, in walked Tom Robichaux.

"Don't know why it is," he rumbled in greeting, "but all I do these days is run errands for Francis."

Waymark brushed the complaint aside. "What did the Board say?"

"They say you're to open negotiations with Simpson immediately," said Robichaux, carefully repeating his message. "Francis has every confidence that you will soon have the situation under control."

He looked around the room, examining its occupants, and relaxed his official manner. "Don't know where he gets that idea, but there it is. This fellow Simpson is nothing but a damned troublemaker."

With a start of alarm, Stanton Carruthers said, "I certainly hope you're not making public statements to that effect."

"For God's sake!" said Robichaux indignantly. "That's fine thanks for the running around I'm doing. You don't think I enjoy it, do you? Why I could be—"

Before Robichaux could get well launched on an enumeration of the alternate activities available and preferable to him, Thatcher intervened with a soothing flow of palliatives. At a moment like this, handling Tom required the infinite patience of a tugboat captain piloting the "Queen Mary," which in many ways he resembled.

". . . very inconvenient, I'm sure. But what I don't understand is what we're supposed to negotiate about. It is customary to have something to give, in order to get something."

Before his eyes, Hugh Waymark ceased to be a Leader of Men and became a cunning guerrilla chieftain.

"It depends how you work it," he said, rubbing his chin craftily.

Stanton Carruthers drew a deep breath, preparatory, Thatcher guessed, to an explanation that a man who had

seized on the Parry crisis with the avidity of a Richard
Simpson could not lightly be detached from television
cameras, public protest meetings and the leadership
of parades. He was forestalled.

"We're not going alone," said Waymark triumphantly.
"We're going to have Nat Schuyler at the meeting."

Thatcher closed his eyes briefly.

But it was too late for the voice of sanity to make
itself heard. By going to the Board first, Waymark had
made a neat end play. Nothing remained but to view the
debacle.

The debacle started inauspiciously. By five o'clock the
next day, Vita Cola was down eighteen points, and people
were playing guitars in the halls of Waymark & Sims. Nat
Schuyler, benevolently satanic, received the news calmly
as he ushered the Committee of Three into a suite at the
St. Regis.

"Yes, bourbon and branch," said Waymark, rubbing his
hands together. "Been quite a day, quite a day. All hell is
breaking loose over at our place." He chortled in high
good humor.

Really, the man was wasted in underwriting when
catastrophe so clearly brought out the best in him.

". . . Berman's making a statement for the TV boys. I
thought that was a smart public relations move. Now, before the others get here, we ought to clear up a few points.
Just the five of us." He waved to include Vin McCullough
by the bar.

"By others, you mean CASH?" Schuyler demanded with
a cackle.

"Naturally."

Just then, the chimes sounded.

"And here they are," said Schuyler with gusto.

Waymark looked confused. Under cover of the opening door, he hissed at Thatcher, "I thought they weren't
supposed to get here until five-thirty."

Thatcher sighed impatiently as they stood up.

The well-known novelist Richard Simpson and
aides accompanied their host into the room. Simpson per-

formed introductions. There was Dr. Matthew Ford, "the well-known sociologist," and Mrs. Mary Crane. Mrs. Crane, it developed, was well known in connection with hostilities recently directed against the Board of Education.

"Oh, I'm really just a wife and mother," said Mrs. Crane, with a steely smile.

A corporate shudder gripped the room.

Carruthers took one look at Hugh Waymark, who was unnerved by the appearance of female auxiliaries, and twitched the reins of control from his hands. He introduced his colleagues, offered CASH Nat Schuyler's liquor and suggested that everybody settle down to the business at hand.

"Good," said Simpson, accepting a Scotch and simultaneously flicking the conversation from Carruthers. "We have to get to the dinner meeting of our executive board."

"Yes," said Carruthers.

Nat Schuyler, carefully crossing spindly legs, looked amused. Before Carruthers could continue, Simpson said:

"You want us to abandon our legitimate protest against the segregationist policies of Wall Street."

He spoke more in sorrow than in anger.

Surprisingly, it was Vin McCullough who protested.

"We won't make any progress that way," he said baldly. "Let's get some facts straight. Mr. Schuyler and I are supporting Ed Parry's nomination. We'll do all we can do to push it. So it doesn't help to call all of Wall Street segregationist."

His emphatic voice brought an impolitic look of surprise to Hugh Waymark, and another smile to Nat Schuyler.

Dr. Ford, the sociologist, nodded. "Yes, we want to be scrupulous about that, Dick." Mrs. Crane simply pursed her lips.

Unrepentantly, Simpson replied, "I stand corrected. We admit that Schuyler & Schuyler is an honorable exception. But you cannot deny that there are racist forces . . ."

He had underestimated Stanton Carruthers. While not precisely denying the existence of racist forces, Carruthers managed to point out that the Stock Exchange was exhausting itself in efforts to be fair.

"Ha!" said Mrs. Crane, causing Hugh Waymark to bridle slightly.

"Owen Abercrombie," added Dr. Ford more specifically.

Hugh Waymark blustered into speech; Stanton Carruthers continued his stately and measured comments on the New York Stock Exchange. Dr. Ford contented himself with sardonic little interjections and Richard Simpson, nettled by Stanton Carruthers' practiced fluency, commenced a moving word picture of the plight of the Negro stockholder in America. Helping herself to another drink, Mrs. Crane joined Nat Schuyler, who was looking on with vast satisfaction.

Under the cover of three, if not four, conversations, Thatcher spoke to Vin McCullough.

"I'm glad you said what you did, but I expected it from Nat, not you."

McCullough smiled wryly. "Because I wasn't crazy about losing money if we took Parry in? Hell, it's too late for that. I'll be damned if I'm willing to dance to the tune of that wild jackass Abercrombie. Do you know, he called me up and tried to threaten Schuyler & Schuyler? Well, nobody pushes Schuyler & Schuyler around—at least not while I'm there. We're going to get Parry a seat on the Exchange if we have to use a cannon to do it."

"That's the spirit!" cried Mrs. Crane, who overheard his remarks. "Fight force with force."

"You're right," said Vin McCullough somewhat grimly.

"Good boy," Nat Schuyler called, sending a knowing glance at Stanton Carruthers.

Who was the idiot who had suggested that Nat Schuyler might be prevailed upon to cooperate? Or Richard Simpson, for that matter?

Simpson, chin up toward nonexistent television cameras, had risen.

"That must be CASH's position. No, gentlemen, peaceful demonstrations and the legitimate use of economic might to further the human betterment of the American Negro cannot be stopped simply because we may embarrass some elements of the community, who prefer to ignore one of the crying shames of this city, and of the whole United States."

His breath control, Thatcher conceded, was remarkable.

"No," said Simpson, although no one had spoken. "We shall persist until the glaring inequities which exist upon Wall Street are eradicated forever. We hope and pray that they soon will be."

Mrs. Crane rose to join him. Filling an alarming bosom with a preliminary breath, she spoke vibratingly.

"In this, his hour of peril, we shall stand by Edward Parry."

Dr. Ford also rose. He issued no clarion calls, but contrived nonetheless to loose a blockbuster.

"Coming, Mr. Schuyler? We're going to have to hurry."

"Eh? Oh yes, yes," said Schuyler, busy playing the aged totterton as he got spryly to his feet.

"Just sitting in on this CASH dinner tonight," he explained airily. "Help yourself to the drinks."

With something remarkably close to a strut, he accompanied CASH to the door, paused for the parting civilities, then left.

The door closed on a stunned and indignant silence.

"Well, I must say!" Stanton Carruthers began. "And what's funny?"

For John Putnam Thatcher and, after a moment, Vin McCullough were laughing heartily.

"The old so-and-so," said Thatcher with approval. "Did you know about this, Vin?"

Still chuckling, McCullough shook his head.

"Nat is one surprise after another."

For a moment he leaned back in an attitude of complete relaxation, then determinedly gathered his forces.

"I'd better get along. I'm carrying Art Foote's work at the office until we can get Parry in. And moving house on top of it. So, if you don't need me . . ."

Within five minutes, the Committee of Three was again in executive session.

"So much for that idea," said Thatcher. "Let me make

a suggestion. Our one function appears to be that of wasting the time of many people—including ourselves. We can't do much to protect the McCulloughs of the world, but we can save our own necks. Instead of acting as a body, why don't we split up?"

While it was too much to say that the profound good sense of this suggestion cheered his companions, it did appear to be persuasive.

"Mmm," said Waymark. "But we'll meet for progress reports from time to time."

"If you think they're necessary," said Thatcher ambiguously. "But not at the Sloan."

"Or Carruthers, Broadside & Pettigrew," said Stanton Carruthers hastily.

"Or Waymark & Sims." Waymark was mildly regretful. "We sent out forty thousand empty envelopes, by mistake, this afternoon."

Silence descended.

"I suppose you've heard about Lee Clark," Waymark remarked idly. "He's preparing a complaint to the SEC accusing Schuyler & Schuyler of simply using Parry to harm Clovis Greene's Harlem business. Says that Nat doesn't have any real intention of getting Parry a seat."

Stanton Carruthers considered this. "A possibility, I suppose. Clark is pretty bitter, I understand. He's joining forces with Abercrombie, as well."

Again silence, then Hugh Waymark produced a small notebook. "Here are some of the public events the Board would like us to attend . . ."

"We'll toss for it," said Thatcher, seeing the light of endless discussion in his eye.

Three minutes later, Hugh Waymark said, "You've won the ADA tomorrow night."

"What do you mean, won? I've lost."

"Stan gets the John Birch Society, and I get the Committee to Clean Up Wall Street."

"Like Richard Simpson," said Thatcher. "I stand corrected. We've all lost."

10 · No Duty Is Too Lowly

BY THE NEXT DAY the press had surpassed itself in idiocy.

Statements from prelates, the Civil Liberties Union, senators and Black Muslims abounded. Everybody disapproved of the present situation, for one reason or another: it was too violent, it wasn't violent enough, the target was too specialized, nothing could be accomplished without open war between the races. A wealthy church in the downtown area had proposed a solution to the problem which involved dividing Wall Street in much the same manner as Berlin, complete with the introduction of checkpoints and the disarmament of bankers. The Police Commissioner's comment on this plan was a model of fiercely controlled emotion.

In the Bronx, an elementary school which preened itself on its model racial mix (thirty percent colored, thirty percent Puerto Rican and forty percent white) burst into print with a smug analysis of its own virtues. It sent a high proportion of its unending stream of graduates to the Bronx High School of Science, the High School of Music and Art, the High School of Performing Arts and Hunter High School and took this occasion to congratulate itself on its unfailing wisdom in confronting racial problems that made weaker men blanch. There followed interviews with three selected students: Julia, aged thirteen and Puerto Rican, intended to go to Music and Art for further study of the oboe before ultimate attendance at Juilliard. Snatching a moment from her arpeggios, she said that anybody who worked hard enough didn't have time for all this nonsense. Howard, aged fourteen and Negro, was going to Bronx Science to be a physicist. He felt that science offered opportunities for those facing discrimination in other fields. Sammy, a master chess player at the Manhattan Club, thought it was a mistake to let human passions intrude into any problem.

Thatcher did not approve of encouraging self-satisfied teenagers, but he was forced to admit that their statements compared favorably with those of their elders. Including, he thought bitterly, his own daughter, who was militantly reacting to Edward Parry's problems in a manner that would have won approval from Elijah Muhammad.

A member of the Board of Education tried to refute accusations that racial minorities were deprived of educational opportunity with statistics showing that ninety-eight percent of the graduates of all elementary schools in Chinatown went on to take doctorates. This discouraging vision of horn-rimmed young Orientals standing in serried ranks before something called Whirlwind xxv left Thatcher unreceptive to the counsels of the Chinese Merchants Association serenely prescribing absolute calm for members of the black and white races. In the face of this detachment, he found their references to "our Fair City" unduly proprietary.

The article concluded its massive survey of turbulence and disorder with the announcement that attempts to gather the views of high city officials had been abortive; they were all vacationing out of the country.

No day with such reading matter is a dead loss. Considerably invigorated, Thatcher slapped aside the last page of this comic relief and briskly proceeded to the task of leveling the gigantic pile of arrears accumulated on his desk.

By five o'clock Herculean inroads had been made, Miss Corsa was mollified by a day's work which would have caused many a woman to hand in her notice on the spot and Thatcher, supported by a sense of accomplishment, could anticipate the evening's approaching agenda with unimpaired cheer.

"Where is this ADA banquet I have to attend?" he asked the departing Miss Corsa.

"At the Grand Ballroom of the Waldorf. Six forty-five," she reported.

"Good heavens, how very substantial."

When Thatcher arrived at the Waldorf to join the Americans for Democratic Action milling around outside the ballroom, he realized that his vision of political progressives was outmoded. This smartly dressed, gaily chattering crowd was indistinguishable from any similar gathering of prosperous reactionaries. On both the right and the left, Thatcher noted as he accepted the drink procured for him by a harassed chairman of the program committee, it was the ladies who sounded the most aggressive. He gazed around him with interest. On second glance, he could discern some differences. The ADA ladies were perhaps a shade more intense than the female conservatives of his acquaintance. And, unless he was mistaken, they tended to be a trifle thinner as well. They sported hornrimmed glasses, not jeweled frames.

He discovered that the chairman's disjointed remarks had been addressed to him.

"I was woolgathering," he apologized, to be rewarded with the news that he had much to be thankful for. Unlike his confreres on the Committee of Three, he was not addressing a specially convened meeting. The ADA banquet had been scheduled many months earlier. A speaker from Washington was on hand.

"And," said the chairman with myopic earnestness, "time will be limited."

"Excellent," said Thatcher.

"So," the chairman continued, "we've had to squeeze you in with the appetizer. I hope you understand."

Thatcher was sincerely delighted. When the assemblage finally trooped into the ballroom and settled down at the banquet tables set up there, his remarks on the Stock Exchange's determination to maintain scrupulous impartiality in the case of Edward Parry's application for a seat constituted an introduction to the shrimp cocktail.

For this Thatcher was doubly grateful. In the first place, he was not intoxicated by the sound of his own voice. Any excuse to keep his statement brief was a source of pleasure. But in the second place, during cocktails he began to fear that the ADA—moneyed, academic and legal—was likely to know a good deal too much about the Securities and Exchange Act as well as the bylaws of the National Association of Security Dealers.

This apprehension was confirmed during the question period following his short statement. References to section numbers and joint committee reports flowed from his hosts in abundance. Thatcher took due notice. When dealing with a pressure group, it is a wise precaution to learn precisely where the pressure is going to be applied. He could now report to the Exchange that the ADA would be camping on Washington doorsteps to demand more extensive federal regulation of the Stock Exchange if Edward Parry were denied his seat. That was not too bad, and, fortunately, hunger kept his audience from laboring the point.

As he left the rostrum, the chairman agitatedly thanked him and said that he was being placed at one of the smaller tables where, the chairman understood, he had acquaintances.

To his surprise, Thatcher found himself joining Charlie Trinkam.

"I didn't know you were a member of ADA," he remarked. If there was one thing noteworthy about Trinkam, it was not the prominence of his commitment to politics of the liberal variety.

"I'm not," Trinkam replied. "Barbara, here, arranged for us to come. Barbara, this is John Thatcher. John, this is Miss Feathers—and Paul and Irene Jackson."

John Thatcher sat down and took stock of his surroundings, brightening as he did so. Any social occasion, however outré, which came about through Trinkam's efforts promised some interest. And the trio with which he and Trinkam were joined was indeed strangely assorted. The Jacksons radiated money, gaiety and knowledgeability. Paul Jackson, smooth-haired and stocky, was, it developed, a thriving criminal lawyer with an extensive and lucrative practice among the city's less desirable citizens. His very attractive wife was a woman obviously deriving considerable enjoyment from life.

Miss Feathers was an economist.

Not for the first time, Thatcher was roused to admiration by the speed with which Charlie Trinkam, given any conceivable public or private problem, could attach himself to a woman with some claim to inside information. Nor were there any limits to his catholicity. Lovely women, social women, intellectual women, dedicated women, family women—all were a source of real interest to him.

At the moment, it was an economist. They were discussing the main speaker of the evening.

"He should have stayed at Harvard," she said, stubbing out one of the cigarettes she was smoking in rapid succession. "But that's the trouble with some of these intellectuals. Stanley is simply power mad."

Thatcher glanced at the head table. Stanley was small, partly bald and possessed of an irritatingly confident smile.

Paul Jackson looked up from his cooling roast beef to remark in jovial accents that he had rarely enjoyed anything so much as Stanley's address to the ADA on the eve of his departure for the White House.

"It was called," he chortled happily, " 'The Challenge to Intellectuals.' "

Miss Feathers' lips tightened as if she reserved to herself the right to criticize Stanley—and all other intellectuals. With his usual soothing instincts, Charlie Trinkam inquired after the subject of tonight's address.

" 'Limitations Imposed on the Intellectual in Washington,' " Miss Feathers replied repressively.

This unhappy, if natural, progression effectively dampened the conversation. The talk, therefore, became desultory, with Trinkam and Jackson exchanging mildly scandalous comments about several friends they had in common and Irene Jackson displaying lamentable frivolity in the face of a lengthy disquisition from Miss Feathers on the subject of the need for More Women in Politics.

"Barbara," said Mrs. Jackson finally, turning to Thatcher, "Barbara is on the ADA action committee to study the Parry situation."

"Oh yes?" said Thatcher. "What . . . er . . . action do you envisage? Apart from urging increased SEC legislation, that is?"

"SEC legislation!" she said with contempt. "That's all right when it's a question of protecting investors. But this whole Ed Parry affair has triggered violence. It's brought out the lowest hoodlum element. The riffraff of the city." She turned to her left and peremptorily broke in on Jackson's exchange with Charlie Trinkam.

"That's right, isn't it, Paul? You're the one who knows all about criminals and violence after all."

Jackson, amused, denied her charge. "Now wait a minute, Barbara. My clients may go in for violence. I don't get called until it's all over."

Barbara Feathers dismissed this hairsplitting.

"That's not what I mean. But you know that we're not dealing with speculators or defrauders—" she broke off and directed a look at Thatcher that made him wonder if she were including him in this select group "—we're dealing with murderers!"

Jackson was not shaken by her earnestness. "You mean those nut boys of Abercrombie's? They're not professionals, if you know what I mean. They talk big, but I don't think they're ready for anything more dangerous than egg-throwing."

With a quick look at Thatcher, Charlie Trinkam gave the ball a push to keep it rolling. "But somebody has already tried to murder Ed Parry—twice. That's dangerous enough, Paul."

Jackson chose his words with care. "I don't think Abercrombie's crowd is ready for mob violence. As a group, they're not prepared to pay the penalty for it. But, on the other hand, a single individual, resorting to concealed murder—well, that's something else again. As you say, we've got double proof that somebody is willing to try that."

Miss Feathers looked at him with disapproval.

"I don't agree with you about mob hysteria," she said didactically. "Even if these people wouldn't start much by themselves, let them sit around inciting each other for a week—and you don't know what will happen. You have to meet the threat of mass action with a display of mass solidarity. That's why I feel that a big turnout at Lincoln

Center is so important. And the committee has finally agreed with me."

Beating down a flicker of sympathy for the action committee, Thatcher asked Miss Feathers if she and the ADA supported Richard Simpson.

"In spirit, we do," said Miss Feathers loftily. "Dick Simpson has a very powerful mind. I don't know if you saw him on the "Today" show, but I personally have never heard a more penetrating analysis of the basically sexual basis of racial bigotry . . ."

"Good God!" said Charlie Trinkam as Mrs. Jackson directed a minatory look at her husband, who obediently broke into speech.

"I think," he said, "the ADA position is that the best way to attack racial discrimination by the Stock Exchange is through pressure on the SEC . . ."

Miss Feathers interrupted him:

"Yes, that's true—as a long-term approach. But when there's violence, we plan to counter it with a massive display of individual support for Ed Parry. We're going to send a thousand members to Lincoln Center Saturday night."

Perhaps sensing John Thatcher's apprehension that the conversation might revert to the sexual basis of racial bigotry, Irene Jackson said brightly, "We wouldn't miss it for anything. It's not every night you can wear your best clothes to a potential riot."

Miss Feathers said, "Charlie is coming with me, Mr. Thatcher. I hope you're planning to attend."

Thatcher framed an evasive reply, inwardly marveling at the sympathetic working of social antennae. Elements as variegated as Gloria Parry, Nat Schuyler, Miss Feathers and the Jacksons all realized that the NAACP benefit was assuming a symbolic significance. Surely it was too much to hope that Owen Abercrombie and his cohorts had not come to the same conclusion.

And what about Owen Abercrombie? Thatcher had noticed that the careful Paul Jackson's statement absolved Abercrombie's followers, while leaving plenty of scope for homicidal action on his part.

And if Owen Abercrombie were capable of dangerous violence, what more appropriate place for it than an NAACP benefit at Lincoln Center?

At this moment, Thatcher's thoughts were interrupted by sounds from the head table that ultimately resolved themselves into a lengthy introduction of the speaker of the evening.

John Putnam Thatcher gave the intellectual precisely three minutes. Then he chose the course of prudence and suspended all thought entirely.

At that very moment, intellectuals were the least of Stanton Carruthers' problems. He hadn't seen anything approaching one for the last two hours. In fact, as he looked at Owen Abercrombie's ponderous, underslung jaw and glittering feral eyes, he was tempted to think that he had receded through several major geological eras and was surrounded by Neanderthals.

The White Association for Civic Intervention (known as "Whacky" the length and breadth of Wall Street) was an offshoot of the John Birch Society, organized by Owen Abercrombie and composed of members disaffected with the moderate views of the parent organization. Its program called for action, and the nature of that action was becoming ominously clear as Carruthers, standing on the flag-draped rostrum before an enormous photomural of the founder, braced himself for questions from the floor.

Or they were supposed to be from the floor. Most of them were coming from Abercrombie himself and started with the phrase: "Do you mean to stand up there and say . . . ?"

". . . I am afraid you may have misunderstood the nature of our committee," Carruthers was saying as he thanked God for a lifetime of self-control under adversarial fire. Only now was he beginning to appreciate the high standards of *politesse* which govern the legal arena. "We want to help promote order during the period necessary for the Stock Exchange to come to a decision with respect to Mr. Parry's application."

Abercrombie, who was also standing, hunched his shoulders forward and let his short arms dangle loosely, thereby emphasizing the simian resemblance.

"You mean to say you people are going to stand back and let them take over?" he demanded.

"The question before the Exchange involves one seat out of over a thousand. That can scarcely qualify as taking over."

"You're opening the door. They'll come pouring in."

Carruthers repressed the desire to ask Abercrombie where "they" were going to get the necessary hundred thousand dollars. Instead he opted for a dispassionate review of the statistics about available seats. It is rare, he pointed out, for more than two seats to fall vacant in any one year.

"Don't try and whitewash this thing with phony numbers!" shouted Abercrombie. "You're trying to cover up the fact that you're scared to stand up for your rights!"

Carruthers permitted himself a tempered coldness. There was, he pointed out, a genuine difference of opinion about exactly what those rights were.

"There's no difference of opinion between honest, God-fearing Americans! We all know there's a Commie line designed to infiltrate our way of life. Are you going to stand up there and feed us Moscow propaganda?"

"I'm afraid I have to contradict you on that, Mr. Abercrombie. The difference of opinion extends to the majority of Congress which passed a Civil Rights Act."

These words were a red flag. A new contestant now entered the fray.

"Civil rights!" shouted Dean Caldwell from the floor. "That's one name for it. I'd like to get this talk down out of the clouds and ask the speaker what he'd do if his daughter wanted to marry one of them. Because that's what it all boils down to! Whether or not we're going to protect the purity of our race and our women!"

In the thunderous ovation which greeted this remarkably offensive question, Stanton Carruthers unexpectedly found himself relaxing, sustained no doubt by the vision of his daughter Fernanda.

With deliberate provocation, he smiled benignly down

at the militant young Southerner and told him that, when he was old enough to have a daughter of marriageable age, he would realize that he had precious little to say about anything she did and probably would be damned grateful to anyone who took her off his hands.

Abercrombie, older in the ways of the world than Dean Caldwell, returned to the attack.

"It may be a laughing matter to you," he said, lowering his voice to a dramatic hiss, "but the defense of our homes and our businesses and our families is something we're prepared to take seriously with every drop of our blood. We are ready for action."

Ovation.

"You come here and tell us you stand for order. You tell us *that* when the Vita Cola specialist collapses and has to be hospitalized—the first casualty on the field of battle. But not the last, let me tell you!"

Ovation.

"Well, we've got something to tell you and your committee. We're the ones who stand for order!"

Here Abercrombie started pounding on the table in a manner irresistibly reminiscent of the United Nations.

"And we're going to protect it and we're going to protect you—in spite of the fact that you're too yellow to stand up and be counted yourselves. We're not afraid to use force against force, are we?"

Arms angled into a stubby vee, Abercrombie received the cheering assent of his supporters. The ugly red tide that had suffused his face when he was exchanging remarks with Carruthers disappeared, replaced by a pale exultant gleam. With his head thrust back he rocked to and fro in a hypnotic interplay of emotion with his audience. He swung forward with each question he asked, and then swayed back under the blast of their maniacal approval.

"Are we going to lie down and take this without lifting a finger?"

"NO!"

"They're all against us. They'll try to muzzle us, try to smear us. Are they going to get away with it?"

"NO!"

"You're the only ones left to defend America. Are you going to let the pinkos take over?"

"NO!"

And then, like a mechanical toy that had been wound tight, he abandoned his dialogue with the auditorium and launched into a wild, disordered peroration, filled with incoherencies and strange quotations:

". . . for the love of God and country . . . no time or place for weaklings, for questioners, for those who would undermine us . . . a solemn duty to which we here pledge ourselves . . . fight force with force . . . let not this cup pass from us . . ."

The evening ended for Carruthers with the frenzied howls of a thousand voices ringing in his ears.

11 · Keep Silence,
All Created Things!

AT FIRST BLUSH it would have seemed impossible that the next day should fail to be an improvement over its predecessor.

Not that Thatcher was deluding himself. No one acquainted with Wall Street's passionate attachment to peaceful, if powerful, anonymity—as well as profits— could reasonably expect that listening to intellectuals detail atrocities suffered in Washington would be the only cross to be borne during the Parry Crisis. With Vita Cola still collapsing—in faithful emulation of its floor specialist —Thatcher knew that the demands on him, however incoherent, would be many and urgent.

Nevertheless, when he arrived at the Sloan the next morning, he was unfavorably surprised to find that Miss Corsa had already received four top priority calls.

"First Mr. Carruthers," she reported, consulting a note.

"Then Mr. Withers. Then Mr. Devane, and finally Mr. Lancer. They all want you to call back as soon as possible."

"Something must be up," Thatcher mused aloud. "Well, it will have to wait. I'm going to check the papers."

Miss Corsa looked censorious.

"After all, Miss Corsa, possibly the press can explain this new emergency—whatever it is."

"Yes, Mr. Thatcher," said Miss Corsa, ostentatiously buckling down to work.

Thatcher withdrew into his own office and scanned the headlines rapidly. He found nothing to explain why the president of the Sloan Guaranty Trust, its Board Chairman, one of the governors of the Stock Exchange and Stanton Carruthers should be hounding him before nine-thirty. This is not to say that he failed to find anything of interest. There was a front page interview with the Deputy Mayor ("We want to assure out-of-towners planning to visit New York that we have not had one single instance of a tourist molested in the financial district."); a plaintive account of the corporate confusion reigning in Vita Cola's executive offices ("But our profits are thirteen per cent above last quarter!"); and a somber announcement that the New York City Police Department had granted CASH a permit for "peaceable demonstration" ("The right to peaceable demonstration is constitutionally guaranteed to all U.S. citizens," police officials grudgingly declared.).

Nor did the police, if the press was covering the situation (and to find mention of the Soviet Union, southeast Asia or Washington, D.C., for that matter, one had to penetrate to page fourteen of *The New York Times*), have anything to say about the murder of Arthur Foote—or the murderous attack on Edward Parry.

With the newspapers uninformative, Thatcher resorted to the telephone. Within minutes he learned of yet another chore. Edward Parry was finally leaving the amenities of Katonah to come to Wall Street and deliver his long-awaited statement. The Board of Governors of the New York Stock Exchange felt that the presence of the

Committee of Three at his press conference would be most advisable.

"Yes indeed," said Thatcher to Stanton Carruthers, who conveyed this information. "It will be a good opening for a few words about the Exchange's scrupulous fairness."

"Yes," said Carruthers, already in the throes of composition.

After learning the particulars—the conference had been scheduled at one o'clock at Schuyler & Schuyler—Thatcher courteously asked about Carruthers' evening with the White Association for Civic Intervention.

There was a long silence. Finally Carruthers cleared his throat.

"Endless and ugly," he said. He debated adding further comment and decided against it. "That sums it up, I think. Well, John, I'll be seeing you this afternoon. And I'll prepare just a few words."

Rather satisfied with his Machiavellian tactics, Thatcher returned his attention to the matters which brought him his substantial salary and gave Miss Corsa and the whole sixth floor of the Sloan Guaranty Trust one of his well-known workouts.

"Well, that should keep you busy," he announced bracingly at twelve-thirty, "I have to be getting along."

Kenneth Nicolls, stunned by the bulk of his impossible assignments, smiled weakly, struggled to his feet and fled. Miss Corsa was made of sterner stuff.

"Where can I reach you, Mr. Thatcher?" she asked.

"Just a press conference over at Schuyler & Schuyler," he replied cheerfully. "I should be back in an hour."

His carefree frame of mind lasted precisely eight minutes—the eight minutes it took him to fight his way through the lunchtime crowds to Schuyler & Schuyler.

There, at the William Street curb, creating pedestrian and vehicular congestion, stood two gaudy trucks. The usual big-city crowd had gathered, well-dressed and to all appearances gainfully employed, rooted to the spot and theorizing freely to account for the appearance of television crews. Fortunately, Thatcher was unable to identify any Sloan employees amidst what he unfairly apostrophized as "brainless time wasters." He pushed his way forward. Around him hypothesis flowed. There had been a bank robbery. There was a new salad oil scandal. Somebody had misplaced securities.

"Probably," said a sleek young woman, "probably some file clerk is threatening to jump from the fortieth floor."

No one, Thatcher noted, looked up.

Well, one thing you could say for Wall Street. If no one was looking up, no one was shouting, "Jump!"

By the time he had worked his way into the lobby a heavy sense of premonition was ripening. By the time he reached the twenty-sixth floor, he found it was all too justified. The Edward Parry conference was being televised.

Schuyler & Schuyler was a madhouse.

"No, no, no," crescendoed a bearded youth with a notebook. "The three camera. I told you, George. If I told you once, I told you . . ."

Thatcher stepped aside for two men manhandling what looked like an irrigation pipe.

"And we'll need more light here . . ."

". . . what about the boom . . ."

"WATCH THAT CABLE!"

"Who are you?"

The last question was directed at Thatcher. It emanated from a large woman with red hair. She did not wait for his reply, but consulted a clipboard and said: "You're Hugh Waymark."

Her conviction made Thatcher regret the necessity for denial.

"Hmm," she said skeptically. "Well, Mr. Waymark—sorry, Mr. Thatcher—you'll have to go to makeup. Willy! Oh, Wil-ly!"

"Now, just a minute . . ."

Thatcher's horrified protests availed him nothing. A harried youth appeared and firmly led him past a gaggle of wide-eyed secretaries, worshipfully watching the invaders.

"In here," said Willy, ushering Thatcher into what in happier days served Schuyler & Schuyler as a conference room. Just emerging was Edward Parry, accompanied by a bitter-looking man who barely reached his shoulder.

Sighting Thatcher, Parry paused.

"Please, Mr. Parry!" cried the bitter-looking man, tearing a cigarette from his lips and grinding it underfoot. "We don't have much time. I'll ask you to read your statement—that's one minute four. Then, when you finish . . ."

Still talking, he led Parry away.

"Here you are, Mr. Waymark," said Willy, indicating a chair for Thatcher.

"I do not propose to let myself be daubed," Thatcher began firmly, just as the large woman reappeared.

"We're running late," she said tersely. Willy burst into agitated burblings and, before he knew what was happening, Thatcher found himself in a chair as a technician advanced upon him with a small tray of cosmetics.

"Oh God!"

For Thatcher was not to be the only victim. Willy was leading Dean Caldwell and Vin McCullough into the conference room. They inspected Thatcher carefully.

"Carruthers," he said with dignity, "neglected to tell me that we were going to be involved in this sort of thing."

Vin McCullough laughed aloud, but Dean Caldwell saw nothing amusing in the situation.

"He's outside," he said sullenly. "God damned circus, that's what it is. What the hell is the matter with Nat?"

Caldwell was still young enough to be submerged by his resentments, Thatcher noted, as he manfully detached his attention from a studious evaluation of his hairline. And, being angry, Caldwell was incapable of hiding it. Despite the technicians moving around, despite the arrival of a sheepish Stanton Carruthers, he continued to voice his discomfort.

"How're we going to get any work done?" he demanded pettishly. "It's bad enough that Nat is steamrollering all of us, but now we have to put on shows for . . ."

"Dean," said McCullough wearily. "Just keep it to yourself, won't you?"

He turned to exchange a mildly ironic comment with Stanton Carruthers.

Caldwell dropped into a chair near Thatcher and hostilely watched the makeup man.

"The whole place is a monkey house," he said in a lowered voice. "And we all know it's Parry's fault that Art Foote got killed!"

Thatcher reflected that the problem of disciplining junior staff members was handled better at the Sloan. He did not, however, propose to concern himself with this petulant young man. Moreover, his bedizenment achieved, he was free to go.

He rose.

"Doesn't know his place," Caldwell was continuing. "And you know what?"

Irritably McCullough moved past Thatcher to take the seat indicated for him.

"What?" he repeated.

Stanton Carruthers was silently radiating disapproval.

"Some people are going to do something about it. And I'm going to be with them."

"Can't someone shut him up?" Carruthers whispered to Thatcher.

"Apparently not," he replied. "Let's get out of here."

But before they could escape, they were privileged to hear McCullough evenly pointing out the advantages of self-control to Caldwell. The technician woodenly continued beautifying both of them.

"No, I'm not getting into trouble, Vin. You'll see."

His slyness would have roused suspicion in a man far more obtuse than Vin McCullough.

"Look, Dean, I'm just trying to give you some good advice. At a time like this, the prudent thing to do is to keep your mouth shut and watch your step."

"That's the trouble with everybody," said the younger man sullenly. "They're so busy being prudent, they forget they're men."

McCullough interrupted impatiently.

"I know you don't want to be slow and cautious. You've got some crazy idea about strutting down to Lincoln Center Saturday night with your friend Abercrombie and making trouble for Ed Parry."

"So you think you know all the ideas in my head, do you?" smiled Caldwell unpleasantly. "Say what you want, Owen Abercrombie is more of a man than anybody else down here. He doesn't run around licking people's boots."

"He doesn't have to," said McCullough dryly. "He's head of his firm. You're not."

"You're a fool if you think Owen wouldn't be man enough to do what he knows is right, whether or not he was a partner."

McCullough retreated from his attack on Caldwell's mentor. "Maybe so, maybe so. God knows he's crazy enough! But, Dean, let me tell you, starting riots at Lincoln Center is no business for an employee of Schuyler & Schuyler, even if he is the best research man we've ever had."

Caldwell preened himself in the mirror as the makeup man finished his ministrations. "It may turn out that Schuyler & Schuyler needs me more than I need them. And, anyway, what's so important about Lincoln Center?"

"It's the NAACP benefit. Half the bigwigs in the city will be there. If you start anything there, the networks will play it up all over the country."

"It's time they did," said Caldwell defiantly. "They've been hiding things from people long enough."

Vin McCullough brought his fist down on the counter. "For God's sake, will you listen to sense! And try to talk some into your friend Abercrombie."

"Pu-leese!" said the beautician haughtily.

Caldwell's reply was lost to Thatcher and Carruthers.

"Well, McCullough tried to talk turkey to that boy. But if you ask me, not a word got through," said Carruthers.

Thatcher grunted disapprovingly. "I don't think any word could get through."

"You're right," said McCullough, catching up with them in the corridor and overhearing. "I suppose it isn't worth the trouble."

"Well, the effort does you credit," said Thatcher, not mincing matters, "but frankly I didn't like the way he seized on Lincoln Center."

McCullough groaned. "I know, I know. But we can't

tiptoe around watching every word we say, for fear that boy will get himself into trouble. He's got to get used to the idea we're going to have a Negro partner."

"Don't we look fine!" trebled Willy, darting up to them. "This way . . ."

Within minutes all chaos was resolved. Thatcher, Carruthers and the late-arriving Hugh Waymark sat at one side of the long table, facing the staff of Schuyler & Schuyler, including a glowering Dean Caldwell. Nat Schuyler, together with Edward Parry and the interlocutor, who was the forceful and bitter man, sat at the head of the table.

Upon a signal that transfixed everybody, Edward Parry cleared his throat. Then, in his pleasant resonant baritone, he carefully read his statement. It was, Thatcher decided, about as much as they could have hoped for. Parry first expressed formal confidence in the New York Stock Exchange's fairness. He was, he continued, opposed to violence and extremism.

Parry spoke calmly and without embarrassment. Thatcher mentally applauded him. He knew enough of the man to know he must detest this whole performance—almost as much as Dean Caldwell, if for different reasons. But Edward Parry had learned self-discipline.

When he finished his remarks, the interlocutor asked Nathaniel Schuyler a question. Schuyler was at his best, exuding venerability, wisdom and saintly tolerance.

". . . and I would be most interested," he said with a straight face, "in hearing the opinion of our distinguished representatives from the Stock Exchange."

When Stanton Carruthers responded without hesitation, Thatcher thought he discerned a fleeting look of disappointment in Schuyler's benevolent eye.

"o.k.!" shouted somebody.

Everybody relaxed.

"Very, very good," said Nat Schuyler, rising stiffly. "I think that was excellent, Ed."

Turning, John Thatcher happened to catch sight of Dean Caldwell watching the head of his firm congratulate Ed Parry.

It provided him considerable food for thought.

12 · I Was a Wandering Sheep

TWENTY MINUTES LATER, Thatcher was returning to the Sloan, a prey to new and unwelcome sensations. Ordinarily devoid of self-consciousness, he now sensed every eye upon him. His ears turned scarlet as a muted giggle broke from two stenographers behind him. Common sense told him they were deep in discussion of their own affairs. But what price common sense, when a man has been subjected to ordeal by television?

Rising to haunt him were the numbers proudly flaunted by networks in pursuit of sponsors. Our daily news program is watched by ten million viewers . . . by twenty million . . . by fifty million. In fact, by everyone between the ages of ten and eighty.

"Good God!" And he almost said it aloud.

For weeks to come he would be dogged by reminders of the horror so recently undergone. Mrs. Corsa, out in Queens, would have something to say. Charlie Trinkam would be more outspoken. There would be the housekeeper of the Devonshire, the elevator operator, taxicab drivers . . . The list was endless.

It almost seemed worthwhile to discover important business in Poona.

Then he remembered the furry hats.

This is the tragedy of our time, Thatcher thought as he strode along. The illusion of refuge is gone. No comfortable sensations of security rise at the thought of Tahiti, the Himalayas, or Arabia Deserta.

Things have changed. Nowadays, Gauguin's family in Paris could enliven dull evenings by following the adventures of their levanting husband and papa among dusky island beauties. The Grand Lama of Shangri-La would conduct a Sunday morning program of spiritual uplift, and

Lawrence of Arabia would be interviewed on camelback about the Cyprus question.

"Tell me, Monsieur Gauguin, what exactly made you decide to give up banking for painting? And perhaps we could introduce this young lady to our viewers?"

"Now, the Reverend Grand Lama—do I have that right, sir?—will give us his views on attaining personal serenity."

"If you could just hold that dynamite a little higher, Colonel Lawrence, our listeners could see exactly how you go about blowing up a train."

There is no sanctuary. A man might as well face it out on Wall Street.

Thatcher's spirits began to rise. If there was nothing to be gained by exile to polar snow drifts or glaring deserts, then he might as well enjoy his notoriety in the comfort of New York, where, in addition to central heating and indirect lighting, he had the advantages of rank and position. Millions of people might be dying to tell him what they thought of his television performance, but the combined efforts of Miss Corsa at the Sloan and the entire staff at the Devonshire should insulate him from the more immediate manifestations of this peril.

Unfortunately, one of the people from whom not even the redoubtable Miss Corsa could protect him was the Sloan's Chairman of the Board. The message to call George Lancer was marked urgent.

"What's this all about, Miss Corsa?" Thatcher asked, frowning down at the memo slip.

With a monumental lack of interest, Miss Corsa professed ignorance.

"But Mr. Lancer's secretary did say it was very important, and would you please call back as soon as you got in."

Thatcher sighed.

For Lancer to be in a flap about something which had escaped Miss Corsa was ominous.

There was only one way to find out. Grimly he nodded to his handmaiden and within seconds was greeting the Chairman of the Board.

"John? Thank God!"

This was scarcely reassuring.

"What seems to be the matter, George?" asked Thatcher, already displaying that tendency to belittle trouble that comes to the best of us, when faced with strong displays of anxiety.

"It's that damned lunatic, Withers. We ought to keep him locked up."

There was a moment of appalled silence. Thatcher knew perfectly well that only extreme provocation could have sparked this trenchant candor.

"What's he done this time?" he asked, treading warily.

"You know about the tour for UN junior staff?"

Thatcher did. An annual event arranged for the benefit of UN financial types new to New York, the tour included important and historic spots in the Wall Street district. Among them, naturally, was the Sloan, where Bradford Withers was in the habit of making a short ceremonial speech of welcome. It was the kind of thing he enjoyed doing, and did well.

"But what can have gone wrong?" demanded Thatcher. "He does it every year."

"Well, this year he had some extra time on his hands, and he insisted on escorting them up to see the new employees' dining room. You know," Lancer added in bitter parenthesis, "how loony Brad is about that dining room. We never should have let him pick out the murals himself. Anyway, as soon as they got there, somebody from Tanzania asked him about segregated eating facilities."

"Oh, God! What did he say?"

"I gather that part wasn't so bad," Lancer admitted grudgingly. "He made some stately remark about the Sloan not tolerating that sort of thing and this wasn't Mississippi. In fact, the whole thing would have blown over except that some little twerp from the Congo insisted that the colored dining room was being hidden from the tour, and finally it dawned on Brad that the guy was calling him a liar."

"And then?" asked Thatcher with sinking heart.

"Then he blew up and said Wall Street didn't want outsiders telling it how to run things, particularly outsiders with plenty of riots themselves. That got picked up by every wire service in the country. Wait a minute . . . I've got the damned thing here somewhere . . . I'll read it to you."

There was a pause while George Lancer could be heard shuffling the papers on his desk and adjusting his glasses. His voice had a savage bite as he continued:

" 'Wall Street wants no outsiders,' declared the President of the Sloan Guaranty Trust today in discussing racial tensions in the financial community with a delegation from the United Nations. Bradford Withers went on to deplore violence among groups seeking admission to the select downtown community' . . . and so on . . . and so on. Got the picture?"

So much for distracting attention from the Sloan by not holding meetings of the Committee of Three on its premises. Thatcher could already hear the guitar-strummers beating at the front door.

"Yes," he said wearily, "I've got the picture."

"So naturally we've got a press conference scheduled. To try to correct the impression that's gone out—"

"You're not going to let Brad talk to them?" Thatcher made no attempt to conceal his alarm.

"Of course not. You and I are taking them on. It won't do any good," said Lancer with defeatist realism, "but it's the least we can do."

Three hours later, with Bradford Withers safely packed off to start a long weekend on his estate in Connecticut, Thatcher found himself giving guarded answers to a young man from Tass. No doubt the interview would enliven the front page of tomorrow's edition of *Pravda*. The young man asked long, involved questions to which there was no innocent answer. Thatcher delivered elaborate statements which were totally unresponsive to any question in the world. Lancer had already performed yeoman service in a more acrimonious exchange with a representative from the official organ of the Rhodesian Association for National Union.

Under Thatcher's right hand rested a hastily compiled file setting forth statistics about the original hiring, subsequent promotion, present salary and future prospects of every Negro employee of the Sloan, as well as past public statements, union clauses and internal memoranda on the subject. Curiously enough the chief emotion exercising Thatcher at the moment was pure, undiluted chivalry. He was prepared to go down fighting in defense of the privacy of a woman he had never met. Her name was Mrs. Joyce Morse, and she was the only Negro teller employed in the main office of the Sloan. Should her existence ever be revealed, she would spend the rest of her life being hauled in front of television cameras, while unctuous young men asked offensive questions about what it was really like in the ladies' room.

"No," he said, sadly shaking his head at the man from Tass as if the necessity for denial were a personal grief. "I am afraid it is against our policy to release a branch-by-branch breakdown of our figures. I can tell you that one hundred and thirty-two Negroes are employed in the capacities you have mentioned. That is for the bank as a whole, of course."

The man from Tass then asked a long question designed to show that, even though the Sloan's dining facilities were not segregated, things were as bad as though they were.

Thatcher countered with an equally lengthy reply challenging the Soviet Union to produce one black bank president, and implying that, if the Sloan knew of a qualified candidate, they would rush out and hire him at once. As he mouthed this inanity, he reflected that they could scarcely do worse than with the president they already had.

With the honors about even, Lancer rose to take on Reuters. In many ways these innings with the foreigners were a warm-up, centering as they did on facts and situations. The domestic press, Thatcher feared, would be much more interested in personalities.

He was right. After the London *Economist, Le Matin* and *Der Spiegel* had had their sessions—and after the man from a Bombay daily had made it clear that, in India, John Putnam Thatcher was a household name—there was a muted hush of expectancy. Then the dam burst.

Where was Withers? Was he hiding? Had the NAACP communicated with the Sloan? Had Thatcher heard what Richard Simpson said about Withers' statement, and did he care to comment? Was it true that Lancer was making a personal apology to Edward Parry? Was the Sloan supporting Owen Abercrombie's attempt to blackball Nathaniel Schuyler from two luncheon clubs? Was City Hall declaring the Sloan off-limits to the UN? Had all the Negro employees of the Sloan been given two weeks' vacation, a bonus and orders to go to Las Vegas? Had the Stock Exchange demanded Thatcher's resignation from the Committee of Three? Did Edward Parry and Bradford Withers belong to the same yacht club? Was the Secretary of State closeted with the Sloan's Board of Directors?

And on, and on, and on. When the last journalist had been ushered out by the still feebly smiling representatives of the Sloan, a great silence seemed to fall on the room.

Lancer's first action was to summon brandy. Then he looked at his associate.

"Well, what do you think?"

"I am past thought," said Thatcher acidly. "All I can rely on now is my will to survive."

Lancer poured two healthy snifters before mopping his brow. "We're going to have to produce Withers," he said unhappily.

"Yes. But in our own time, and in our own way. That's all we could hope to gain."

"I suppose so. If we could just prevent questions . . ."

Thatcher pondered. He was reminded of Nat Schuyler's trafficking with CASH. A little of the same kind of duplicity seemed indicated.

Meanwhile, the Chairman of the Board was dispiritedly reviewing the possibilities within the Sloan's staff.

"It's useless to think we'll get any help from the public relations people. They're the ones who organized this massacre." He stared around the recently vacated room balefully.

"I don't think that's the right line to pursue," said Thatcher slowly.

Lancer looked at him hopefully. "You've thought of something."

"Yes," admitted Thatcher. "You may think this is crazy. But the man who could help us is Edward Parry."

Soundlessly the chairman whistled. "Well, it's a different approach all right. What exactly were you thinking of?"

"We could get Parry and Withers together on a platform somewhere, with Brad more or less appearing under Parry's egis. Ed Parry would understand the kind of occasion we want—something where Brad can do a public *mea culpa* in sympathetic surroundings. God knows Parry must have occasions by the handful right now."

"Would he do it?" asked Lancer doubtfully.

"I don't know. He might. This isn't the kind of publicity he wants, any more than we do. And," concluded Thatcher in the tones of one summarizing the thirty-nine Articles of Faith, "he is a banker."

The chairman brightened. "Then I'll leave it to you. If you can find the right way to approach him—it will have to be done delicately, you know—then go ahead. But, if it's going to do us any good, it'll have to be done pretty fast."

One thing Thatcher was learning from this whole mess: every horror can be outstripped by some subsequent outrage. For the past week his life had consisted of events, any one of which should have been a climax of discomfort to be recovered from at leisure, lingering in the memory as an eminence towering above its surroundings. But at the pace he was now living, recollection could barely stretch back for two hours.

Thus when his daughter's call came through, interrupting his appraisal of possible approaches to Edward Parry, he was momentarily bewildered by her opening remarks.

"Daddy? We watched your show. It was grand."

What in the world was she talking about?

"What's that? What was grand?"

"Your television show, Daddy. At lunch today," she added impatiently. "Timmy wanted to know why you looked so stern."

In the host of diabolic viewers he had envisioned, he

had never imagined his ten-year-old grandson. No wonder family authority was breaking down everywhere. Briskly he counterattacked by demanding to know why Timmy was watching television instead of attending the fifth grade.

"Oh, he saw the rerun at four o'clock. I saw it live. Mr. Schuyler must be a fascinating man."

Thatcher agreed that he was. He could think of other descriptions, unsuitable for his daughter's ears.

"I'm *so* looking forward to meeting him," trilled Laura in the tone Thatcher recognized as preliminary to an unwelcome request. Even so, he could not resist following up this statement.

"When are you going to meet him?"

"At the benefit at Lincoln Center. That's what I wanted to talk to you about."

In some ways Laura and the young man from Tass had a great deal in common. She too phrased her questions so that there was only one possible answer. After much beating around the bush, it developed that Dr. Benjamin Carlson was going to be busy the day after tomorrow and Laura would thereby be deprived of her husband's escort that evening. She wanted her father to step into the breach.

"That's what you get for marrying a surgeon," said her father brutally. "If you want to go to this Donnybrook, it's your business and your problem. I have enough of my own."

"Oh, Daddy!" Laura was used to sweeping over *pro forma* displays of opposition. "It isn't just that I want to go. I have to go!"

"What do you mean, you have to go?" he demanded suspiciously.

"I'm a patroness. Together with Mrs. Parry. I must have forgotten to tell you. And everybody knows I'm your daughter. Can't you see what people would say if your daughter backed out of supporting Mrs. Parry at a time like this?"

Thatcher could see all too vividly. Nor did he credit

Laura's forgetfulness for one minute. She had him in a cleft stick, and they both knew it.

"Can't you get anybody else?" he asked, fighting to the last ditch.

"But it can't be just anybody else. Not on a night like this. And Gloria Parry likes you. She told me so."

Dimly a plan took shape in Thatcher's mind. Much as he disliked the whole idea of benefit concerts at Lincoln Center, he began to see that it might be his duty to attend. In fact, Laura had given him the answer to his problem. And he had never deceived himself with the hope that the solution was going to be attractive.

But he had his paternal position to maintain. It was with a great show of reluctance that he let Laura force him down the path of compliance, inch by inch.

It was not until ten minutes later that she was saying: "Oh, thank you, Daddy. I knew I could count on you."

13 · Or Roll of Stirring Drum

IN TRUTH, John Putnam Thatcher was happy that his children still counted him among the strong buttresses of life. He did, however, regret that rendering support to his daughter, Laura, so often required formal attire. The check he had mailed that morning to one of his sons was, in many ways, a smaller price to pay.

"A very, very successful evening."

The speaker, a portly middle-aged Negro, was decked out, like Thatcher, in white tie and tails. He was surveying the great lobby of the concert hall, tonight aglitter with the hard brilliance of crystal, the honey gleam of marble, the shimmer of fluid satin and the sparkle of diamonds. His gaze encompassed elegantly gowned women, floating like butterflies through the iridescent beauty of the setting; even among their escorts there was an occasional peacock. Tonight, Thatcher saw, ribbons were being worn; silhouetted against a column was the magnificence of a rich purple turban; just sweeping in through the great glass doors was the crimson splendor of ceremonial African robes. And, to light and sound, there was added the special, unforgettable scent of powder on bared shoulders, the attar of a hundred perfumes, the rich leaf of tobacco, and the smoky pungency of furs touched by the fog's damp fingers.

"It is indeed a successful evening," said John Putnam Thatcher. He had fallen into this stilted conversational exchange after Laura, resplendent in a black taffeta gown that may have explained why her husband was finding it necessary to work hard these days, spied an acquaintance and swept away for a moment. Thatcher's chance companion, while projecting substance and a certain proprietary satisfaction, had the look of a man similarly cast adrift by a woman. Before he could continue their exchange, he was reclaimed.

"There you are, Fred! Where have you been?" a pearled matron emerged from the crowd, collected Fred in a practiced fashion and bore him away. As he passed, his eyes met Thatcher's with an expression age-old to man, regardless of race, creed or color.

"Women," it said.

"There you are, Daddy," said Laura. "I've been wondering where you were."

"I haven't moved an inch," Thatcher replied mildly.

Strong-mindedly, Laura ignored this.

"Isn't it wonderful that the evening's so successful," she said, nodding regally to a passing couple. This moment of graciousness was immortalized by a photographer who exploded a blinding flashbulb at them. Thatcher only wished he could believe that he would appear on the Society Page. But, since Bradford Withers' gaffe, he very much feared that a vice-president of the Sloan Guaranty Trust was front page fodder.

"I've been saying the same thing as a matter of courtesy," he said irascibly, "but with my own offspring, I feel constrained to point out that it's a little early to decide this is a successful evening, in view of the fact that it has barely begun. And why, may I ask, is it necessary for us to promenade about?"

Like her mother before her, Laura had a splendid way of dealing with this kind of fractiousness. She smiled brilliantly.

"Oh, Daddy," she said in perfunctory protest. "Good evening, Mrs. Bertolling . . ."

As Thatcher escorted his daughter through the crush, exchanging civilities with acquaintances, then fell back to let the ladies discuss civil rights (or, occasionally, culture), he had plenty of time to think.

Without a doubt, if volume were the criterion, the NAACP gala was a success. Over intervening heads, Thatcher could see that the endless string of limousines was still debouching magnificently attired concert parties at the door. Unfortunately, he also saw four raincoated policemen, guarding the barricades that kept the corridor under the canopy free of idle sightseers—or worse. Out of sight, but not out of mind, beyond further barricades, were the inevitable pickets, undeterred by foggy drizzle or by the police caution which was keeping them far distant from the festivities. Glum and depressing, they stood in the rain beneath placards which were also depressing:

CIVIL RIGHTS FOR WHITES
NO MINORITY RULE

And, inevitably:

IMPEACH EARL WARREN

Of course, these poor wretches posed no threat to the assemblage of wealth, prestige and power (black and white) gathering in the stylish premises of Lincoln Center, to attend a concert, then a late supper, to swell the coffers of NAACP, and to support civil rights in general, and Edward Parry's rights in particular.

But were there any other threats? Thatcher looked around. It was hard to believe that anybody in this animated gathering—and he saw a U.S. senator laughing in a hearty professional way—felt any threat imminent. Negro or white, the dignitaries were smiling unconcernedly, conversing happily, exuding fellowship, optimism and goodwill.

But, Thatcher knew, many things are hard to believe. Some of the men and women floating grandly up the stairway to the balcony had had firsthand experience with the dark forces of hatred and bigotry—and recently. Could anyone—say, Owen Abercrombie—be planning further damage? Something more meaningful than ugly words on placards, carried by life's rejects?

John Putnam Thatcher profoundly hoped not. The ladies were excited enough already. Add an "incident" perpetrated before their eyes, and the ailments afflicting Wall Street would include enraged Carry Nations, marching in and out of brokerage houses, axing ticker machines.

"Mrs. Parry," said Laura. "Hello, Gloria."

Thatcher roused himself. The first thing to meet his eyes was a vision of calculated and artful magnificence. He spoke the words that came into his mind.

"You are in great beauty tonight, Mrs. Parry."

This old-fashioned formulation delighted Gloria Parry, who briefly gleamed the smile of a warm, vital woman instead of a poised and disciplined public personage. Laura dimpled her approval, rather as if her father were young Timothy, doing something precocious and, for a change, socially acceptable. Yet Thatcher spoke no more than the truth. Mrs. Parry wore a gown of amber lace with emeralds. The effect was impressive.

Thatcher glanced around to see if Edward Parry's composure were equal to the trying task of escorting a really dazzling woman. A word with Parry, he reminded himself, could go far toward relieving the Sloan Guaranty Trust of its current embarrassments—and so render tonight's discomforts a simple extension of his professional obligations.

"Ed's talking to Mr. Kingsley over there," said Mrs. Parry, reading his thoughts. What she really meant, Thatcher knew, was that she had dispatched her luckless husband to take care of her furs, then blithely sailed away into the crowd, leaving him to search for her.

"Have you met Mrs. McCullough?" Gloria Parry continued.

"I wonder where Vin is?" Mrs. McCullough replied after greetings had been exchanged. She looked around, vaguely expectant.

This was the only way in which Mrs. McCullough resembled her companions. A tall, slim woman, she wore her hair in the long blond sweep that had, no doubt, made her an exceptionally attractive college girl some twenty-five years earlier. She was not evincing pleasure in the gaiety of the occasion, like Laura who was becoming more organization-minded with every child. Nor did Mrs. McCullough have the aura of enormous physical attraction coupled with superb (and expensive) plumage that marked Gloria Parry. She was, it soon developed, another, not uncommon, type of American woman.

". . . just about dead on my feet," she said in a firm voice.

"Oh, really?" Laura began. But despite her four children, she was too young to have perfected social armament against the Julia McCulloughs of this world.

"We went to Arthur Foote's funeral today," Mrs. McCullough continued commandingly. "So depressing. Of course, Virginia is prostrate, poor dear. But I understand that Art had very good insurance, which is something. . . ."

Gloria Parry was old enough to be able to deal with this phenomenon. Moreover, her upbringing had brought her to a finer cutting edge (socially speaking) than would ever be necessary for a Laura Thatcher Carlson. But she, too, was effectively immobilized. Anything concerning a Schuyler & Schuyler partner—even a murdered partner—was necessarily interesting to Edward Parry's wife. Gloria Parry was not a politician's daughter for nothing.

Nevertheless, she indulged herself with an alarmingly intelligent look at Thatcher, before murmuring:

"What a tragedy . . ."

"Just awful . . ." Laura echoed dutifully.

". . . but of course, there are the children, which makes

it hard," Mrs. McCullough forged on, her voice quarantining her unwilling audience from the general surge of bright social chatter, the graceful semiwaltz movements of the fluid festive crowd and, Thatcher saw with sudden indignation, from the champagne cocktails being made available (rather than served) at a table beneath an extraordinary ton of metal which was, it was to be presumed, a piece of statuary.

"I know how it is. My sister's husband died just last month, and Vin and I had to support Carolyn through the whole thing. And it wasn't the money . . ."

"No, indeed," Gloria Parry said through a glaze of boredom.

Laura, Thatcher regretted to see, was incapable of even this.

". . . because he was a doctor and left Carolyn quite comfortable, thank God! But Vin was executor, and there was all the trouble of settling his effects, and closing up his office—and so suddenly. Then, telling the boys was simply terrible. I said . . ."

Without compunction, Thatcher withdrew his attention. At a distance he sighted Nat Schuyler. Nat was looking subdued. Was he worried, Thatcher wondered. Or, was it simply the small round woman at his side (black velvet and lace, a plethora of chains and other hangings, and completely improbable black hair)?

Idly, Thatcher's gaze wandered on. There was Tom Robichaux, with an extremely decorative blond young woman. Was that Celestine, returned from the sinister Greek yacht?

As Thatcher recalled—and he was the first to admit that he might be in error—the current Mrs. Robichaux was a striking redhead.

"John! Good to see you!"

Clearly Charlie Trinkam had not let social niceties keep him from the champagne cocktails. He was enjoying himself thoroughly. In his way, the man was a marvel. Beside him, looking handsome, if severe, in black brocade was Miss Feathers.

"I'm glad to see that the Sloan Guaranty Trust is out

in full force tonight," she observed after a round of introductions.

With a raised eyebrow, Charlie inspected the crowd. "Brad here? I haven't seen him, have you?"

"God forbid!" said Thatcher under his breath.

Fortunately, his words were lost in a lecture from Miss Feathers:

"In view of the really appalling situation developing on Wall Street, I can only say that if the large institutions . . ."

Her earnest tactlessness—and the real terror of what she might feel impelled to say—galvanized Gloria Parry and Laura into protective measures. As of one accord, they turned to Mrs. McCullough, and cooingly said:

"And you're moving too, aren't you?"

"Oh, moving is such a chore!"

Mrs. McCullough, who had looked Miss Feathers up and down and decided that she did not like what she saw, sighed dramatically. The enlargement of her audience did not, however, materially alter her peculiarly confiding tone.

"I am just about frantic. We're selling the house, now that the children are grown up . . ."

Miss Feathers, as befits a lady intellectual, interjected a comment designed to inflate Mrs. McCullough's troubles into a sociological generalization.

"Have you noticed how housing starts are shifting heavily into multiple dwelling units . . .?"

Even the normally imperturbable Charlie Trinkam was moderately taken aback; Mrs. McCullough simply raised her voice slightly.

". . . a terrible wrench, leaving Stamford. Not to speak of how terribly rents have risen. You wouldn't believe what we're paying for a simple six-room terrace apartment on the East Side. I told Vin he'd have to take care of selling the beach cottage himself. Really, what with talking to real estate people, and trying to get everything into storage and getting rid of the second car—and then having to go to funerals, I am thoroughly exhausted. Not that Carolyn . . ."

Her detailed recital continued. Mrs. Parry merely endured. Laura allowed herself the luxury of nodding to fortunate passing friends, and Miss Feathers listened as if Mrs. McCullough were an aborigine encountered on a particularly arduous field trip.

"By God!" said Charlie Trinkam in a low voice. "Look over there, John."

Thatcher glanced toward the entrance.

Just strolling in was a small party of men, all decorously attired in evening clothes. In their midst, enormously pleased with himself, was Owen Abercrombie.

"Do you think that means trouble?" Charlie asked in an undertone. "Lee Clark is here, too."

"Lee Clark is no threat," Thatcher said, keeping his voice down. "He's just trying to protect his Negro business. But I don't like this. . . ."

He broke off when he noticed that Gloria Parry was following this exchange, quiet as it was. She too had seen Owen Abercrombie enter. She raised her chin fractionally.

Good girl, Thatcher applauded mentally.

She was smiling her beautiful smile as Ed Parry made his way through the crowd to her side.

"There you are," his wife said calmly. "I was wondering where you were."

"Yes," said Ed Parry. "Well, I think we should be getting inside. . . ."

In the ensuing stir, John Thatcher managed to have a few quiet words with Parry concerning a brief talk between the two of them at some point during the evening.

"I'll bet it's about Withers," said Parry with an appreciative grin.

"It is," said Thatcher.

"We'd better talk about it. We can have coffee together after dinner," Parry said, still smiling.

He was as impressive as his wife, Thatcher decided.

Because Edward Parry, too, had seen Owen Abercrombie, and he knew what that meant. He was remaining not only calm, but cooperative.

"That'll be a help," said Charlie Trinkam, as a discreet stirring showed that the assembly was being shepherded into the concert hall.

"Where on earth is Vin?" Mrs. McCullough asked the world. "Oh, there he is . . . Vin! Vin!" Smiling kindly, she bade them a general farewell and plunged off toward her husband.

"You've got the tickets, Daddy?" Laura asked anxiously, after making punctilious *au revoirs* to the Parrys, who were moving toward the farther entrance.

He did.

Using them, however, took time. Progress down the aisle was slow, interrupted by greetings, brief conversations and general confusion. Only when they had finally located their seats (next to the head of the State Liquor Authority) did Laura whisper a confidence.

"Wasn't she a perfectly dreadful woman?"

"Mm," said Thatcher, noncommittally, idly flicking through the fat program. He had met worse but he did not say so, knowing this would only elicit a lecture from Laura. She turned to reply to friends yoohooing across two rows and her father, to ensure himself against meeting any eyes, continued leafing through a compendium of advertising and good wishes from every major commercial institution in New York City.

He smiled wryly. Clovis Greene Bear Spencer & Clark sent best wishes to the NAACP. CASH did not. Possibly they had been formed too late to make the publication deadline. Robichaux & Devane also sent good wishes. The Sloan Guaranty Trust, Thatcher discovered with approval, sent nothing; it had merely taken two full pages.

On the whole, he was inclined to think that the NAACP was the group to value this above quarter-page "good wishes." Particularly when, as he found riffling on, good wishes were also emanating from Dibbel Abercrombie.

Well, fund raisers, like public relations people, couldn't be deflected by little things like reality.

"Oh, my God!" It was an involuntary exclamation, made as the last of the violins finished his cacophonous wailing and joined the rest of the orchestra in staring at the audience, willing it to still the magpie chatter that was keeping the maestro in the wings.

"What's the matter?" Laura asked as the lights began to fade.

He had stumbled on the evening's program, sandwiched between eloquent statements of faith from Chock Full O' Nuts and Macy's. Pre-intermission he was safe: Bach, Brahms and Schumann. But post-intermission? He read it again.

INTERMISSION

ROOTS   *AARON BOATMAN*
to a text by Richard Simpson

Soprano: Lucine Asmara
Tenor: Jan Arrow
Bass: William Barlick
Narrator: Alicia Pontandante

PREMIERE

"*Roots*," fluted Program Notes, "is an orchestral 'happening' by Aaron Boatman, the musical rendering of the mellifluous verse by Richard Simpson. It is scored for twelve violins, fourteen trumpets, a marimba and the full percussion section of the orchestra with arias by the soprano, tenor and bass, contrapuntally painting the pastel musical nuances of the long anguish of suffering humanity evoked by Simpson's agonizingly immediate word images. First, the Narrator reads Simpson's powerful and moving "Where Are My Roots?" against the background lament of the richly conceived atonal choral . . ."

"Do you mean . . . ?" he began with deep indignation.

"Sh!" said Laura. She determinedly stared ahead, applauding the arrival of the conductor. Her father eyed her. Without turning, she laid down the law:

"And Daddy, we are staying after the intermission!"

Thatcher fell back, strangely relieved. Obviously Fate could have nothing worse than *Roots* in store—at least this evening.

14 · And Only Man Is Vile

Two HOURS and thirty-four minutes later, the music crashed into its penultimate bar. The only thing sustaining Thatcher was the dim air of *finale* that had crept into the otherwise unidentifiable melodic workings of the evening's last selection. There was a shattering dissonant chord for three beats, a quarter rest, another chord, a half rest and finally a vast tumult that defied definition as a chord, suggestive as that word is of some relationship between individual notes.

Then a horizontal flick of the conductor's baton brought silence, blessed silence. But not for more than ten seconds. Too long had human beings been coerced by mere instrumental chaos. A mighty clamor arose from thousands of human voices, hands, feet. From the balcony, a demented claque from Julliard howled for the composer. The conductor bowed alone, then graciously lofted the orchestra to its feet with one sweeping gesture.

Wild applause continued. Thatcher himself was still clapping, he realized. It was understandable. No matter what the critics might say, this was enthusiasm for release, or, more simply, the human propensity to raise cain in any socially acceptable manner. Functionally speaking, *Roots* was not music but an outlet that left everyone happy without constituting a threat to life or property. Presumably, at a performance by a teen-age idol, Thatcher reflected as the ovation continued, it was at this point that high-strung adolescents proceeded to wreck the premises. Although he wondered why the young were always described as supercharged dynamos perilously close to eruption. The ones he knew personally, those employed by the Sloan as file clerks or messenger boys, displayed a languor profound enough to approach the pathological.

Twenty minutes later, Thatcher was still lapped by the tide of well-being, but the tide was ebbing fast. The audience had been marshaled back into the great lobby for supper. Now, against the dramatic backdrop of glass planes and other geometric complexities, there twinkled a myriad of tables resplendent with crystal and silver damask. As the guests seated themselves, each table assumed a distinct personality. Thatcher saw Charlie Trinkam and Miss Feathers join the Jacksons to fill out a circle of NAACP notables. The Schuylers and Parrys were throwing the mantle of Wall Street over their own little enclave. Unfortunately, Thatcher could not join them or have his discussion with Edward Parry during supper. His own table, alas, was heavily musical, housing, as it did, the composer of the evening, Aaron Boatman.

But the food was excellent and the wines even better. Much could be forgiven. While the woman on his right insisted on discussing the technical merits of a tone poem that he intended to forget as soon as possible, on his left, Mrs. Boatman was interested in nothing more alarming than finding an apartment in Manhattan suitable for small children.

Diligently working his way through a crumbling paté, a memorable lobster bisque and veal as it is too seldom encountered, Thatcher contented himself with small nods of comprehension to the right and rather more helpful comments on real estate to the left. The wine waiter was assiduous in attendance, and the end was in sight.

It was with the appearance of artichokes in *sauce vinaigrette* that Thatcher's attention was wrenched back to the menace at hand. Mrs. Boatman's comments had turned his private thoughts to banker's calculations. Once their children were grown, many people, like the McCulloughs, were moving from the suburbs back to the city and cooperative apartments without lawns. Construction was meeting this demand. But what about the Boatmans, with their small children? Were they an isolated instance, or the newest of *nouvelles vagues*? Perhaps new building was required. Deep in real estate syndicates, construction bonds and first mortgage holders, Thatcher was only distantly aware of his right-hand neighbor swaying to one side to allow a change of plates.

"Oh, dear, there he is!" she cried.

Thatcher murmured something politely interrogative.

"Henry will be furious if there's trouble. He didn't want to come, but I said that he was always looking for an excuse to get out of concerts. And I said, 'Henry, this is Aaron Boatman's latest!'"

Without understanding her, Thatcher experienced a marked fellow feeling for the unknown Henry.

"That did it, I suppose?" he suggested helpfully.

"Well, no," she admitted. "He still said it was dangerous. So we made a bargain. We decided to come as far as the door, and see. Henry said that if there was a mob we'd go straight home. But there wasn't, was there?"

She appealed to him with large, watery blue eyes.

He composed his face into an expression of manly reassurance, but Mrs. Boatman took the bull by the horns.

"Do you mean Owen Abercrombie?" she demanded. "That *awful* man. Aaron was so worried that he might try to ruin *Roots!*"

To avoid a comment, Thatcher turned. Owen Abercrombie and his party were dining at an inconspicuous table near the far wall. Thatcher inspected them. He wished to be fair-minded but they did not look like music lovers. There was an air of rented livery about six of the evening attires.

"A friend of yours?" he asked his neighbor to the right, wondering if these were now fighting words.

"Certainly not," she said coldly. "But I did see him on television yesterday."

Hastily, Thatcher turned the subject. He did not succeed in turning it from Abercrombie.

Mrs. Boatman was glaring at Abercrombie's group. "Philistines!" she said. "And those men with him look more like a bodyguard than anything else!"

Clearly, any threat to *Roots* brought out the beast in Mrs. Boatman. Since Thatcher could think of nothing pleasant to say about the composition, he was at a loss.

Fortunately, Mrs. Davis again contributed her mite. "Oh dear! You don't suppose that it's true what *everybody's* been saying? That he'll try to kill that *dear* Mr. Parry again?"

Thatcher waggled his eyebrows furiously at his daughter. The ladies had drawn the attention of the whole table, and worse still, the attention of Owen Abercrombie himself. Noticing their unwavering interest, he was now staring back with imperial arrogance. Across half the width of the room, Thatcher could feel the lordly self-satisfaction.

The man was aching for a scene. For the first time, Thatcher wondered if Abercrombie were certifiably insane.

In the meantime Laura Carlson was proving herself worthy of her descent. As titular hostess she raised her voice into a sweet clarion, addressed a question to Aaron Boatman and then remorselessly involved the entire table in a discussion of the inspiration for *Roots.*

"Only now are we beginning to understand the mainsprings of the baroque . . ."

". . . suitably modified by the demands of a mechanistic age . . ."

". . . but, Mr. Boatman, isn't automation the most important facet . . ."

"Too long have we allowed a slavish adoration of the romantic . . ."

"The time has come to recognize we are in the midst of a new Renaissance. The twentieth century *is* the sixteenth century. What the *cinquecento* was to art . . ."

Thatcher watched it all with relief and some amusement. His daughter, as nearly as he could tell, was going to skip being a young woman entirely. Incredibly, she had managed to remain a girl, albeit an attractive and considerate one, until the birth of her fourth child. Then, without pausing for breath or putting on an ounce of weight, she had started to unfold matriarchal petals. He was not sure that he approved. He remembered the thirty-five-year-old women of his youth nostalgically. It had been an interesting time of life.

And what of his own role in all this? Matriarchs, he felt, should have managed to shed at least their ancestors, and better still, their husbands. What future was there in being the father of a dowager? With extended life expectancy, one generation after another would soon be impinging on each other's jurisdiction. Modern society would have to create new forms to absorb the ever-extending period between extreme youth and extreme age.

Entrancing as these speculations were, he did not forget his duty. He agreed seriously with Mrs. Davis that we have much to learn from the East. The West had been too absorbed with the diatonic scale. Counterpoint had preoccupied some of our ablest men to a grievous extent. There was the simple charm of single notes to be rediscovered. Mrs. Davis, it developed, had been to Tokyo. Even worse, she knew from *Time* that Thatcher had been to India. While he would not, offhand, have assumed that a short trip to help open a dam made him an authority on yoga and Shinto, it was enough to convince Mrs. Davis of certain sympathies. Inevitably the conversation broadened.

"Nowadays everyone realizes that theirs is a much more gracious way of life. Don't you agree?"

"Oh, absolutely."

"All those rock gardens and almost no furniture. It gives the mind so much more room."

"Just so."

"Then one can concentrate on the really important things. It's not surprising that they're so far ahead of us in things of the spirit, is it? Why, I do believe that it's time for coffee. The time has just flown talking with you, Mr. Thatcher. It's so rare to meet someone who understands. Of course, I say it's impossible unless you experience it yourself. And you have to be receptive. There's no point unless you can open yourself to new impressions. Henry, I'm afraid, isn't . . . Oh, he's waving at me. You'll have to excuse me. We're taking coffee with Mr. Hornstein, the concertmaster, you know."

Thatcher assisted her to rise and watched her sweep off on the arm of the unfortunate Henry. That, of course, was one way of passing the middle years. He went to the head of the table to claim his own.

"Ready, Laura?"

"Yes. And there comes Mr. Schuyler." She waved at the Schuylers and Parrys, who were threading their way forward as Thatcher pulled out her chair. Her eyes laughed at him. "Now you can be comfortable. And, remember, I took care of Aaron Boatman."

Nat Schuyler overheard her last remark. "Did you get stuck with the composer, Thatcher? We got the chairman of the NAACP finance committee. Tonight was a great success from his point of view."

Thatcher was too relieved at his deliverance from Mrs. Davis to comment on Schuyler's ability to land on his feet. He congratulated him on his luck and Mrs. Parry on the financial prospering of the evening. He did not get far before he was interrupted by alarmed cries.

Turning, he saw Owen Abercrombie and his followers bearing down on them. Abercrombie was in the lead, shouldering his way forward with a reckless disregard for the comfort or safety of his victims which augured ill for his intentions. Several women were already clutching the arms of their escorts in the wide wake that the group was leaving. Abercrombie's dark eyes glittered under the busy eyebrows, and a vein in his neck twitched visibly over the starched white collar. Out of the corner of his eye Thatcher saw two stolid men close up on Edward Parry.

Abercrombie stepped forward and grasped Nat Schuyler's sleeve.

"Just a minute, Schuyler! We've got some business with you and your playmates," he growled.

Schuyler was superb. He stood still, unalarmed and quietly disdainful. His face expressed only inquiry at this rupture of the evening's decorum.

"I'm sure you have a great deal to say, Owen. But I have no intention of helping you create a brawl. You can come to my office Monday morning and say anything you want."

"You can't get away with that! You and your protégé have to take what's coming to you. We've had just about enough of your troublemaking. The time has come to settle things."

Abercrombie was so engrossed by this exchange that he could not check on his subordinates. They were in some disorder. Two of them, eyeing the approach of several uniformed policemen from the corridor, were uneasily trying to slip away.

"You're making a fool of yourself, Owen. Now we're leaving."

As he spoke, Schuyler broke his arm abruptly free from Abercrombie's clasp and stepped forward. Unfortunately this left Abercrombie face to face with Edward Parry. Without pause, he closed the gap, grabbed Parry's shoulder and gave a bull-like roar that sent spittle streaming down his jaw:

"Well, *you're* not getting away, my fine colored friend. Think you're somebody, don't you? I'll show you just what you are . . ."

Parry did not try to emulate Nat Schuyler's contemptuous hauteur. Instead he doubled a workmanlike fist. But, at that moment, the two stolid men behind him oozed forward. One of them firmly removed Abercrombie's hand from Parry's shoulder.

"Now, we don't want any trouble here tonight, Mr. Abercrombie . . ."

"HOW DARE YOU TOUCH ME?"

The strong hand on his wrist seemed to rupture Owen Abercrombie's tenuous hold on sanity. The twitch spread from his neck to his face, working convulsively from jaw to brow. With an inarticulate shriek of encouragement at his followers, he shook loose from the detective and began to flail against him. The second detective instantly grasped his left arm, uttering professional injunctions to take it easy and come along quietly.

These were lost. With his right arm thrashing wildly,

Owen Abercrombie suddenly fumbled in a pocket, then brandished a small black revolver.

"Hey!" shouted the detective, pushing forward.

There was one deafening shot.

Knocked off balance, Abercrombie had fired while he was still struggling. The bullet hit one of the chandeliers. There was a cascade of tinkling glass. And from somewhere came a frightened wail.

"Let me alone . . ."

"Watch it, there . . ."

"Get back, get back . . ."

With a madman's strength, Owen Abercrombie, still clutching the revolver, struggled against the two burly detectives, struggled to level his gun on his enemy.

Then Edward Parry shook off restraining hands and stepped forward. With a clublike fist, he smashed a blow down on the gun so savage that Abercrombie's high, thin scream of pain almost blanketed the thud of heavy metal striking the marble floor.

15 · Tell Me the Old, Old Story

FOR A MOMENT that seemed to extend itself into an eerie vacuum of sound and movement, everybody was immobile, staring dully as the revolver bounced along the tiles and shards of falling crystal rang a series of notes that spaced themselves further and further apart. It was almost as if they were waiting for a second finale.

Then, abruptly, there was a convulsive milling as the uniformed police pushed their way forward, hurrying to the scene. By the time they arrived, Owen Abercrombie, restrained by Edward Parry and one of the detectives, was shrieking and raving, twitching and sobbing, mouthing inarticulate exhortations and obscenities. The police shouldered Parry aside and grasped Abercrombie competently, before turning their attention to his companions. These, they lined up and searched on the spot.

"Two more guns!" was the final tally.

"Aiiihheee . . . !" Abercrombie's unearthly screech made Thatcher's skin crawl.

"Leave him alone!"

The shout, urgent and angry, rose above the growing buzz of conversation.

"I said, leave him alone!"

Dean Caldwell paused in his struggles against constraining arms to watch disbelievingly as a gibbering Abercrombie was moved swiftly toward the exit. Then he resumed his defiance.

"Who do you think you are? You can't do this to him, you filthy . . ."

The officer in charge broke in. "Oh yes, we can. And you're next, buddy."

He nodded a command, and two of his men efficiently frog-marched Caldwell away to the waiting riot car.

They passed in front of Thatcher so that he saw the blank stupefaction descending on the angrily twisting face of the Southerner.

It was all over in minutes.

"My God!" somebody said. "Abercrombie tried to murder him in front of a thousand people . . ."

"I tell you he's crazy . . ."

"Oh, Henry . . ."

"Daddy!"

Laura, white-faced and suddenly defenseless, had moved close to him.

"It's all right, baby," said Thatcher, tucking her hand reassuringly in his arm. "Just a passing ugliness."

But it was more than a passing ugliness. Gloria Parry, breathing hard, was stroking the sleeve of her husband's coat to reassure herself that he was still there. Mr. and Mrs. McCullough, who had hurried over, stared blankly at the door through which the police and their prisoners had gone.

Thatcher looked down at his daughter. "No, don't talk

about it. Let's have some of that coffee we were aiming at."

Mrs. Parry seconded him. "Yes," she said, and her voice shook only slightly. "Yes, I think I'd like some coffee, too."

But once the initial shock was over, Owen Abercrombie's arrest cried aloud for comment. The NAACP banquet, once recovered, discussed it in a brittle near-hysterical way until late into the night.

As Wall Street did, on Monday morning.

According to the Sloan's Chief of Research, no arrest unconnected with storage tanks had aroused so much talk for decades. Walter Bowman was having the time of his life, trumpeting into the telephone, sounding old contacts, opening new pipelines of information. His subordinates were lashed into a frenzy of activity.

"The New York City Police Department employs over forty thousand people," he thundered. "One of you must have a contact. Think!"

He refused to admit that very few budding young bankers do know a cop. Neophytes in the Research Department, accustomed to appraising their circle of acquaintance in terms of potential tipsters to mergers and acquisitions, suddenly found themselves remembering that dim daughter of their mother's Cousin Susan who was rumored to have married somebody in the police public relations office. Irately they reviewed their relatives, their classmates, their neighbors. Wait a minute! Didn't their roommate at the Business School have a brother who was a pathologist, somebody who did autopsies? Spiritually, the Research Department rang with cries of "Mush!"

In spite of this self-flagellation, very little meat was added to the bare bones of the official press releases. These were massively uninformative. Owen Abercrombie had been formally charged with violating the Sullivan Act by carrying concealed weapons, with breach of peace, malicious mischief and a host of misdemeanors and minor felonies. Bail, however, had been denied, indicating that a more serious charge was in the offing. His cohorts had also been the subject of miscellaneous holding charges. Indeed, two of the thugs were wanted in Rhode Island for armed assault. Dean Caldwell was out on bail.

"And that's about it," Bowman summed up for Thatcher. "Not much so far. But we'll keep working at it. By tomorrow—"

He was interrupted by the entrance of Charlie Trinkam, who beamed at them in high good spirits while draping himself on the windowsill.

"Hashing over this Abercrombie business?" he asked. "I just got all the dirt from Paul Jackson."

Thatcher nodded approvingly. A criminal lawyer had the contacts they needed. He would know everything there was to know. But perhaps it was more than a question of knowing the right people. So far there had been no announcement of an attorney for the defense. This delay had inspired the White Association for Civic Intervention to an angry denunciation of incommunicado tactics by city officials and confused mumblings about *habeas corpus*, which had hitherto been incapable of provoking "Whacky's" recognition, let alone its approval. The Police Commissioner had wearily countered by disclosing that the defendant had already seen his wife, his son, his doctor, his partner and three lawyers whom he had refused to retain.

"Is Jackson going to undertake the defense?" asked Thatcher.

"They asked him to, but he said no."

"Good man," murmured Bowman.

"Oh, it isn't that." Charlie shook his head. "He'll act for anybody. But he says that it's a million to one against this coming to trial, so it's not his cup of tea."

Bowman began to protest this view of the situation, but Trinkam held up a restraining hand.

"It's all very interesting," he said. "You know Abercrombie is a rich man. Well, he threw out his son a couple of years ago when the boy decided to go and be a poet in a beach shack out in California. They'd been having trouble anyway, since Owen's second marriage."

Rapidly Walter Bowman scanned his mental files on the personages of the financial community. "That's right. He got married about five years ago. To that model."

"Exactly. And the honeymoon's been over for some time. Personally, I think Owen lost interest in sex when he discovered segregation. So, guess what happened as soon as the news hit the radio. The boy flew into town in the middle of the night, and he and the wife put their heads together. Their theory is for Owen to beat the rap by being pronounced insane."

"Ah-h-h," Thatcher was appreciative. "Then he'd be legally incompetent to handle his estate."

"Sure. They get themselves appointed guardians, then they hold the purse strings, and the beauty of it is that Abercrombie doesn't have any financial liabilities. He's piled up a mess of criminal charges but there aren't any civil damages, no big tax bills, nothing. It's just a question of putting him quietly away in a private sanitarium for a couple of years. Hell, he's going to have to spend more than that in jail anyway if he doesn't agree. Public opinion won't go along with a suspended sentence, particularly when it comes out that those two thugs from Providence got their guns from him. And that's even if they don't get him for the two earlier attempts on Parry."

"Yes, it doesn't seem as if Abercrombie has any choice. But you say he's resisting the idea?"

"The way I hear it, he's barely able to get out a coherent sentence. When his own lawyer advised an insanity plea, Abercrombie threw him out. Sure, he'll fight it at the start. But then he really hasn't taken in the fact that he's a criminal. The wife and the son have got the old man in a squeeze. He doesn't have any choice. And even if he does contest it all the way, the family isn't going to have any trouble producing a string of witnesses. Quite apart from his performance last night, a lot of people think he's loony."

"Then that takes care of Abercrombie for the duration,"

said Walter Bowman out of the depths of his experience. "The courts can settle a lot of things fast when they want to, but the one thing that takes months, if not years, is a family quarrel about control of an estate. And part of that estate is his partnership interest in Dibbel Abercrombie. Had you thought about the mess this is going to make over there?"

Everyone present agreed that even customers with a strong enough stomach to deal with Abercrombie *qua* broker during the past few weeks were going to fight shy of a house that managed to foul itself up into a situation worthy of *Jarndyce v. Jarndyce.*

Thatcher's interest, however parochial, was not confined to this aspect of Owen Abercrombie's arrest.

"Are they going to charge him with the other attempts on Parry?"

"Not if he sets up a successful insanity plea."

Thatcher waved away this technicality. "Of course not. But do the police think he did it?"

Charlie shrugged. "They don't know, according to the poop from Jackson. They tried to check his alibi for the shooting, but you can guess what they came up with. The wife doesn't get up till noon, and Owen drives to the station himself. He lives in the same town as Parry, after all, and the whole thing took place during commuting hours. He could easily have slipped over for half an hour and then gone on his way to New York. But that holds true for everybody in that neck of the woods. All of Westchester and the Connecticut shore."

"Connecticut? How does that come in?"

"While the police had their hands on Dean Caldwell, they decided to run a check on him too. He lives in Greenwich, and he has the same itinerary as Abercrombie. Solitary drive to the station and time of arrival in New York unprovable within an hour or two. I think what the police are really pinning their hopes to is finding the rifle. They've got both the bullet and the cartridge case. And the way Caldwell has been talking makes him a good second-string suspect. Personally, I think it's a lot of hot air. At least he wasn't carrying a gun last night."

"That doesn't mean anything," Bowman objected. "He had a good motive, and the attempt in Katonah was pretty safe. He'd be smart to let Abercrombie take the spotlight at Lincoln Center where no one but a nut would try anything."

"Maybe so." Charlie was still unconvinced. "But look, John. If you really want the latest, why don't you have lunch with Jackson and me. I fixed it up with him for one-thirty."

"I'd like to," said Thatcher, "but right now I'm interested in what you said about a motive, Walter. I thought young Caldwell was simply giving vent to his spectacularly unpleasant racist feelings."

"Don't you believe it," said Bowman wryly. "Sure, he's from the South and he thinks exactly the way he talks. But what really put the bite into his venom was the situation at Schuyler & Schuyler."

Both men turned to him respectfully and Bowman visibly expanded under their attention. Trinkam might know criminal lawyers, but when it came to what was going on behind the scene at any brokerage house in the world . . .

"You've got to go back to the time when Ambrose Schuyler died. That's a small house they have over there, but even so it was obvious that they were going to need a new partner. Even before Art Foote died they were understaffed. Now, that kid Caldwell's got a swollen idea of his own competence. He decided that he was going to be the new partner. Normally that idea would have been squelched damned quick when it became obvious that Nat Schuyler was talking to all sorts of prospective partners. But Nat played the whole Parry scheme close to his chest, and the negotiations dragged on for a couple of months, even after Nat located his man. In the meantime Caldwell convinced himself he was as good as in. I saw him around that time and tried to get him to back-pedal a little, but it was useless. Then, when he finally found out what was going on, he exploded. As far as

Caldwell is concerned, Ed Parry stole something that was his. And he doesn't have a doubt in the world that, with Parry out of the way, he could have it back."

Thatcher frowned. "You say you tried to discourage him even before you knew about Parry? But how did you know he was wrong, Walter?"

"Because nobody in the world would have offered him a partnership. He was never even in the running. Dean Caldwell is a good enough research man," replied Bowman with all the serenity of a man who knows that he is the best of all possible Chiefs of Research and has no further ambition, "but there are others. And he's lacking on almost every other score. He has no pull, he's not a salesman, he doesn't get on with people and he doesn't have the judgment to be a particularly good trader."

Trinkam whistled at this comprehensive indictment.

"I wonder if the police know about this," mused Thatcher.

"Jackson will be able to tell you," said Bowman handsomely.

"Sure, they've dug up all that business about Caldwell's bid for a partnership," said Paul Jackson, spearing his butter with a breadstick. "All these people seem to be complete blabbermouths. Caldwell must have spent his entire working day complaining to people about how Parry did him dirt."

Jackson did not approve. His own clients were noted for taciturnity.

"Amateurs," Trinkam murmured indulgently.

"You said it," agreed Jackson heartily. "They're having a hell of a time finding out whether there's a gun missing from Abercrombie's collection. It seems they found an arsenal at his place in Katonah—rifles, shotguns, machetes. The only thing he was short on was pocket weapons. I guess that's why he only outfitted two of his boys."

"I'm surprised the others didn't march into Lincoln Center shouldering shotguns," Thatcher observed.

"The boys wouldn't go for that." Jackson was perfectly serious. "But the fact remains that the bullet and cartridge don't match anything in the Abercrombie house now. I understand they're sifting through the Katonah dump. It would be just like that lunatic to toss his rifle there."

Trinkam was sympathetic. "Hell of a job."

"Oh, I don't know. It's a model dump. Won a prize or something," Jackson said, displaying yet another piece of esoteric information. "Just the sort of thing Katonah would have."

"Then it's the kind of dump that will probably have vaporized this rifle within twenty-four hours."

"No," said Thatcher and Jackson simultaneously. Charlie Trinkam every now and then displayed a powerful ignorance of life as it is lived outside the confines of a metropolitan district. He would have been far more at home in the center of Peking than in South Orange, New Jersey.

"Scavengers," explained Thatcher clearly. "In fact, in Katonah, it's probably antique dealers who inspect the throwaways."

"That's right. A good rifle would be picked up right away. One of the dealers got a fine Oriental off the trash heap up in Westchester."

Charlie moodily pecked at his salad, unprepared to contemplate this strange and exotic way of life. Jackson tactfully turned the conversation.

"The police are pretty hot on the idea of Caldwell as their boy. They figure it this way. Practically everyone at the poison party lives within striking distance of Katonah. In fact, Nat Schuyler is about the only one they care to cross out. He lives in Princeton, and hasn't driven his own car in years. Even so, he could probably still have done it if anybody can think of a reason why he would want to. So, unless they can find the gun, they've pretty well had it on the shooting. But then, there's the poisoning. And that's where you come to an interesting point."

"But everyone at the party could have done that too," Thatcher protested. "It still leaves you with the same group of people."

"Not exactly. First of all, they've compiled a monster timetable of movements at the party. They were lucky there. They got to people right away, the next morning in fact, while the details were still fresh in everybody's minds. And they figure they got as much as they ever will by that route. So they haven't been around again. But they've been working on it."

Thatcher realized with a start that he had almost forgotten that gravely deferential young man who had interviewed him so efficiently. But Centre Street had not forgotten. All through these past days people had been sitting in offices piecing his statement together with seventy others and amassing a very accurate picture of that ill-fated party.

"And poison isn't like a gun," Paul Jackson was continuing. "This won't be a case of someone having nicotine around the house for years. If they ever pin this one on anybody, access to the poison will be a part of the case. Anybody can have a rifle innocently. It's a lot harder to pull that as a defense with nicotine."

"People in cities don't have rifles," said Trinkam, still obsessed with his unfortunate glimpse of exurbia. "And anyway, I thought people in these estate areas had weed killers and insecticides by the ton. That's what the pharmaceutical firms are always saying."

"Foote wasn't killed with any weed killer," Paul Jackson replied. "It was the pure alkaloid. You don't come across that often, and it's damn hard to explain away."

It was apparent that Jackson was already readying himself for the arduous task of defending the poisoner, if and when brought to trial. His dark eyes glinted with interest and he elaborated further.

"The police will really have something to sink their teeth into if they can find a solid motive—and I don't mean one of these 'Let's Keep Wall Street White' things —and access to poison. I assume they can prove opportunity with their charts."

"That still doesn't narrow things down at all."

"Ah, but if you think of it as a rational crime, then you

get to the point about the confusion of the glasses. That's what I meant about the police being onto something interesting. They're concentrating on the people who had reason to know that Foote was on the wagon. Someone who wouldn't have been put off by finding four men with three glasses."

"Does that narrow it down much?" asked Thatcher dubiously.

"Does it ever!" replied the lawyer exuberantly. "What with old Nat Schuyler spending all his time squiring Parry around, and someone having to take up the slack in the office, poor Art Foote was pretty well chained to his desk, except when he was helping on the Parry bit. His contacts were much more restricted during his last week than normally. And practically everyone he saw was at the reception. Of course there was one group that heard about his ulcer morning, noon and night, and that was the people at Schuyler & Schuyler." He ended on a triumphant note.

Thatcher was forcibly reminded of canny old Nat Schuyler's comments on the use of Owen Abercrombie as a stalking horse. He said as much.

"Of course it makes sense. Anybody could play these racists like a piano. And there's not much doubt that somebody's been doing it from Schuyler & Schuyler. Abercrombie was a gift from heaven to the murderer." Jackson grinned brilliantly around the table. "And he's going to be even more of a gift to the guy's lawyer."

16 · Day of Wrath!
O Day of Mourning!

JOHN PUTNAM THATCHER set off for his office Tuesday morning in high spirits. Since no sane observer could derive satisfaction from the current state of affairs, this left him to conclude that he was an unregenerate earth-ling, as opposed to the rare Eastern spirit Mrs. Davis had apparently discerned. An excellent breakfast, including first-rate eggs, bacon and hashed brown potatoes, real coffee and the other necessities, was followed by the dis-covery that the sun had finally reappeared, bathing the world outside the Devonshire with a vitality which end-less days of gray drizzle and fog had drained from it. After this, Thatcher found it impossible to let the exist-ence of Owen Abercrombie affect him.

Except favorably. Was it possible, he asked himself as Brewster summoned a taxi, that the Abercrombie arrest had eclipsed Bradford Withers' *bêtise*? Was it too much to hope that gunfire at Lincoln Center had diverted CASH's attention from the Sloan Guaranty Trust?

After all, Owen Abercrombie's maniacal outburst did tend to monopolize attention. How long had it been since anybody thought of that quite likable man, Arthur Foote? Of course the police were still pursuing his murderer, but there was no doubt that Wall Street was much more in-terested in the attack on Edward Parry.

To the extent of assuming that Arthur Foote's poisoner and Edward Parry's assailant were one and the same man.

But were they?

And if so, why?

No good answer suggested itself, so Thatcher leaned back and watched the sun brighten the colors worn by the clerks and secretaries streaming up from the IRT. Indefatigably nature touched the aridity of even this man-made desert, nourishing the human spirit as surely as it fed flowers and bushes.

It rapidly developed, however, that nature had an up-hill fight. Thatcher got his first intimation of this when the taxi turned off Broadway, only to be waved to a halt by a uniformed policeman.

"What the——?" demanded the driver, who gave no evidence of having breakfasted well.

Usually Thatcher let these little exchanges complete

themselves without his participation. Today, however, a general predisposition toward peace and harmony caused him to hitch himself forward. But before he could contribute to the conversation, a squad car screamed to a halt beside them. As they turned to watch, three blue-coated policemen flung open the doors and pelted down to Exchange Place, nightsticks in hand.

"——do you want me to do?" the cabby snarled.

The policeman was willing to tell him in some detail. After completing a picturesque recitative, he withdrew.

"Officer," Thatcher called out, handing his driver a bill and hurrying to alight. "What's going on?"

The policeman, busy fending off other taxis who were now creating a tangle that would last for some hours, had time for only four words.

"Trouble at the Sloan!"

"Good God!" said Thatcher.

He started to struggle through the huge crush, at the same time mulling the possibilities. Embezzlement? Then, why the police horses, dancing dangerously down Exchange Place, with grim-faced riders, wielding sticks, shouting commands that the surging mob get back?

Fire? Then where were the fire engines, the alarm bells? Only the whine of police sirens rent the air. Thatcher was jostled slightly as another team of uniformed men, breathing hard, charged past him. Above the din of thousands of people trying to see, trying to get to work, trying to move, there were shouts and confused noises from ahead. From, John Putnam Thatcher realized, the Sloan Guaranty Trust.

"Here, there, you can't . . ."

A human chain of policemen behind a barricade of wooden horses barred the approach to the Sloan lobby.

"What's going on?" Thatcher demanded.

"Just move on."

With a spurt of rage, Thatcher elbowed his way to the red-faced policeman who was shouting directives.

"Now listen here. I'm a vice-president of the Sloan," he began in icy tones. "And if . . ."

The harassed policeman capitulated immediately. "o.k., o.k. Let him through. Get in there, and see what you can do!"

Thatcher barely had time to digest these ambiguous words as he slid past the policeman and hurried the twenty-five steps to the great glass doors (intact) of the Sloan Guaranty Trust.

Without pause, he pulled them open—then stopped dead in his tracks. The nature of the problem was instantly and painfully clear.

The lobby of the Sloan Guaranty Trust (terrazzo with mosaic inlay) was totally obscured. Kneeling on every available surface were, perhaps, five hundred Negroes (with a sprinkling of white faces among them). They were singing, very beautifully and very softly. Instead of the muted clacking and cheerful clicking of a busy bank, the great glass lobby with its tortured friezes and elephantiasis-ridden foliage was—except for the muted hum from outside which became a punctuating burst whenever the doors were opened—echoing with the solemn harmonies of devotional anthems.

Well, there was one question answered. cash had not forgotten.

The staff, naturally, was confused. But respectful, thought Thatcher, edging inside. He noticed Henley, the office manager, back to the wall, fix horrified eyes on four young girls at his feet as they clapped their hands softly and reverently.

"Well, here you are, John!"

Even Everett Gabler was whispering. He came sidling along the wall to Thatcher. As he did, he inadvertently trod on a brown hand.

"Oh, I'm so sorry," he said anguishedly.

"That's quite all right. Didn't hurt a bit," replied a pleasant-faced matron. She resumed her singing.

Gabler whipped out a handkerchief and mopped his brow.

"What is all this?" Thatcher inquired.

"A kneel-in," said Gabler.

"A *what?*"

"A kneel-in," Gabler replied. "The minute the doors opened this morning at eight o'clock, these people marched in and started all of this—praying and singing! Shocking thing to do in a bank, but it is imposing in its way, don't you think?"

Thatcher agreed that it was and suggested retreat to the Sixth Floor and the Trust Department, leaving Commercial Deposits to handle its own problems. As he spoke, Henley, the manager, finally reached their side. Behind him, looking baffled, was a policeman, resplendent in gold braid.

"Thank heavens you're here, Mr. Thatcher. Mr. O'Hara is in Washington, and I don't know what to do!"

"We can clear 'em out," said the policeman in a low growl. Then, conjuring up violence and bloodshed, he gloomily added, "That is, if that's what you want!"

Thatcher sighed inwardly. It was not, technically speaking, his responsibility to deal with this. But Henley was clearly out of his depth (and O'Hara, fortunately in Washington, would also have been out of his depth, he thought uncharitably). It was obviously unthinkable to let Bradford Withers handle this. Henley, wringing his hands, broke in:

"I understand they're protesting Mr. Withers' remarks," he said, looking anxiously over his shoulder at the congregation. He was not mistaken; the tempo of the singing was picking up.

"Perhaps we should try to get to your office to talk," Thatcher suggested. At this, Henley registered enormous relief; well might he. He had just shifted his burden to other, stronger shoulders.

Reaching the office was not easy. All available floor space was packed. Standing behind the counters, looking beleaguered, and rather bemused, was the depleted staff.

"A lot of people can't get in," said Henley apologetically over his shoulder as he led the way. "Oops! Oh, sorry, sir!"

"Quite all right," caroled back an elderly black gentleman, without breaking the beat. "Rock, chariot, I told you to rock!"

"Oh dear," moaned Henley, picking his way forward.

They followed him, Indian file, until they had reached the comparative comfort of the tellers' area. There, Thatcher noted with a gleam of amusement, one of the young women had momentarily forgotten that her first allegiance was to the Sloan Guaranty Trust. Caught up by the rhythm, she was tapping her foot, and softly joining in:

> "Rock, chariot, I told you to rock!
> Judgment goin' to find me!"

As the dignitaries passed, she put hand to mouth in an endearing gesture of guilt. Neither Henley nor Everett Gabler noticed her. John Putnam Thatcher did.

With a sudden grin, he winked at her.

He was, however, grave and sober as he marched into Henley's office and listened to his plaints, and to the ominous, though less voluble, prognostications from Captain Bielski.

"Well, it seems clear enough," he said decisively. "If these people are determined to stay, we certainly are not going to throw them out."

Bielski looked relieved. So did Henley, until he thought about the day's business.

Thatcher cut his lament short.

"The major problem seems to be order outside," he said.

"Don't worry," Bielksi reassured him. "The riot squad is on its way."

They looked at him in silence for a moment.

"Ah . . . yes," said Thatcher. "Well, that should convince the staff of the value of physical fitness, if nothing else does. Now, Henley, all you have to do is hold the fort down. We'll try to work something out."

At some stage, Thatcher knew, the singing would end and Richard Simpson would emerge.

"Yes, yes," said Henley, perceptibly reviving. "What about the employees who are late today?"

With an effort, Thatcher reminded himself that Henley, in the last analysis, was a clerk, not a banker.

"I'd just forget about them," he said gently.

Henley was disappointed.

"Low level tyrant," Thatcher said to himself, pondering this unattractive type as he and Gabler escaped to the executive elevator bound for the sixth floor.

He missed Everett Gabler's critical remarks on Walter Bowman's latest research report.

"Sorry, I didn't hear you," he murmured as they stepped out of the elevator. Here, too, there were gaps in the familiar ranks normally stationed behind files, calculating machines and typewriters. But since the trust officers to a man preferred using the executive entrance, they were all present. Thatcher entertained no illusion that they were working. Predictably, only Everett Gabler could rise above five hundred Negroes singing spirituals in the lobby.

"Pharmaceuticals," he was saying with spinsterish disapproval. "Now, John, you know as well as I do that the drug houses are already overpriced. I see no reason . . ."

"Do I detect a moral disapproval of oral contraceptives?" asked Thatcher, leading the way to his own office in time to shock Miss Corsa yet again. "No, Everett, I don't have time for that right now. We've got a lot of things to do. . . ."

Just then Charlie Trinkam arrived, reporting cheerfully that the throngs on Exchange Place were growing. And the television crews had arrived.

"That's another thing," Gabler began disapprovingly as Miss Corsa rang through. Bradford Withers was on the line.

"John!" The voice was vague and faintly aggrieved. "John, what is all this? I don't know if you've noticed, but there's some sort of fracas going on downstairs. Somebody should do something about it."

Thatcher counted to ten. Then:

"The police are doing what they can," he said carefully, ignoring Trinkam's broad grin.

"The police? What is all this . . .?"

"Brad, we're having a kneel-in. Yes, K-N-E-E-L- . . . yes, protesting your remarks . . ."

The telephone erupted into turkey gobblings.

Rather sharply, Thatcher retorted, "No, I don't think it would be a good idea for you to go down. Yes, we're keeping an eye on the situation. Yes . . . yes . . ."

He hung up and sighed. With considerable tact, his subordinates did not comment.

Instead, they started a brief consideration of Bowman's critique of the pharmaceutical industry. This, unfortunately, caused Thatcher's attention to revert to one of the day's earlier musings—the poisoning of Arthur Foote. It was not so odd that it had slipped from the center of attention—not when Wall Street was being reminded of the attacks on Edward Parry by kneel-ins, trade-ins, by television interviews—and by the dread specter of the coming March on Wall Street.

"Good God!" he said aloud. "If a kneel-in can disrupt one of the Sloan's divisions, can you imagine what a full scale March on Wall Street will do?"

Trinkam raised his eyebrows. "To be honest, I haven't been able to think of anything else."

Determinedly, Thatcher brought a fist down on his desk.

"We've got to strike back!"

"But how?"

For a moment Thatcher pondered.

"They're singing the 'Battle Hymn of the Republic'!" said a new voice.

Ken Nicolls stood in the doorway. It was evident that the junior trust officers, delighted to have their routine interrupted, were making periodic reconnaissances of the lobby situation.

Suddenly Thatcher snapped his fingers and smiled broadly.

"That's it!" he announced.

Trinkam, Gabler and Nicolls stared at him.

"That's it," he repeated. "Now, Charlie, I want you to get over to Philborn and tell him to get the glee club ready. Nicolls, call the custodian . . ."

With a martial air that Hugh Waymark would have envied, John Thatcher dispatched his junior officers to a number of urgent tasks.

"And hurry!" he said in parting. "Now, Miss Corsa, I want you to get Ed Parry for me. No, I don't know where he is but . . . what's that?"

"Mr. Robichaux," she countered briskly.

"No, I don't want Robichaux," said Thatcher authoritatively.

"He's on the line," she reported.

There was no escape.

"Tom, I'm in a hurry . . ."

"Understand you've got trouble over there," Tom shouted.

"To be precise," Thatcher replied, "a kneel-in."

There was a long pause.

"Well, good for them," said Tom Robichaux astonishingly.

Thatcher removed the receiver from his ear and inspected it. What was Robichaux saying?

"You know," the hedonist continued, "I had a little talk with Francis last night, and by God! It hit me."

"What hit you?" Thatcher inquired with genuine interest.

"Why, this civil rights business," said Robichaux. "Never really saw it before. But, dammit, I'd be kneeling-in myself . . . No, I'd be breaking your glass windows, that's what I'd be doing. . . ."

In a world gone mad, it was not particularly strange that Tom Robichaux was going mad with it. The picture of him heaving rocks through the Sloan's great windows was, in fact, irresistible. But Thatcher was still curious to discover how the wily Francis Devane had managed to engage his partner's support for the civil rights movement. Robichaux was happy to explain.

"Well, Francis put it to me. 'How would you like it,' he said, 'if you had fourteen million dollars, and they wouldn't let you buy a seat on the Exchange, simply because you're a Negro?' Well, that hit me, John, I don't mind admitting it. Never thought of it in that light before. But for God's sake, what does color matter when a man has fourteen million dollars—that's the way I see it."

"I'm sure you do," said Thatcher. There was much to be said for an uncomplicated outlook.

Robichaux' voice dropped into a confidential range. "Of course, this may cause me trouble. But I'm a man of principle . . ."

"Trouble?"

"Celestine. She's big in the UDC—United Daughters of the Confederacy, you know. She comes from Macon. But on a thing like this . . ."

"Who was that lady I saw you with last night?" Thatcher could not resist asking. Robichaux did not recognize the quotation.

"You mean Saturday night? A very interesting woman, Zelda. She's a social worker, would you believe it?"

Thatcher, who would not, indicated again that he was in a hurry.

"Yes, well the reason I called you was that I wanted you to hear the latest. They've just told Francis. The SEC is going to come out with a statement later today, something about investigating racial bias in the New York Stock Exchange, with a view to legislation. The Governors want to beat the timing."

Nicolls stuck his head in the door, nodding.

With an uplifted hand Thatcher held him motionless as he continued to listen to Robichaux.

"That's fine, Tom. It works in with something I have in mind. You'll have to clear it with Francis. Now, listen, this is what I want you to do . . ."

A moment later he was turning to Nicolls and listening to his report.

"Fine," he said, consulting his wristwatch. "We don't have much time. Now, you'd better root out the electrician and be sure we have the microphones ready."

Nicolls nodded and listened to further instructions. Over his shoulder, Thatcher saw Trinkam dispatching clerical help on errands.

"We'll have to hurry," Thatcher said.

"Yes, sir!" said Nicolls, suppressing a salute in the nick of time.

"And, Nicolls," said Thatcher, "I need scarcely tell you that if that kindergarten of yours in Brooklyn Heights does not turn out to be fully integrated, your employment at the Sloan is hereby terminated."

With a brisk wave, he strode down the hall toward Walter Bowman's office.

Nicolls stared after him blankly.

Miss Corsa, handling three telephone calls simultaneously, took pity on him.

"Don't worry. That was one of Mr. Thatcher's little jokes."

17 · Sing Ye Heavens and Earth Reply: Al—le—lu—ia!

AT THAT VERY MOMENT, Richard Simpson was cleaving his way enthusiastically toward the Sloan.

He had a very clear idea of how the next two hours would shape themselves. The early morning kneel-in, coupled with a careful leak from his own staff about an important announcement, had ensured the presence of all the major networks. Cameras would abound, while young men with microphones hung deferentially on his every word. Against a solemn background of choral spirituals he would deliver an eloquent statement about the rights of man and the sanctity of selling off Vita Cola.

Then there would be a few stern questions, cast in a rhetorical frame, addressed to the iniquities of Bradford Withers.

Perhaps at this point the Sloan might produce some mindless helot to stammer out a few transparent evasions. It didn't matter. At this peak of dramatic crescendo, possibly with a single basso intoning "Deep River," he would signal the timing of the March on Wall Street for the day after tomorrow. Then there would be a powerful fade-out of his right profile looking firm and exalted. In fact, a good deal of Richard Simpson and precious little of anything else.

It was not to be. Simpson, happily riding the crest of a situation created by others, failed to realize that the opposition had not yet begun to fight. Like many an agitator before him, he was about to learn that it can be difficult to control the powers one has unleashed and virtually impossible to upstage them.

John Putnam Thatcher's blood was up. The invasion of the Sloan had touched off emotions normally associated with the desecration of the home. Like a good general, he first planned his strategy. Then he alerted his intelligence, deployed his troops and summoned reinforcements. The nature of his tactics might have come as a surprise to an orthodox military mind—say, that of Hugh Waymark, last heard from in the clutches of the Committee to Clean Up Wall Street.

Thatcher's conference with Walter Bowman apprised him of the exact nature of Simpson's forthcoming announcement. The trouble with contrived leaks is that anybody can get hold of them. Bowman's information merely confirmed Thatcher's intuitions.

"And I think," he declared, "I think we're taking the right steps."

These steps were many. Workmen moved to the front lobby the giant television set in the Directors' room used for closed-circuit communication with the Sloan's scattered operations. It boasted a thirty-six inch screen. Meanwhile, the members of the Sloan Glee Club, together with their musical director, were hastily summoned from their desks and assembled on the balcony overlooking the lobby, where they were in the habit of serenading holiday crowds with Christmas carols during the yuletide season. They were not a group to be despised, as even the critic of *The New York Times* had admitted after their ambitious rendition of Handel's *Messiah*. Messenger boys were returning from all the local bookstores with every available collection of Civil War songs. All employees had been given permission to join the festivities. And best of all, Tom Robichaux, the light of conversion beaming from his vagrant eye, was hurrying to the scene of battle.

Thatcher's aim was quite simple. The Sloan Guaranty Trust was going to steal Simpson's thunder. The spirit of Mahatma Gandhi was going to be displaced by that of John Brown. People who got up at dawn to take the A train the length of Manhattan to Broadway and Nassau had feelings to rouse. What Julia Ward Howe had done for the Union, she could do again for the Sloan.

A scant two minutes before Simpson's arrival, Thatcher stepped into the lobby, flanked by his ADC's. Summoning the press to him, he declared in stentorian tones that he was in momentary expectation of an important message from the Stock Exchange. A representative would be with them immediately. Then, dead on time, he wheeled to the doors and welcomed Richard Simpson with a ringing speech which placed the Sloan so far in the vanguard of the civil rights movement that it left Simpson looking like a Ku Klux Klansman. There was a tumultuous ovation from the lobby and then, as the CASH leader collected his scattered wits to reply, seven hundred voices thundered forth, "The Battle Hymn of the Republic."

In the face of this welter of noise the television cameras, understandably enough, abandoned the principals and panned over the singers. There was much to reward any cameraman. The kneelers were singing with passion, their eyes lifted upward. And as the lens followed their gaze into the architectural heights of the lobby, it came to the glee club, equally exuberant, and being conducted with demonic energy. Pages fluttered as chorus after chorus unfolded. Then down came the camera to another enthralling scene. Tom Robichaux had come through the doors and, after taking in the picture before him, reverently removed his homburg to lay it across his breast while he stood at attention.

> Glory! Glory! Hall-e-lu-jah!
> Glory! Glory! Hall-e-lu-jah!
> His Truth goes marching on!

With the last chorus echoing through the marble halls, Thatcher and Robichaux relentlessly advanced on the microphones, where Robichaux announced that the Board of Governors of the New York Stock Exchange would meet on Thursday morning to deliver its decision on the transfer of a seat to Edward J. Parry.

This news had two happy results. It sent the entire financial press scampering from the scene to attack the President of the Exchange in his lair, and it cut the ground from under Simpson. By the time he could get to the microphones to paralyze his listeners with a call to the great March on Thursday, he sounded like a man determined to have his March whether or not there was any reason for it. As he incoherently accused the Exchange of deliberately undermining his schedule, he sounded neither firm nor exalted. He sounded petulant.

Thatcher let him maunder on until the conductor reclaimed the attention of his chorus. Then, to a telling accompaniment of "We Are Coming, Father Abraham," Thatcher really let himself go. In rip-roaring accents he reminded the kneelers, the television audience and most of Exchange Place of the gigantic rally at Madison Square Garden the next evening for all March sympathizers.

"And we of the Sloan Guaranty Trust, including our president Bradford Withers, will join with you—and Edward Parry—for this occasion!"

Ovation!

The proceedings were then brought to a climax by a

final anthem. Emotions had reached new heights. The elevators, the halls, the stairways were crowded with employees joining in. If that fire-proof, water-proof, earthquake-proof building had any rafters, they rang as never before. Not until he saw the young woman teller from Commercial Deposits openly laughing at him did Thatcher realize he himself was singing. Like many a farmboy from New Hampshire in 1862, he could not resist the "Battle Cry."

> We will rally from the hillside,
> We will rally from the plains,
> Shouting the battle cry of freedom!
>
> We will fill the vacant ranks
> With a million free men more,
> SHOUTING THE BAT-TLE CRY OF FREE-DOM!

With the Sloan achieving the spiritual renaissance that figured so largely in the supper conversation at Lincoln Center, with sandwich boards demanding "Justice!" in the corridors of Stanton Carruthers' law firm, and a hootenanny in progress at Waymark & Sims, the Committee of Three found it difficult to select an unobtrusive site for the deliberations which would produce the press release being promised to the *Wall Street Journal* at this very moment by Francis Devane. They had long since become resigned to their hoodoo impact on their surroundings. No normal commercial establishment could be expected to welcome them with open arms.

These considerations, plus the prevailing atmosphere of insanity which was beginning to topple strong minds, explained why, although the blustering November afternoon had ominous gray skies overhead and a brisk breeze whipping in from the northeast, Thatcher and his colleagues were assembled on the pitching deck of the Staten Island ferry plowing their way endlessly back and forth across New York Harbor. Nor were they united by any common reaction to their plight.

Thatcher himself was so uplifted by the success of his give-'em-hell tactics that morning that he could have taken an entire armada in his stride. Repressing a tendency to burst into "Anchors Aweigh," he buoyantly reminded his companions that he had a great deal to do. He still had to see Edward Parry, check Bradford Withers' speech so that it was foolproof, absolutely foolproof, and—as a concession to Francis Devane—invite Lee Clark to join the Sloan and Schuyler & Schuyler in appearing at the March on Wall Street Rally.

"Let's get down to business," he urged.

But Hugh Waymark wasn't going to do anything until he had relieved himself of his accumulated grievances.

"That Committee to Clean Up Wall Street," he sputtered angrily, "it was all a fraud."

Thatcher pointed out that it didn't matter what they were. The only reason for speaking to them was to prevent uncontrolled action.

"You don't understand. They didn't care about Parry. They were nothing but . . ." He cast around wildly for the *mot juste*. "Nothing but nonbelligerents. In fact, civilians," he concluded, much as Rommel or Montgomery might have described a stray Bedouin wandering over the fields of Alamein to a water hole.

"But I thought they wanted to clean up Wall Street," objected Carruthers, emerging briefly from his reverie.

"They mean it. Literally. They want trees on the sidewalks and a flower box in every window." Waymark's voice rose in scornful mimicry. "A sapling now will provide shade and spiritual comfort to future generations." He resumed his normal tones. "It seems there's some sort of a deal you can set up with the Department of Sanitation. They provide the tree and care for it during the first year. Then it's yours. Not a bad idea, really. I wouldn't mind having one in front of my place uptown. But is now the time for that sort of thing?"

No one could say that the Committee of Three wasn't learning about life, thought Thatcher. He had found out all about the prizes won by the Katonah dump, and

Waymark would soon be tending an infant oak in Sutton Place. But perhaps the strangest result of their flight to the sea was to be found in Stanton Carruthers. He was standing by the rail, inhaling deeply.

"Haven't been on this ferry in years," he said expansively. "Really it's a great place to get away." He gazed yearningly at the Statue of Liberty in a posture suggestive of the newly arrived immigrant, one leap ahead of the Gestapo.

"Yes, yes," said Thatcher impatiently.

But Carruthers also had things to get off his chest. He told them in loving detail about his little ketch at the Greenwich Yacht Club, lamented Vin McCullough's sale of a fine schooner consequent upon this removal to the city, and said that young men today were faddists. Always taking things up, and then dropping them. One year it's sailing, and the next year it's birdwatching. Sad, sad. No stamina, no fixity of purpose. For those with the sea in their veins . . .

In the end Thatcher wrote the release himself.

Francis Devane no doubt meant well when he suggested that inviting Lee Clark to join the Sloan Guaranty Trust and Edward Parry on the rally dais would be both courteous and politic. Clark didn't see things that way at all.

"It's an insult, that's what it is," he growled at Thatcher.

"Oh, come now. The Board of Governors knows that this has been a hardship on Clovis Greene. This would give your firm an opportunity to publicize your connection with the Negro community."

"Connection!" Clark twisted his knuckles until they cracked. "We're just another victim. Schuyler & Schuyler is responsible for this whole mess—and they're reaping a damn big profit!"

Thatcher was not going to indulge in meaningless platitudes.

"They certainly hope to do so. But Devane thought you might be able to stem the wave of withdrawals with a personal appearance. We all know that you can't recoup your losses completely."

"You can say that again. But you don't understand what the damage has been so far. Look, we've picked up a couple of clients from Schuyler & Schuyler. Some of their Southern customers who dropped McCullough when they heard the news. Well, they've had to wait two weeks for their portfolios. And you know why? Because they're so busy over there handling the new business. We've lost over five hundred accounts. So what do you think a little speech from me is going to accomplish?"

Possibly losing another five hundred, Thatcher yearned to say. Instead he repeated the invitation.

Clark showed his teeth in an unpleasant smile.

"Oh no. Nat Schuyler and I are going to have a reckoning. And that reckoning doesn't include smoking any peace pipes in front of all of Harlem."

Thatcher had saved his conference with Edward Parry for last, because he expected it to be the least taxing of his many duties that day. But there he neglected to reckon with the eddies of passion swirling through the corridors of Schuyler & Schuyler. The first thing he heard as he stationed himself before the receptionist was the voice of Dean Caldwell, raised somewhere in the nether regions to a shrill yell of defiance.

"So you think you can throw me out and wash your hands of me! Well, you've got another think coming!"

Dim, inaudible rumbling intervened. They did not sound particularly placatory. The receptionist, Thatcher noted disapprovingly, did not measure up to Miss Corsa's high standards of indifference. Visibly nervous, she asked Thatcher to take a seat.

"I don't know whether Mr. Schuyler and Mr. Parry are free right now," she babbled distractedly, giving Thatcher a good idea of the identity of the disputants.

"I haven't gone through all this to be given the boot for some nigger! You can't get away with this!"

The voices were coming nearer. Evidently the disturbance was roiling its way to the exit. A good thing in many ways, but Thatcher could find it in his heart to wish that his own movements had detained him from the house of Schuyler for another fifteen minutes.

Caldwell burst through a door into the reception room. He came backward, whether because he was turning to yell at his companions or because he was being hustled along, Thatcher could not tell. Ed Parry and Nat Schuyler were right behind.

"You planned it, the three of you!" shrieked Caldwell. "You and Art Foote and this colored boy. You ganged up on me. That's what you were after all along, to get rid of me!"

"That's enough, Caldwell," said Nat Schuyler sharply. "You're hysterical and you're upset. I have some sympathy with you. But if you're not out of this door in two minutes, I'm going to call the police."

Schuyler paid no attention to the other occupants of the room. Nor was he making any attempt to hide the fact that his lapels and shirt collar were rucked up, as if violent hands had been laid on them.

For a moment Caldwell glowered silently at him but, as Parry stepped forward and Schuyler turned to the girl at the switchboard, the Southerner suddenly let out his breath and his shoulders sagged.

"All right, all right," he muttered, stumbling toward the door.

But with his hand on the doorknob he seemed to recover some of his defiance. He turned for one parting shot.

"But you haven't heard the last of this. I've got plenty of friends, and I'm not taking this lying down!"

The door banged behind him.

The girl at the switchboard kept her hand on the dial, unwilling to recognize that the crisis was over. Parry and Schuyler looked at each other helplessly. Then Nat became aware of Thatcher's presence.

"I'm sorry," he said sheepishly, as if embarrassed at a display of emotion unseemly for a brokerage house. "I have to get cleaned up. You can probably figure out what happened, Thatcher. Anyway, Ed'll tell you all about it. You'll have to excuse me. In spite of everything, I can't help feeling sorry for that boy."

Then, moving very slowly, but still erectly, he left the room.

There was a moment of silence.

"Whew!" breathed Parry at length. He took out a gleaming white handkerchief and mopped his brow. "Sally, we'll be in my office. Send us some coffee, will you? And find out if there's anything Mr. Schuyler wants."

He ushered Thatcher back into what had once been Ambrose Schuyler's office. There were lines of worry around his eyes. "I hope all of this isn't doing Nat any harm. He's not a youngster, you know."

"Did Caldwell attack him?" asked Thatcher bluntly.

Parry shied at the word. "Well, the boy jumped him," he admitted unhappily. "I pulled him off. Nat fired him."

"Under the circumstances, that can scarcely have come as a surprise to Caldwell."

"You'd think so. But then you weren't here. I could swear that he was completely taken aback. It sounds impossible, but I don't think he expected Nat would. I guess he thought he was indispensable." Parry shook his head. "He went berserk. As if the whole world had suddenly turned upside down."

Thatcher tut-tutted sympathetically, recalling Walter Bowman's opinions of Caldwell's self-esteem.

"Maybe he'll calm down once the shock has worn off," he suggested.

Parry looked dubious. "I've been hearing a lot about him lately. You know, when I first agreed to join the firm, the people I saw were Nat and Art Foote. I worked out the deal with Nat and did a lot of office work with Art Foote. He spent most of his time here filling me in on the house's business. It's only recently I've gotten to know Vin McCullough and this Caldwell kid. Vin and lots of others have let me in on how Caldwell feels. I don't think it's going to die down. In fact, it seems to be growing stronger and stronger."

Here was more confirmation of the police view as expounded by Paul Jackson. Look at Schuyler & Schuyler, they said. These were the people who knew about Art Foote's drinking habits. These were the people who had something really riding on Edward Parry's admission to the firm.

And, it developed, these were the people who thought in terms of assault and inciting others to assault.

It was an effort to return to business.

"Now, about the rally," he began.

"Oh my God!" said Edward Parry from the heart.

18 · Hasten the Time Appointed

TWENTY-FOUR HOURS later, John Thatcher recalled this comment.

"Where to?" asked the cabby.

"Madison Square Garden," said Thatcher. One thing, and one thing alone, could be said for his current peripatetic rounds; he was revisiting many New York City landmarks. After all, how many years was it since he had last taken the Staten Island ferry? Or been to Madison Square Garden? He remembered the long count, but nothing since. Probably it was time that he revisited Madison Square Garden.

At this point reality broke in. Were there any solid reason for a return trip to Madison Square Garden, a hockey game would be infinitely preferable to a CASH March on Wall Street Eve Rally.

Featuring, as his baser self cravenly pointed out, placatory remarks by Bradford Withers, designed to dissipate the Simon Legree attitude he had foisted on the Sloan.

"Geeze, I hope there ain't no trouble," the cabby remarked turning right on 50th Street behind a bus emblazoned: PASSAIC CASH JOINS MARCH ON WALL STREET. It was the last of a long string of buses. "I mean, just look!"

Handing him a bill, Thatcher looked. The sidewalk, as far as he could see through the tangle of buses, cars and trucks, was thick with Negroes, well-dressed but determined-looking. Their placards also were determined:

> FREEDOM AND EQUALITY
> NO SECOND CLASS CITIZENS
> THE TIME HAS COME

With difficulty, he began to struggle indoors. The lobby, too, was thronged. From the auditorium there thundered great organ crashes, with ringing voices uplifted in accompaniment:

> "There's a little black train a-comin',
> Get all your business right;
> There's a little black train a-comin',
> And it may be here tonight!"

Thatcher stood aside to let a large family party pass him hurriedly. The father, anxiously surveying his brood, had a mischievous little girl perched on his shoulder. The mother, lips compressed with silent but firm control, was supervising two frankly rambunctious boys, perhaps ten and twelve. And, also in Sunday best, the grandparents forged ahead.

It was not Richard Simpson's labored exhortations that were propelling thousands upon thousands of Negroes into Madison Square Garden tonight, to listen to speeches and songs (The music within had moved on:

> "Joshua fit the battle of Jericho,
> Jericho, Jericho!
> Joshua fit the battle of Jericho,
> And the walls came tumblin' down!")

Thatcher was, accordingly, deep in unrewarding thought, when he heard his name called.

"John! There you are!"

He looked up. A frowning Vin McCullough waved vigorously, then plunged cross-stream against the inflowing tide to join him.

"Brad's here," he reported, suggesting that he, at least, had had some doubts about Withers' appearance on the scene. "He's down in one of the offices with some of the officials. We might as well get on down. . . ."

If there was one thing Thatcher could have done without, at the moment, it was officials. Nevertheless he followed McCullough along battered, utilitarian halls, where hawkers were selling huge buttons: CASH MEANS RIGHTS, into a small bare room where he first saw Nat Schuyler, deep in converse with Dr. Matthew Ford, the noted sociologist. Well, he was getting plenty of grist for his mill. Nearby stood Bradford Withers.

To do him justice, he did not look intimidated by the muted distant roar, transformed by some acoustical oddity from simple musical enthusiasm to the screams of Romans eager for Christians.

"No," he was saying, "I still don't like it. . . ."

"Please, Mr. Withers!" His vis-à-vis, a thin, balding young man, was a member of the Sloan's legal staff, Thatcher recalled. For some reason, he seemed to be on the brink of tears.

"Still think . . . oh, hello there, John."

Bradford Withers was sounding very like himself, Thatcher saw. That, of course, was both good and bad.

". . . I still think that I should just get up and explain, informally, don't you know?"

"Please," the lawyer pleaded emotionally. "Please, Mr. Withers, just read the statement. I'm sure . . ."

"Well, dammit, it isn't fair . . . oh, hello there, Stan . . ."

Hard on John Thatcher's heels, the rest of the Committee of Three appeared. Stanton Carruthers, he was glad to see, though sorely tried, still felt that he must rally to the aid of a junior (and outmanned) member of his profession.

"Hello, John. Now, Brad, what isn't fair?" he asked in the heavily soothing voice common to lawyers and dentists. Outside, somebody was performing a stirring march with trumpet flourishes and great responsive shouts. Both Nat Schuyler and Dr. Ford were looking smug.

"Dammit, nobody can claim that I'm anti-Negro," said Bradford Withers heatedly. "Oh, hello there, Parry. Listen, when this is over tonight, I'd like a word with you about that shipyard. . . ."

Parry's look of strain momentarily gave way to the flicker of incredulous amusement that Bradford Withers so often evoked. A tremendous thundering from the auditorium quickly erased the amusement. He looked troubled as he nodded his greetings and moved over to join Schuyler and Ford.

"Nobody claims that you are anti-Negro," said Stanton Carruthers with care and no accuracy. "It is merely that your remarks lent themselves to misinterpretation. . . ."

"Well, then, if I just explained . . ."

"Which is precisely what the statement does," said Carruthers, plucking it from the young lawyer's nerveless fingers and quickly scanning it. "Yes, perfectly clear . . ."

It was true, John Thatcher knew—and suspected that Edward Parry knew, if nobody else in the room did. Bradford Withers simply divided the world into two groups: Witherses and non-Witherses. The appalling misfortune of being born a non-Withers overshadowed such minor disabilities as race, creed or color.

Thatcher settled back to let Stanton Carruthers continue his good work. He discovered that he was sharing a battered desk with Napoleon after Waterloo.

Or possibly Robert E. Lee, bidding farewell to the Army of Northern Virginia.

"After our long efforts," said Hugh Waymark, gazing bleakly into the jaws of defeat. "And, God knows, we strained every sinew. Yet we haven't been able to save the day."

Ford and Schuyler were deep in a conversation that

Thatcher had no desire to join. Vin McCullough and Edward Parry stood exchanging desultory remarks, both of them flinching at each full-throated roar that reached their ears.

"It sounds like another one of those damned sonic booms," Thatcher heard McCullough say in a strained voice.

Parry nodded absently.

"Just a few friendly words," Bradford Withers was saying earnestly. Stanton Carruthers allowed himself a slight frown.

"Perhaps the statement might be more prudent . . ."

"How," Thatcher asked Waymark, "how have we strained our sinews in vain, Hugh?"

Waymark shook his head sadly.

"We've played our last card. I don't think that there's any doubt about it. Tomorrow . . . tomorrow there's going to be a March on Wall Street!"

In view of the fact that nineteen thousand people had assembled to listen to speeches, songs and organizational details concerning tomorrow's March on Wall Street, Thatcher was tempted to make an acid retort. Then, casting his mind forward to the horrors yet to come, he decided to hold his fire.

". . . sad for our comrades-in-arms," said Waymark. Clearly he was ready to organize a Veterans of the March chapter.

"Oh, John!" called Stanton Carruthers, as Thatcher had known that he would. "Perhaps we could have your opinion . . ."

In the end, it took the united efforts of Thatcher, Stanton Carruthers, Hugh Waymark, Vin McCullough and Nat Schuyler to convince Bradford Withers that he should not depart from the script prepared by the Sloan Guaranty Trust's legal and public relations departments. (And there, thought Thatcher, was a collaboration that made the blood run cold.) They were just in time.

"I think," said Dr. Ford, consulting his watch with a deprecating smile, "I think we should be getting up to the platform."

One thing can be said for the financial world. It teaches discipline. To a man, they rose.

"Can we trust that damned fool?" Nat Schuyler did not bother to lower his voice as he joined Thatcher.

"You don't really care, do you, Nat?" Thatcher replied with acerbity.

Schuyler took this as a high compliment. He was still wheezingly chuckling as they filed out of the office and began the long walk down the aisle to the bunting-draped platform in the center of the Garden floor.

"Oh my God!" Thatcher heard Edward Parry say again. He could well understand it.

Noise, like a hammer blow, smote their ears: the blare of horns, the explosion of flashbulbs, the monotonous incitement of drums and the abandon of thousands of human beings, roaring in defiance, in enthusiasm or in sheer exultation. Completing the grotesque distortions were the wild careening of spotlights, stabbing the darkness with blinding gleams of light. As they moved into the auditorium, the world narrowed to a tangle of arms and hands, waving or pointing at them, in one instance grasping at Parry's jacket. The party proceeded into the pandemonium through a weird human arch.

Bradford Withers, who was leading the way with Dr. Ford and Nat Schuyler, simply sailed on, superbly untouched by this tumult, as by the rest of life. Both Vin McCullough and Edward Parry, however, lacked his natural insulation. Both of them were visibly shaken.

Bringing up the rear was the Committee of Three. Stanton Carruthers, mindful of the Chief Justice of the Supreme Court, was weighty and dignified. Hugh Waymark, that gallant officer-gentleman, smiled bravely in defeat.

Thatcher was last to clamber up the wooden steps to the platform. It was already crowded with Richard Simpson, Mrs. Mary Crane, two ministers, two rabbis, a quartet of spiritual singers, the deputy mayor, three technicians and Miss Feathers.

In subsequent days, Thatcher was to maintain that this

exceeded all of the nightmares to which he had been party. As they took their seats—rickety folding chairs—the noise did not abate. Nor did it abate thereafter. Thatcher looked out on an endless sea of faces, shuddered inwardly, and tried to withdraw into his own thoughts. The kaleidoscope of sound and light made this easier than might have been expected: the official program, to those seated on the platform, was nothing more than unintelligible electronic booms, followed by frenetic responses.

". . . March on Wall Street!" shouted Richard Simpson into the microphones, flapping a telegram in the air.

A tidal wave of noise broke over their heads.

Thatcher felt Vin McCullough stir beside him.

"Impressive, isn't it?" said Thatcher.

"Terrifying."

But it was Edward Parry, on his other side, who had replied.

". . . and education!" screamed Mrs. Mary Crane, who had succeeded Simpson. From nowhere, four drum majorettes appeared bearing a huge banner:

READING, 'RITING—AND RIGHTS!!!

In the upper level there was an explosion.

"Just a balloon," Hugh Waymark said, in effect dismissing anything less than a howitzer.

With some apprehension, Thatcher glanced toward Bradford Withers, sitting near the lectern. Once again he was pleasurably surprised; Withers had managed to reduce this holocaust to a social occasion. He was deep in conversation with a bishop of the African Methodist Church. Unless the cleric was a sailor, it was hard to conceive what they might be discussing, but they seemed to be getting on famously.

". . . housing!" bellowed the latest speaker.

The roar that greeted this made McCullough stir again.

"Well, I've done my bit," he said. "Sold the house today, to a Negro doctor."

Thatcher was not sure that he approved of small talk

under the circumstances. On the other hand, sitting there and being yelled at was very difficult.

"Did Nat approve?" he asked.

"Happened too fast," McCullough said as somebody in the balcony hurled tons of confetti into the air, further confusing the whole scene. "I haven't had a chance to mention it to him yet."

Edward Parry, forcing himself to speak lightly, leaned forward. "You can give the doctor my name as a reference," he said. "I may have some tips for him."

But McCullough and Edward Parry could not sustain casual conversation. The spectacle of the emotion-packed auditorium, veritably pulsing with life, and hope, was palpably daunting.

". . . Sloan Guaranty Trust!" shouted somebody.

Thatcher refused to betray tension. He knew that, while the audience was raptly watching Bradford Withers, who was ponderously taking his adieu from the bishop and moving with statement in hand to the improvised lectern, eyes on the platform, particularly those of Richard Simpson and Mrs. Crane, were fixed on him.

He had no trouble masking his reaction to Withers' speech. This was because he had none. The words were totally inaudible. Despite his heavy responsibilities to the Sloan Guaranty Trust, Thatcher was profoundly grateful.

Withers spoke at length. Whatever he said provoked an outburst. For one terrible moment, Thatcher feared that the president had cast prudence to the winds and had indeed just spoken a few words from his heart; in which case he was to have the rare opportunity of seeing a president of the Sloan Guaranty Trust torn to pieces by a howling mob.

But, watching Withers punctiliously shake hands with Simpson and Dr. Ford, he concluded that the *mea culpa* had been, if not effective, at least inoffensive. Stanton Carruthers, he noted, while not moving a muscle, managed to exude vast relief.

". . . Caldwell," said Edward Parry.

"What was that?" Thatcher was forced to ask over the

combined voices of two hundred choristers from Howard University.

"He came into the office today to clean out his desk," said Parry. "I'm a little worried about what he's likely to do tomorrow, during the March."

"And now, ladies and gentlemen," said Richard Simpson. "About the March!"

Despite Hugh Waymark, Thatcher regarded the worst as over. It was not humanly possible to follow the rest of the proceedings, although they consumed another hour.

So, in the midst of emotional whirlwinds, benumbed by the eloquence of speaker after speaker, Thatcher did, at last, withdraw into private communings.

About Arthur Foote.

About Edward Parry.

About Dean Caldwell.

And murder.

"Of course," he murmured softly to himself, waking to virtual silence.

The bishop, an immense figure, had his arms outstretched. In a deep beautiful voice, he was praying.

With sadness, Thatcher listened to him.

". . . and forgive our enemies. Let us seek peace and understanding. And let our needs and hopes teach us to understand the needs and hopes of others. Thy will be done. Amen."

"Amen," said thousands of voices.

"Amen," said John Putnam Thatcher.

Then, as the platform came to life, he moved swiftly to intercept the man he needed—Nathaniel Schuyler.

"Great evening."

Thatcher looked at him.

"No clowning, Nat. Listen . . ."

As he spoke in a low urgent voice amidst the satisfied hubbub surrounding them, he saw the color drain from Schuyler's face.

"No!" Schuyler protested when Thatcher had finished.

Thatcher said nothing.

Schuyler bowed his head for a moment. Then, straightening with an effort, he said:

"Do you want to go now?"

"I do," said Thatcher grimly.

They were going to the offices of Schuyler & Schuyler.

19 · The Day of March Has Come

IT WAS VERY LATE. The usually bustling office lay in shadowed silence. Nat Schuyler closed the last folder.

"Another one," he said harshly, handing it to Thatcher.

Thatcher took it and ran his eye over the neatly typed contents memo, then tossed it onto the large pile of similar folders on the desk.

"You were right. No escaping it," Schuyler said. There was no remnant of his original shock at Thatcher's revelations; hour after hour of proof had forced him into bitter acceptance of the identity of the murderer.

"Question is, what do we do now?"

Thatcher, himself a little tired, raised an eyebrow. Nat Schuyler was old enough to take a philosophical view of life and death, having seen too much of both to respond emotionally to any single incidence of man's inevitable end. Was he extending this same tolerance to murder— and to a murderer?

Schuyler answered the question for him.

"Too late to call the police now," he muttered, rising stiffly. He gathered the pile of documents on his desk. "I'm going to put these in the safe. He'll know—but by that time he'll know anyway."

Thatcher watched him suit action to word, then turn to add:

"I propose to meet you first thing tomorrow morning. Eight-thirty will do. Might as well get this cleaned up before business tomorrow."

"I suppose you're right," said Thatcher doubtfully, also rising. Delay did not seem desirable but it was already past three o'clock. Alerting the police now would serve only to take horror into an innocent home. Better let the arrest take place in the impersonality of Wall Street.

It was, after all, a peculiarly Wall Street murder.

"All right, eight-thirty," he said, stifling a yawn. "Shall I meet you here?"

Nat Schuyler drew his spare frame upright. "No," he declared. "Not here. At the Centre Street police head-quarters!"

This was not precisely how John Thatcher would have chosen to proceed, but he did not protest. In a manner of speaking, this was Nathaniel Schuyler's show. It was only courteous to let him, temporarily, retain the illusion that he was still calling the shots.

Unfortunately, it had slipped his mind that eight-thirty tomorrow morning was going to be a very busy hour.

Indeed, by seven o'clock, the quiet suburbs and the somnolent exurbs were already humming with preparations for the day.

"I wish you didn't have to go in today," said Gloria Parry.

Edward Parry looked at her, but she did not give him a chance to reply.

"I know," she said. "You think it's your duty! You think this whole noble March is because of you, so you're going to go in. But, Ed . . ."

Gloria Parry rarely let herself get upset, and never let herself sound upset. Parry reached across the breakfast table to grasp her hand reassuringly.

"Now, Gloria," he said, "I promise to be very careful. I promise not to take any risks. And I'm sure the police will be watching me like a hawk!"

"That doesn't comfort me!" she flashed back.

"Me neither," he said with a half smile. "But I do have to go in today. No, it isn't just heroics. There's something important I've got to do at the office."

Twenty miles away from the luxurious environs of Katonah, a variant of this scene was being enacted in Greenwich.

"I wish you didn't have to go in today," said Mrs. Dean Caldwell, automatically fluttering her eyelashes while at the same time efficiently shoveling oatmeal into her younger son's mouth.

"Now, Varena," Caldwell replied. Hysterical youth though he might be in the office, in his own home he was very much the *paterfamilias* (if not the Old Massa). In fact, a good deal of trouble would have been avoided had the rest of the world accorded him the respect and admiration that Varena did. There were drawbacks to this role: Dean Caldwell was still wondering how to tell Varena that he was now a member of the Great Army of the Unemployed.

"I just get so worried, Dean honey," she continued, carefully wiping her son's chin. "And, young Dean, you finish your toast!"

Old Dean looked around his kingdom, recalled Robert E. Lee's moving observation about his footsteps guiding the young and, persistent in error, attempted something equally memorable.

"A lot of colored rabble can't make trouble for a Caldwell," he declared with quiet dignity. He remained pleased with the apothegm until young Dean spoke up.

"Then what can, Dad?"

The accent (Greenwich, Connecticut) and the spirit (dispassionate inquiry) were alike offensive to Caldwell.

Quickly, his wife said, "Now that's enough from you, young man!"

"Gee, what'd I say?"

Only after an ungenteel wrangle could Dean Caldwell resume the subject.

". . . and besides, Varena. I have to go in today. I've . . . got something important to do."

Four miles away, Mrs. McCullough called to her husband, who was rummaging through the closet for his coat.

"I wish you didn't have to go in today."

"Oh, the March will be orderly," he murmured.

Julia did not hear him. Nor, it developed, was she concerned about his well-being. She rarely was.

"The storage people are coming for the crates. Then I promised the real estate people that I'd get an estimate on that garage door, and if that isn't enough, I've got to have lunch with Dot Pervin, and you know what that means! She'll be furious about our selling the house . . ."

"I've got something important to do at the office," McCullough said.

Julia was still talking when he left.

And as the clock crawled on, the access routes to Manhattan began to swell, to choke and to jam with the millions of toilers in that vineyard. They came by the IRT and the BMT, by the Independent and the Hudson & Manhattan tubes, by the Long Island Railroad and the New York, New Haven & Hartford. They came on roads, through tunnels and over bridges, and in their midst they floated thousands, coming for another reason.

At Union Square, one of the preliminary rallying points, the last of the Connecticut buses had arrived by eight o'clock.

"You're in the group over there," shouted a young Negro, hurrying up and consulting a master plan on his clipboard. "They've already got your banners."

Three hundred people started moving toward the standard:

CONNECTICUT CASH WANTS CONFIDENCE IN WALL STREET

They passed the Washington, D.C., representatives, already milling around in place.

CAPITOL CASH FOR CAPITAL WITHOUT COLOR

Having arrived on the five-thirty Pennsy, Washington, D.C., was raring to go, and scornful of late-arriving Connecticut.

"C'mon, let's get this show moving!" shouted one of its members (owner of a substantial amount of IBM).

His exhortation was drowned out by the roar of three

large open trucks that came lumbering in and ground to
a noisy halt. Approximately seventy-five Negroes began
clambering down.

"Is that the best that Delaware could do? I mean,
trucks?" asked the assistant director for New Haven; he
was still smarting from D.C.'s scorn.

"Delaware!" the young man with the clipboard shouted.
"Oh, good! We were afraid that breakdown with your
bus might have held you up. You're over there . . ."

He gestured to a distant placard:

DELAWARE WANTS COLOR-BLIND DIVIDENDS

"Oh, I don't like that . . ."

"Now's no time . . ."

"ATTENTION!" boomed an authoritative voice through a
megaphone. "We're about ready to get started!"

A chorus of cheers rose from the ranks.

". . . we're picking up the New York representatives at
our rendezvous point on our way downtown . . ."

Cheers, laughter, cries of "Hurray for New York!"

"Now, before we get started . . ."

"C'mon let's go, go, go!" This was a shout from Delaware. The delegation, though small, was spirited.

"ATTENTION! Now, I just want to review some last minute reminders . . ."

"We know, we know . . ."

"First, keep together while we're at Washington Square.
There'll be a lot of students, and we don't want to be
separated. That's our official starting point, and each state
will be notified of its position in the lineup. Second, remember the route. Down Broadway, over to Foley Square,
through City Hall Park and then right on down to Wall
Street. And last, keep in ranks until we get down to the
Exchange itself. Orderly ranks. The police will be lining
the route so there probably won't be any trouble, but if
anybody starts anything, it's up to you to stop it as fast as
possible."

The assorted stock and bondholders listening to him

nodded vigorous agreement, but there were faint catcalls from a small clutch of white folk singers who, though totally devoid of any investment in American business, were bringing up the rear. They, frankly, were itching to encounter the American Nazi Party; they were folk singers second, the University of New Hampshire football team (second squad) first.

"Fine. Now, if anybody feels faint, or gets overcome by the heat . . ."

Since it was a clear, bitterly cold morning that promised to become a clear, sunny and cold November day, this caused a Cleveland, Ohio, dentist to turn to his neighbor, a teacher from Philadelphia.

"What's he talking about?"

"He learned the ropes at the March on Washington," the teacher explained knowledgeably. "I'll bet he doesn't realize that this is a roast beef crowd. That's the trouble with these specialists."

He was right.

"Red Cross stations are at Washington Square, City Hall and Trinity Church," said the speaker. "Now what else? . . . oh yes! Lunch at Battery Park after the March. No chicken, egg or tuna sandwiches . . ."

The assemblage had already been instructed to the point of exhaustion. Moreover, it possessed mimeographed sheets presenting essentials both more clearly and in greater detail than the speaker. It stirred restively.

Even though he was not particularly sensitive (and a man who makes a career directing demonstrations cannot afford to be too sensitive), the speaker registered this reaction.

"o.k. That's all. I just want to tell you that there will be over ten thousand of us marching . . ."

Deafening cheers!

"And I've just received news that we're not alone. Our friends in Paris are staging a sympathy sit-in at the Bourse. The eyes of the world are on us!"

On signal, the band struck up "Marching through Georgia." Eagerly the ranks surged forward.

At eight-thirty on the dot, John Putnam Thatcher was struggling into Centre Street Police Headquarters against a similar eager surge—this time, blue-coated, determined policemen charged with the onerous task of keeping order on Wall Street.

"Without anything which could, under any circumstances, be construed as brutality—by anybody!" the commissioner had said emotionally, thus contributing to the general thanklessness of police chores.

The powerful wave of blue had wedged Thatcher into a corner when suddenly a flashbulb exploded at him.

"*New York Times!*" shouted a voice above the others. "What are you doing here, Mr. Thatcher?"

"I have nothing to say," he barked, jamming himself forward as a circle of newsmen turned their attention from the police to him.

"Is the Sloan expecting trouble?"

"Why are you here today?"

"Nothing to say!' Thatcher shouted.

"Can we quote you?"

Thatcher turned to snarl, and in so doing caught sight of a disheveled Stanton Carruthers.

"John!"

"Not a word here," said Thatcher, indicating the *New York Times,* busy demonstrating its superiority by abandoning the police and sticking with a vice-president from the Sloan Guaranty Trust.

"Certainly not!" said Carruthers, offended.

A few low words with the desk sergeant told them what they wanted to know.

Not until they had driven off the *Times* and were alone in the dusty second-floor corridor, did Thatcher discover why Nathaniel Schuyler had abdicated in favor of Stanton Carruthers.

"It was Min Schuyler. She got the whole story out of Nat when he got home and decided that it wouldn't do to have him come down here. She said," Carruthers quoted carefully, "that the excitement might harm his health."

Thatcher snorted.

A full-scale riot wouldn't disagree with leathery old Schuyler. What Min really meant was obvious; she didn't want a Schuyler mixed up with the whole distasteful affair. He personally wished that a Thatcher weren't mixed up with it. And a fat lot of good that was doing him.

". . . so I came along to help," said Carruthers. "Once we lay this information before them, we can let the police . . . er . . . do their disagreeable duty, and . . ."

"Get back to our own business," Thatcher finished for him.

"Certainly not. We'll join Hugh Waymark at the Exchange."

At first this program moved smoothly. It took but ten minutes to lay certain financial facts before the poker-faced individual behind the desk. Scrupulously, Thatcher simply outlined technical information, without once mentioning murder—or Arthur Foote.

"We wondered about him. Everything was clear—except the motive," the policeman said, after giving him a long hard look. He spoke slowly, but he was pressing buttons in his intercom. He snapped orders into it. "And now you've given us the motive. We'll pick him up before he gets into the building," he said.

And that, it appeared, was that. After the officer hurried out, both Thatcher and Carruthers delayed leaving; it is no little thing to deliver up a murderer.

"Well, we'd better get over to the Exchange," said Thatcher, recovering.

It was precisely thirty minutes later that he first began to wonder if he had indeed delivered up a murderer.

He and Carruthers were still on the fringes of City Hall Park, trying to battle their way down Park Row. The sidewalks were solid with humanity, not the inadvertent solidity of men and women hurrying from different directions to a standstill, but the contented motionless solidity of viewers and spectators. The narrow streets were given over to official vehicles; there were squad cars, ambulances, motorcycles, two Red Cross mobile units, three television trailers, several radio transmitter cars, a Civil Defense truck and—for no reason that John Thatcher could dredge up—a Brinks armored car.

Over the talk, the occasional mysterious noise of officials communicating with each other, and the roar of the motorcycles, the beat of a band was distantly audible. A brass band. A marching band.

By strenuous exertions, Thatcher advanced about six paces.

"We made a mistake," he said to Carruthers.

"What was that . . . oh, sorry. Yes, Madam, I am truly sorry that I trod on your foot . . . good heavens! What did you say, Thatcher?"

"We made a mistake," Thatcher declared. "The police won't be able to get to Schuyler & Schuyler in time. When he sees that those files are gone, well, he'll know . . ."

His hat knocked rakishly over one eye, Carruthers pointed out that giving the police certain financial information (which, incidentally, enabled them to identify a murderer) was really the extent of their duties. Apprehension of the miscreant today, or in the near future, was a police problem.

". . . and it doesn't concern us, at all, thank God . . . ouch!" In a savage undertone he continued, "I wish you would tell me why that woman needs an umbrella on the finest day in weeks."

His grumbling was submerged by a clash of cymbals as the CASH band strutted by, on the move again, followed by the stern leaders of the movement—including Richard Simpson and Mrs. Crane, Thatcher saw over intervening heads. Mrs. Crane was in precise step with the music. Simpson, all too predictably, was not.

Next came a uniformed group representing veterans (who were presumably also stockholders); then a contingent of school-children; then, as far as the eye could see, row upon row of other marchers.

"We've got to get to the Exchange before they do."

With judicious use of the elbow and aided by a general seepage southward, they managed to inch themselves through the crush while CASH members from fifty states, so it seemed, strode by in stately array on Lower Broadway, which was being kept clear for this purpose by at least four hundred policemen. Across the street, far behind the police lines, Thatcher could see a small group of pickets. They had no more chance of disturbing the parade than did the distant (but also hostile) governor of Mississippi. Vin McCullough had assured his wife that the March would be orderly, and it was.

The trouble period, however, was still ahead, at the technical terminus of the March where ten thousand marchers would be assembled, however peaceably, before the New York Stock Exchange, an area definitely not designed to accommodate such gatherings.

Would Richard Simpson be able to resist the temptation to say a few words?

Thatcher very much doubted it, although the police had expressly forbidden any speeches before Battery Park.

Yet, under the circumstances, what would the police be able to do?

And, more germane to John Thatcher's responsibilities, what would the Stock Exchange do?

"Sorry, I have to get through," he said frigidly to a stenographer who was audibly wondering who he thought he was, shoving that way.

Their painful voyage to the Stock Exchange was accompanied by other freely voiced criticisms. Accordingly, neither Thatcher nor Carruthers was feeling particularly peaceable (or even orderly) when they reached the first of twenty concentric semicircles of security forces well ahead of the March.

"My God, they're not planning a siege!" Thatcher shouted in exasperation to an obtuse and unyielding member of the Exchange's own guards. Fortunately, at this moment, Hugh Waymark emerged.

"Let 'em through, Powers," he ordered. "Good man, Powers," he continued, dropping his voice. "I've deployed only veterans out there. Come on in . . ."

With the density outside approaching disaster proportions, Thatcher was happy to do so.

Hugh Waymark had been assigned or had assumed the military precautions at the Stock Exchange. Within the building, Thatcher discovered, somebody else had decreed that it was to be business as usual.

Somebody, Thatcher decided, following Waymark upstairs, without much horse sense.

"Volume's way down," Waymark remarked over his shoulder.

Thatcher glanced into the pit; there were traders and specialists as usual, if perceptibly fewer; there were the familiar druggists' jackets. But business? No. This site of so many frenzied scenes, normally abuzz with men rushing in and out, with buy or sell orders falling like snow onto the Floor, was a study in lethargy.

"How's Vita Cola?" he asked.

"They haven't opened yet . . . what is it?"

For Stanton Carruthers had suddenly stepped forward to grip Waymark's arm, halting him.

"Look!"

Following his pointed finger, they saw a member of the New York Stock Exchange stroll onto the Floor.

"Why not?" Waymark asked curiously.

"Because he's a murderer, that's why!" Thatcher said grimly. He had been right. One look at the looted office had been enough to sound the murderer's alarm. He had fled—into a street swarming with police. And now—here.

Hugh Waymark instantly became the leader of a posse. "We'll just go down . . ."

Stanton Carruthers kept his eyes fixed on the trim figure. "He's behaving quite normally," he said. "Possibly he doesn't know the police are after him."

"I doubt that, Stan," said Thatcher.

"I do too," said Carruthers. "And, Hugh, this man is a murderer. This is police business."

Waymark, looking mulish, launched into protest but Thatcher was thinking rapidly.

"There's no use calling the police," he said, turning to

return to the stairway. "If their lines aren't jammed, ours certainly will be. The thing to do is to get some of those men outside."

"I'll do it!" Hugh Waymark cried, bounding athletically ahead, briefly so transfigured that he forgot one of his favorite possessions, his tricky heart.

With resignation, Thatcher watched him sprint ahead. This, as he was subsequently quite ready to concede, was one of the most serious errors he had ever committed.

Waymark reached the heavily guarded entrance just as the last of the March on Wall Street had snaked ten thousand members of CASH (actually 8,495) onto New Street. Richard Simpson had assumed a commanding position in the shadow of the Stock Exchange's angled brass doorway, and was now turning to face his followers.

Police, on the one hand unwilling to let him flout the law, and on the other hand extremely sensitive to the delicacy of the whole situation, were trying to close in on Simpson, and move him off, without actually touching him. Just as they began their deliberate stalk, Simpson seized his advantage; flinging his arms wide, he bellowed:

"We demand to be heard! We must talk to the Board of Governors! About rights—for Edward Parry!"

A huge roar went up from the multitude, including those on the steps of the Treasury Building, those around the corner on Broad Street and those hanging out of every window in the district.

At this moment, the forbidding doors swung open. Instantly, all noise ceased. In the almost painful silence, Richard Simpson turned.

Hugh Waymark strode outdoors. Masterfully ignoring Simpson (and his 8,495 followers), he sought the nearest high-ranking police official. His eye fell on a harassed captain, not ten feet away.

"We need you in here," he said in clear carrying tones. "We've got your killer!"

There was a moment—a brief one—during which Hugh Waymark's second heart attack could have been averted. Then, he simply disappeared beneath the tidal wave.

A subsequent SEC investigation revealed the following facts:

a) 1,847 unauthorized personnel rushed into the sacred precincts of the New York Stock Exchange. 138 of them managed somehow to get onto the Floor.

(The uniformed forces caught up in the onslaught caused less distress than others.

"But, Madam!" shouted old Bartlett Sims shortly before she shoved him to his knees, "WOMEN ARE NOT ALLOWED ON THE FLOOR OF THE EXCHANGE!")

b) For three hours and twenty-eight minutes, no business —at all—was transacted.

(In Iron Mountain, Michigan, Mr. Fred Lundeen called his broker.

"What's the latest on Bessy?" he asked, prepared [he thought] for the worst.

The broker sounded drunk. "We haven't had a single quote for the last fifty-eight minutes."

"Oh, I see," said Mr. Lundeen, hanging up. He reflected deeply, then sadly spoke to his son, who was in business with him:

"Duane, those bastards have dropped the Bomb!")

c) Approximately $28,405 damage was done to the N.Y. Stock Exchange's physical plant.

("There he is!" shouted a policeman, carelessly propelling a tally clerk through a plate glass window. The murderer, after one comprehensive inspection, had ripped off his jacket and was moving toward the stairs leading to the balcony.

"What do we do now?" an enthralled Stanton Carruthers inquired.

"Remove ourselves," Thatcher replied. This was only prudent; hard on the murderer's heels was a motley crew, some bearing placards, some swinging nightsticks, all of them pounding along like stampeded buffaloes.)

d) Almost one million dollars in commissions was lost during the period of the disturbance, see prorated transactions schedule, Appendix A.

(The murderer, realizing that he had inadvertently
started a wild race that was only drawing attention to his
own flight, ducked into a convenient cubicle [a statue was
being replaced] and let the mob surge past. Then, with a
quick look for watchful eyes, he slowly begin to sidle
downstairs again. The Floor was a cauldron, but in its
disrupted pandemonium he could be momentarily safe.
He quickened his steps, past two policemen intent upon a
short pugnacious order clerk. In so doing he cannoned
into the U.S. Steel specialist who had, somehow, lost his
tie and a portion of his shirt. He was also bleeding slightly
from a small cut over his left eye.

"What the hell is going on?" he demanded, breathing
hard.

"God knows!" said the murderer. He sounded frightened and panicky, but so did the steel specialist.

"There he is!"

Incredibly, a policeman had sighted him again, a
policeman who recognized him.

The steel specialist at that moment sustained a painful
swipe in the neck from a fiercely brandished placard
[CASH WANTS PEACE AND JUSTICE]. He turned angrily and
saw a new covey of police who were ignoring offenses in
their immediate vicinity to struggle toward him.

"My boy," he said softly, "I don't know why they want
you, but . . ."

With that, he pivoted and landed a competent rabbit
punch. He followed this up with a short, powerful jab.
The murderer folded. [He did not slump to the ground
since he was held erect by the crushed tangle surrounding him.] The U.S. Steel specialist might be sixtyish and
overweight, but he had not boxed at Dartmouth for
nothing.

Moreover—he looked around, shuddered and moved
aside to give a nearby fistfight decent room—this sort of
thing was Letting the Exchange Down.)

The SEC report, combining schoolteacher disapproval with maternal anguish, continued its list of outrages connected with the March on Wall Street for many pages. It did not, however, contain two interesting items:

1) At 10:32 (approximately eighteen minutes before Hugh Waymark disappeared, and some four minutes before the March reached the Exchange), the Board of Governors completed its formalities and approved the application of Schuyler & Schuyler to admit its newest partner to the Exchange with all the rights and duties of a full member.

2) At 11:16 (approximately nine minutes after Hugh Waymark regained consciousness, but long before order was restored), another Schuyler & Schuyler partner was removed from the Floor by four burly policemen.

His name was Vincent McCullough.

20 · There Is a Line, By Us Unseen

"SO IT WAS Vin McCullough all along." Edward Parry shook his head. "From the way Nat talked, I was almost sure it was Dean Caldwell. Seems incredible. But then everything has, this past week."

He was not the only one finding it difficult to reemerge into a workaday world. The financial community, which had survived the threat of race riot and the reality of murder, suffered its greatest casualties in the termination of the great March on Wall Street. As the news had spread into every side street and alleyway that Edward Parry was now a member of the Stock Exchange and his would-be murderer under arrest, the March had mushroomed into a celebration. Wall Street, whose meanest resident was something of a connoisseur of ticker tape parades and welcomes for the returning hero, had never seen anything like it.

A mad, impromptu fiesta sprang up with dancing in the streets, confetti and, of course, music. Everywhere there were stirring marches, moving spirituals and ribald folk songs. As catchy marimba bands on Broadway vied with devotional gatherings in Bowling Green, the scene resembled some enormous cross-breeding between a Latin American gala and a Salvation Army crusade. The infectious enthusiasm of clapping, laughing, stamping, sobbing proved too much for the denizens of the concrete barracks towering overhead. They poured forth into the streets, leaving behind companions to fling out the refuse of thousands of punch card machines, tickers and typewriters, until a blizzard in rainbow-colored hues floated down from the heavens.

Thatcher was to retain many hectic memories of that day, not the least of them being Miss Corsa and Everett Gabler, driven into temporary alliance, looking on in outrage as Kenneth Nicolls swung his secretary in a lusty square dance. Perverse thoughts inevitably germinated in this fertile soil. What would happen if he asked Miss Corsa to rhumba?

Unthinkable. After all, he had obligations to the unknown Mrs. Corsa in Queens.

With such a carnival of merrymaking and revelry on Thursday, Friday reeled under the monumental after-effects. Thatcher took in stride the Sloan's massive list of absentees, and even his own brief notoriety as a leader in the civil rights movement. His composure was undiminished as he declined an invitation to address an investment club of Negro women in New Rochelle, arranging for Nicolls to appear in his stead. What was really wanted, he reflected, was a special Lenten season for Wall Street. Forty days of fasting and shriving would set everybody to rights and had the further merit of historical tradition. Instead, he began to receive calls from Washington. It was these that brought him to the luncheon table looking like a veteran of street warfare.

"There is not the slightest justification for it. I have been willing to take a good deal, but this," he announced incisively, "this is outrageous."

The lunch was also a celebration. The three men were eating at the Stock Exchange Club, and Thatcher was present as the guest of its newest member, Edward Parry. The occasion was a gesture and, for the sake of the gesture, they were all prepared to put up with the food.

"What's so outrageous?"

Thatcher explained that Washington wanted to appoint him ambassador to a small, new African country.

"There'll be a lot of that sort of thing coming your way," said Ed Parry wisely. "With me, they always tried to push the UN."

Nat Schuyler waved away these irrelevancies. He was displaying the resilience that had brought successive generations of Schuylers unscathed through every major American crisis. Five short months ago he had had three partners—his cousin Ambrose, Arthur Foote and Vincent McCullough. All three were gone, and now he had one— the man across the table. But business was coming in as never before.

"Have you heard anything more about McCullough?"

Thatcher reported that Paul Jackson had undertaken the defense, but it seemed a hopeless task.

"The trouble is that once McCullough was suspected, the evidence was lying around, waiting to be picked up."

"I never did understand why you and Nat raced away from Madison Square Garden that way," interjected their host.

"It was McCullough telling me he sold his house to a Negro doctor."

Parry grinned.

"So?" he challenged softly. "What's so incriminating about that?"

"It certainly wouldn't have alerted me," Nat admitted. "I might have been furious, but I would have assumed he had gone crazy. Almost everybody else did, in one way or another."

"But that's the point. McCullough's posture was that of a man who resisted Ed's admission into the firm on perfectly businesslike grounds. Then, when the whole issue became fraught with racist ramifications, he began to cooperate with you, Nat. That was credible. He certainly wouldn't do anything to hurt the firm. But selling his house to a Negro could have been disastrous, simply by distracting attention from the central issue. Anybody could have predicted you would be furious. You had all you could do the other day to keep quiet—when Mrs. Parry said she was going to Lincoln Center. Every single person responsible for this Exchange seat transfer has been anxious to keep it simple, to keep it undistracted. The reason we objected to Richard Simpson was that he insisted on clouding the issue. And, in a different way, so did Owen Abercrombie. Now, Gloria Parry had a good reason to insist on Lincoln Center. But Vin McCullough didn't have any apparent motive for introducing an additional complexity. Particularly at a time when he depended on you to make up for his lost clients. In anybody else, you would say that he sold that way because it was an easy, fast, profitable sale. Right?"

They both nodded.

"And then, when you started thinking in those terms, we had been hearing a lot about McCullough selling things. A house, a boat, a summer place, a car. What did it all add up to? Vin McCullough needed money desperately and quickly. His wife said that the rent they were going to pay was high. That meant he wasn't making an investment in a cooperative. Nothing was being replaced, and a great many things were being converted into hard cash, under cover of a move into the city. It was clever of him to realize that so many sales could be made to appear normal that way. You expect a change in life when people move into an apartment. And what Carruthers said about faddists was true, also. If a man is moving downtown, you're not surprised to have him change from an outdoor type to a city type. The theater and nightclubs quite naturally replace country clubs and yachts. But once you started to think of McCullough as a man in urgent need of money, a lot of things came floating to the surface. Most suspiciously, the slowness with which he was returning portfolios to his customers."

"Now that I hadn't heard about," Schuyler broke in to say. "My ears would have pricked up if I had."

"Exactly. Lee Clark got it from some of the customers themselves. He thought it was a departure from normalcy because of your newly acquired business."

"Nonsense! The last thing in the world a brokerage house wants is a reputation for not delivering on request. It's as if a bank couldn't come up with funds to meet a legitimate withdrawal. The next thing would be a run on the bank. The same thing would happen to us. Let people once get edgy about whether they can withdraw, and they will."

Even now, with all danger past, Nat Schuyler waxed indignant at the possibility of such a rumor spreading forth and undermining the house of Schuyler & Schuyler. It would take him several moments to recover his equanimity.

"And then there was something else." Thatcher turned to Ed Parry. "Everybody accepted the fact that two tries had been made to murder you, as indeed they had. Well, why did they stop?"

"I was just grateful that they did," Parry admitted. "I suppose, if I thought at all, I thought it was police protection, my isolation in Katonah, that sort of thing."

"Yes, and there was a good deal of merit in that position. If you had come into the city within the next few days, something would have been tried. All right, so far as it goes. But after Lincoln Center, you did start coming in again. You were here when Nat threw out Caldwell, you came in before the Madison Square Garden rally. But nothing happened. It looked as if somebody had lost interest. Why?"

Parry frowned in thought. "You're right. Not only did I come in, but all the most obvious suspects knew about it."

"And that takes us back to the original motive. McCullough didn't want you in the firm for the very same reason he gave you. Because it would spark many of his customers into withdrawing. What he didn't add, was that he was in no position to return their portfolios, because he had stolen them. And it didn't make any difference to him whether the Stock Exchange ultimately denied you a seat, or deliberated about it for two years. Just let there be enough publicity about Schuyler & Schuyler wanting you, and the damage was done. His fraud would be revealed, and he would be discredited. And that would be the end for him—discovery, prison, no future. The thing that infuriated him the most was that it was all a question of timing. He had stolen to get the cash for a really big plunge. He had what he thought was a sure thing. Two months more and he would be in the clear. That's why he started off by urging Nat to go slow, advising caution, trying to delay things. When that didn't work, he took steps to end the threat to himself. He went to the reception with nicotine in his pocket and tried to poison you."

"And instead got poor Art Foote," said Schuyler with sad solemnity.

"And was just as badly off as ever," added Parry. "Or even worse. Now he had to worry about exposure for murder as well as fraud."

But Thatcher shook his had. "Things weren't that simple. Although he thought so at first. That's why he tried to shoot you first thing the next morning. He was in a desperate hurry. Already customers were backing out. Thanks to that sonic boom, he missed. You remember that the police were satisfied Caldwell could have been responsible for that attempt. But McCullough lived in Stamford—which hasn't been troubled with sonic booms, by the way—next door to Caldwell in Connecticut. The geography was as easy for him. But that failure sent you into isolation up in Katonah, and McCullough had time to look around. Then he discovered a very odd fact."

"What? I presume that's what made him stop trying to kill me. Or was it that, by the time he had another chance, the damage had been done?"

"There was that of course," agreed Thatcher. "But the

real thing was that Nat, here, gave him Art Foote's portfolios. After all, while he couldn't easily get at you in
person in the city, there was nothing to prevent his sending you poison packages or blowing up your house. He
had already shown he was unscrupulous in his methods.
No, the thing that did it was the discovery that Art Foote's
death was almost as good for his purposes as yours would
have been. True, his customers withdrew, but he used
Foote's portfolios to make up the difference. Supplied the
actual shares when they were the same, or sold off and
converted when they weren't. And in so doing left a
damning record behind him. Because all of these transactions were recorded on the books, if you knew what to
look for—name of share, amount, date of purchase. Take
Continental Can, for instance. One of his customers held
two hundred shares which he had stolen. There were
some in one of Foote's accounts. So he supplied those.
But the records show that he supplied shares purchased
two years after those bought on his account. And it's
even easier where he wasn't able to make a replacement
from Foote's inventory."

Parry nodded his comprehension. "So that's why you
and Nat rushed off to the office after the rally."

"Yes. We spent most of the night going over the
records, and we matched over forty-seven transactions."

"He could never have kept it up," said Schuyler. "We
would have had the usual audit after a partner's death."

"That explains the need for cash, and that's why I said
the timing was so important. It's one thing to have
people howling for something you can't deliver. It's
another to go out and raise money before a routine audit.
He managed to accumulate well over a hundred thousand
dollars in cash from his sales. With his credit standing
and position, he probably could have borrowed another
hundred thousand. That would have seen him through,
even if he didn't make his pile before the audit."

"It's a good solid motive, all right."

"Oh yes. But the police have a good deal more than
motive, you know. First, they found the rifle. His treat-

ment of that was simple enough. Instead of making any attempt to destroy it, he let his wife send it into storage along with all their excess belongings—furniture that wouldn't fit into the apartment, boating gear, country clothes. He thought, and quite rightly, that as long as he wasn't suspected, all he had to do was get it out of sight. If he was suspected, there was so much other evidence against him it wouldn't matter much. I wouldn't be surprised if he didn't plan suicide in the unlikely event of the police probing into his accounts. Of course everything happened too quickly in the end, and he just panicked."

Schuyler looked worried. "Suicide? Do you really think so?"

"I don't know. Not any longer, I expect. Paul Jackson has a way of heartening his clients. But I suspect that he's just heartening this one into a good frame of mind for his prison sentence. He can never explain away the poison."

"That was something to do with his brother-in-law, wasn't it?"

"Yes, McCullough was executor for his brother-in-law's estate. And his brother-in-law was a doctor. There were all the poisons any murderer could want, right at hand. And the police have gotten hold of the office nurse and the poison log. They're in a position to show that there's nicotine missing. The pure alkaloid, too, whatever that is."

Damning, agreed Parry. "But the thing that's so hard to believe is that he could do all that, then settle down to being a hardworking broker again."

"Oh, he didn't just settle down. That's when he began his career as an *agent provocateur*. It wasn't comfortable for him to have a full-scale investigation into the murder going on. He felt reasonably safe about the shooting. But the poisoning was a different matter. If the police continued their painstaking inquiries, their suspicions would be roused, then they would be onto the question of access to nicotine."

"I don't see how," grumbled Parry. "I probably did as much thinking about it as anybody, and it never occurred to me to suspect Vin McCullough."

"You did a lot of thinking in the absence of facts," Thatcher corrected him. "Inevitably, that means you were thinking about who would want to kill you. And that led you into the whole morass of the race question. But the police, very sensibly, thought in terms of opportunity. Probably going on the assumption that almost anybody there might want to kill you. And that worried McCullough. Everybody knew the police were working on a timetable, and the possibility of confusion about Foote's drink. Well, the one thing that emerged was that the people at Schuyler & Schuyler had the best chance to know about Foote's regimen."

Ed Parry raised his eyebrows. "I hadn't thought of that one."

"Once the police had gotten that far, what else would they discover? That Vin McCullough had arrived late. Everybody else from your brokerage house was present long before Foote took that glass of tomato juice. And Foote was with your group most of the time. Assuming the murderer had kept an eye on his potential victim, if only to be able to locate him, he could scarcely miss the fact that Ed walked over without a drink to join Foote, who did have a glass. The tomato juice was actually ordered in front of Lee Clark and carried back to both of you. Caldwell was in the room. It's barely conceivable that he might have missed this activity, but one thing was sure. McCullough was certain to have missed it, because he hadn't yet arrived. You recall, he didn't come in until you were all huddled together over the press release. Then there was the business of Owen Abercrombie charging over and being pulled off by Caldwell and Lee Clark. Clark was virtually cleared, unless it was Foote he was aiming for all the time. The other two might have done it. But the one with the best opportunity was McCullough, and that's the kind of situation that makes the police think. McCullough wanted to short circuit that line of reasoning. And that's where the whole race question became a godsend to him, just as it had promised disaster earlier."

"You mean because it was so easy to divert attention?" probed Schuyler. "Yes, I can see that. But he was still extraordinarily lucky that Abercrombie and Caldwell made such fools of themselves."

"Luck, I think, had very little to do with it," replied Thatcher dryly. "McCullough was not the man to sit back and wait for fortune to bestow its favors. You were on the right track when you first suggested Caldwell might be using Abercrombie, but you had the casting wrong. Caldwell, in his own perverted way, was sincere. It was McCullough who was the mainspring, and he was much more subtle than young Caldwell could ever have been. He played the role of trying to save Caldwell from himself. I caught him at it during the television broadcast. He was warning the boy not to be fool enough to try anything at Lincoln Center. It was obvious that, up to that moment, Caldwell hadn't even thought about the concert. I remember asking McCullough if it was wise to let Caldwell know. He looked a little self-conscious, but said that he wanted to give the boy some good advice. At the time I accepted the explanation in good faith. The world is filled with people doing the wrong thing from the best motives. But McCullough had accomplished just what he intended. First, he had conveyed information. Then he also made sure that Caldwell and Abercrombie would do something surpassingly silly by waving a red flag at Caldwell. By the time he was done with his propaganda effort, he was virtually certain that they would draw attention to themselves in some way."

"But he couldn't know that Abercrombie was going to pull a gun," protested Parry. "Even Caldwell didn't know that he was carrying one, and I doubt if he intended to use it. It's hard to explain, but I think he was carrying it simply to show . . ."

"To show how warlike he was," supplied Schuyler, who was not going to shilly-shally around for terms defining Owen Abercrombie's eccentricity. "Undoubtedly that incredible lunatic had talked himself into a frame of mind where it seemed the manly thing to do."

"And never dreamed of using it until that detective injured his sense of *amour propre* by touching him."

"Exactly. Except for that intervention, Abercrombie would probably have harangued you in abusive terms and made a number of vague and disagreeable threats. Which would have suited McCullough very well. You have to realize that he had no thoughts of anybody being convicted for his actions. No one knew better than he the unlikelihood of proving access to poison for Abercrombie or Caldwell. But if the two of them persisted in adopting a consistently homicidal attitude, he had every reason to hope that the police and the public would ultimately assume one of them was the murderer. It would be another case closed for lack of hard evidence. There would be grumblings from civil rights workers until the next big headline came along, and that would be that. McCullough was in a paradoxical position vis-à-vis the race question. On the one hand, he saw himself forced into murder because of his clients' reaction to the problem; but on the other hand, he had a very strong protection against anyone spotting his motive, for just the same reason."

"That may be the way Vin sees it," said Schuyler loftily. "I prefer to say that he was forced to murder because he chose to rob clients of our brokerage house."

The other two men bowed their assent. The head of Schuyler & Schuyler was understandably unsympathetic to such activities.

Parry, after a moment's silent propitiation of these sentiments, returned to the original question. "But still he had luck. He must have been hard put not to stand up and cheer when Abercrombie went mad at Lincoln Center."

"Oh, he had luck," Thatcher agreed. "More than he expected and more, even, than he realized. Jackson tells me that, when the police started to investigate Abercrombie with a view to poisoning, they didn't find anything. But when they tried the same thing with Caldwell, the first thing they hit was a visit of his to some pharmaceutical firm two weeks ago. They were bending every

effort to find out if he could have picked up some pure
nicotine while he was there."

"Good heavens! I'd forgotten about that," exclaimed
Schuyler. "I sent him to Downbill's myself. They're going
public, you know."

"Well, Downbill's maintained he hadn't been anywhere
near their stock of nicotine, but it was enough to keep
the police interested. And, of course, nobody could have
expected Abercrombie to be mad enough to lose his instinct for self-preservation."

"Is he really mad?"

"That's his story. He's entered a plea of insanity on all
those charges, you know. His son, I understand, is giving
up California. Now it's a villa in Majorca."

"It would be. Next thing we know, he'll be publishing
his poems in little lavender volumes."

Schuyler nodded knowingly. "You remember Owen's
Uncle Basil?" He shook his head sadly. "And now Owen.
Terrible, the way these old families go to seed. The boy
will probably end up the same way. Blood tells, you
know."

Parry grinned cheerfully. "It may be that the air of Wall
Street goes to their heads. Anyway, the beatnik strain has
something to recommend it. I hear that the boy has sent
a check for five thousand to the NAACP."

"Wait until he hits Majorca," advised Schuyler darkly.

"And what about Caldwell? Any sign of atonement
there?" asked Thatcher, genuinely curious.

"I wouldn't know," said Schuyler distantly.

Parry brayed his laughter. "Not on your life! He's got
a job with a broker in Atlanta. I think he may intend to
tangle with my father." A deep chuckle rumbled. "He
doesn't know what he's taking on. Well, live and learn."

Sight unseen, Thatcher was prepared to credit the
prowess and acumen of any Negro who had marched into
Atlanta in the 'thirties and emerged a multimillionaire.

"It may be the making of the boy," he agreed gravely.
"By the way, do you hear something odd going on out
there?"

Out there was the vestibule. And, indeed, there seemed

to be some sort of low-keyed disturbance in progress. There were cries of: "But it's all over!" "Hey! You can't go in there!" "Not with the guitar, sonny!"

And then they streamed in. The Troubles had left in their wake a small and determined band that had found a new way of life. When the sun rose each morning, like cocks crowing, like magnets turning to the north, like lemmings entering the sea, they took to the IRT and headed for Wall Street. So finally, Thatcher was able to gratify his ambition. The tune was the "Battle Hymn of the Republic"; the lyrics came through loud and clear as the little group followed its bearded, strutting leader: and "The Three Wise Men" resounded once again:

> There's a mighty storm that's blowing on the Street
> that's known as Wall,
> Where the fat cats with their bowls of cream
> are heading for a fall,
> With a broom that's new, we're going to brush
> the rascals one and all,
> Helped by Three Wise Men!
>
> Waymark, Thatcher and Car-ru-thers!
> Waymark, Thatcher and Car-ru-thers!
> Waymark, Thatcher and Car-ru-thers!
> Wall Street's Three Wise Men!
>
> We are marching for Ed Parry, we are Marching
> for the Seat,
> We are tearing triumph from the banker's howls
> of defeat,
> Tempered by the flames of justice, we are
> turning on the heat,
> Helped by Three Wise Men!
>
> Waymark, Thatcher and Car-ru-thers!
> Waymark, Thatcher and Car-ru-thers!
> Waymark, Thatcher and Car-ru-thers!
> Wall Street's Three Wise Men!
>
> Let the brokers count their money, let them
> count it day and night,
> Let the lawyers and their lawbooks try to keep them
> lily white,

There are thousands of us ready who are girding
   for the fight,
Helped by Three Wise Men!

Waymark, Thatcher and Car-ru-thers!
Waymark, Thatcher and Car-ru-thers!
Waymark, Thatcher and Car-ru-thers!
Wall Street's Three Wise Men!